Seducing the Laird

Seducing the Laird

Lauren Marrero

Black Lyon Publishing, LLC

SEDUCING THE LAIRD
Copyright © 2011 by Lauren Marrero

Our books may be ordered through your local bookstore or by visiting the publisher:

www.BlackLyonPublishing.com

Black Lyon Publishing, LLC
PO Box 567
Baker City, OR 97814

This is a work of fiction. All of the characters, names, events, organizations and conversations in this novel are either the products of the author's vivid imagination or are used in a fictitious way for the purposes of this story.

ISBN-10:   1-934912-40-9
ISBN-13:   978-1-934912-40-9
Library of Congress Control Number: 2011938988

Cover Model: Brannon Charles

Written, published and printed in
the United States of America.

Black Lyon Historical Romance

To my mother.
Thanks for your unconditional love
and encouragement.

Chapter 1

England, 1502

Laird Cairn McPherson urged his mount to greater speed, ignoring the foam falling from the horse's mouth. Heavy rain poured around them. They were both nearly blinded by it, crashing wildly though the dark forest, unheeding of the branches that slapped painfully against their sides. Laird McPherson didn't dare slow his speed for a moment. He bent his head close to the horse's ear, whispering a litany of encouragement and asking forgiveness for his abuse. He had no choice, for Cairn McPherson was running for his life.

The icy wind from the late autumn storm cut through the fine wool of his tunic. He wore no gloves or cloak to protect him from the elements and the cold turned his fingers and ears to ice. Still Cairn didn't take his fingers away from the reins for a second lest the beast slacken its speed. He ignored the numbness creeping across his exposed body, ignored the pain as each ungainly stride of his borrowed mount brought a rush of pain from the wounds covering him from head to toe. He ignored everything except what lay ahead and the sweet promise of freedom beyond the trees.

The horse stumbled over the uneven, slippery ground and Cairn McPherson nearly lost his seat. He held on grimly, determined not to fail after he had come so far. Only a few short hours ago he languished in the English Lord Gundy's dungeon praying for this opportunity to escape and he wasn't going to waste it.

Lord Gundy's and Cairn's holdings sat opposite each other on the border between England and Scotland, but though there had always been animosity between the two, Cairn didn't expect such treachery. He came at Lord Gundy's request to negotiate a permanent peace, yet on his arrival Cairn's party had been attacked and the wounded survivors thrown into a dungeon.

Three men were captured with Cairn yet he was the only one to escape alive. Gundy thought Scotland was weak because of the Scottish King's defeat after supporting the pretender to the English throne, Perkin Warbeck. He thought the McPhersons were weak because of the recent death of Cairn's father, but Cairn was determined to prove him wrong. He was free now and nothing would stop him from exacting his revenge.

The ill-kept road was overgrown with weeds, and treacherous stones threatening to trip his exhausted horse. Claw-like tree branches reached for Cairn in the dark, scratching his face and arms. The horse lost its footing again and Cairn allowed it to slow its furious gallop. He was miles from Gundy's castle and didn't know if the alarm had yet been raised.

The frightened horse's eyes rolled wildly at the howling wind. He reared twice as a large branch crashed to the ground behind them. The heavens reflected Cairn's dark mood and lashed at the earth with all its might. A flash of lightning lit the sky and for a moment Cairn was able to clearly see. The path was briefly illuminated showing a long, dangerous stretch of road that would eventually lead him back to Scotland.

In the two days since his capture Cairn had not eaten or slept and his alerted senses began to play tricks on him. He imagined eyes watching from the shadows ready to pounce and drag him back to Langthorne. He imagined the grim satisfaction of the guard as he told Cairn he was lucky to suffer only light torture by water.

He looked up to see a large shadow dart through the trees beside him. The horse reared once more, catching sight of the sudden movement. Cairn's frozen hands were barely able to hold on until the terrified animal was under control.

Around him the forest began to shift. Shadows darted through the trees, keeping pace with him. Surely Lord Gundy's men wouldn't pursue him so. Gundy's men would have stopped Cairn with a challenge or a well-placed arrow. Cairn saw neither glint of armor nor the bright colors of livery, only the obscure gloom teasing the edges of his sight.

England was surely driving him mad. Who would watch the roads on such an abysmal night? Cairn blinked rapidly to clear his deceiving eyes. But just as he rounded a sharp bend in the road one of the shadows disengaged from the surrounding forest and slammed painfully into Cairn's bruised chest.

He could feel himself flying backward off the horse. He felt the impact of his landing on the muddy road and heard a guttural sound that might have been his own grunt of pain. As Cairn drifted in and out of consciousness he was aware of being dragged off the road. He heard the urgent whispering of several voices and felt hands skimming lightly over his body.

Somehow Cairn found the strength to push the hands away and for a moment the whispering ceased. Then the hands returned and Cairn pried his eyes open to see the figure of an old man kneeling above him. He was arguing with someone and Cairn looked up to see a younger man scowling down at him. Cairn scowled in return; too groggy to understand the words of their debate but knowing he was the subject.

Again Cairn lost consciousness and awoke to find another hovering above him. This time it was a woman. Her hair was so black it was almost blue contrasting sharply with luminous sapphire eyes. Her full lips pressed tightly together as she peered down on him with a look of concern.

To Cairn's delirious mind the woman's beauty seemed unearthly. He wanted to touch her to make sure he wasn't dreaming. He wanted to brush her hair aside, pull her lips to his and taste their softness. As if reading his thoughts the woman licked her lips and Cairn's pulse quickened. He wondered if they were as soft as they looked and if she would taste like strawberries or cherries or some exotic flavor all her own.

"Don't worry," she said in a soft, low voice. It was the tone one uses to calm an injured beast or frightened child. "You are safe now."

Cairn wanted to believe her, but there was something in the woman's voice that worried him, some strange inflection he couldn't fully grasp. He didn't know if she were real or a vision or perhaps an angel sent to carry his soul away. Once again he felt oblivion calling him. Cairn fought to keep his tired eyes focused, not wanting his vision of this creature to fade, but the last few days had taken their toll.

Her tiny hand closed gently around Cairn's and he grasped it tightly. Despite the autumn cold her fingers were warm and solid in his grip. He squeezed her hand as the darkness once again overtook his sight. Cairn didn't know who this creature was, but he suddenly knew with the solid pressure of her hand that he would survive.

Chapter 2

"This will never work," Owen predicted as he glowered at his two companions.

"Hush!" Verena cautioned. "You'll wake him."

By "him" she referred to the unconscious man who imprisoned her hand in his vice-like grip. She didn't know what prompted her to place her work-roughened fingers in his. She thought he was unconscious—he certainly should have been after that fall from his horse. His eyes drifted open for a moment and when he looked at her, he smiled. It was hard to believe this was the man she was sent to capture.

"Wake him?" Owen asked. "We shouldn't be anywhere near him. For all we know this is a lost traveler."

Verena studied the man critically. Though his leonine features were puffy with bruises there was no disguising the sooty eyelashes and high cheekbones that cut a steep line to his firm mouth. When he opened his eyes she felt pierced by their amber depths which sparkled like jewels. His hair was the most intriguing shade of brown, but Verena suspected it would appear golden in the full light of the sun, with deep waves that her fingers itched to trace.

Judging by the length of his frame and the muscles bulging beneath the fine wool of his tunic, this man had an impressive size. He was easily as tall as Owen, though he lacked Owen's muscular girth. At three times her size and more than a head taller than her, Owen was definitely the muscle of their operation—a position he held with pride.

"Look at his clothes," said their other companion, Hadran, a gruff older man with surprisingly intelligent eyes despite the many wrinkles and age spots covering his withered frame. "A red tunic, a chestnut mare ..."

"All of which he could have exchanged between here and the castle," insisted Owen. "As we would have."

"Yes," agreed Hadran. "But not everyone is like us."

The three conspirators shared a look of solidarity. They had worked together for many years, fulfilling the dark ambitions of their Lord Gundy. They knew each other's strengths and weaknesses, but most importantly they knew their value. Hadran's small family of spies had turned Lord Gundy into one of the most powerful nobles in England.

"I will check his wounds," Verena said to pacify her friend. "If we have the wrong man we will know soon enough."

She gently used her knife to cut his shirt at the seams and wet the cloth where the dried blood caused it to stick to the wounds. Lord Gundy had left no chances; describing everything from the clothes Laird McPherson would be wearing to the horse he 'stole' during his staged escape from the Langthorne prison. And just in case the McPherson was able to change before Verena and her crew found him, they also had a description of his wounds in detail including the distinctive cross-shaped scar below his right rib. She even knew of the tiny mole on the Laird's left buttock.

"There is so much blood," she said in wonder. Looking at the ghastly scars she would have a hard enough job keeping the man alive.

"It is him," Hadran said soberly. "This is much worse than we were told. We could have killed him knocking him from his horse like that."

She agreed, but they didn't have a choice. The man rode as if Satan was chasing him and looking at his injuries Verena understood why. It was a painful reminder of the kind of man they worked for. Though she didn't put him in Gundy's dungeon, Verena couldn't help but feel partially responsible for this man's fate. It was her team that made this possible. All too soon the McPherson would realize he had escaped one trap only to fall neatly into another.

"He will survive," she said with conviction. She was sure of it. Verena had seen the strength in his eyes. She remembered the strong pressure of his hand and his smile.

Gathering their hidden supplies Owen quickly started a fire, hanging a small pot of water over it to boil. Hadran prepared a healing poultice of herbs and fat while Verena cleaned and sewed the most dangerous wounds shut. They worked with silent efficiency over Laird McPherson's unconscious form, each praying for his recovery.

This man held the key to a fortune beyond her wildest dreams, and Gundy coveted it like nothing else. It was believed that no one alive knew its location, but Verena knew where and how to look. She just needed a way into the Scotsman's castle.

Hadran had trained them incessantly for this assignment but all of that planning would be in vain if the Laird died in the forest. Somehow she would keep him alive. She would find the Scotsman's treasure and return with it to England.

Chapter 3

Pale sunlight streamed through an open window and caressed Cairn's cheek. The feeling of warmth was so unusual after the last few days he was instantly awake, distrustful of the reprieve. Too much had happened since crossing the border into England and Cairn wouldn't feel safe until he was home.

The young woman he had glimpsed earlier sat beside the bed on an ancient stool, observing him with concern. He had somehow been transported to a small cottage, but the girl was alone. How had she managed to carry him to this place? Even in his weakened state she looked too frail to lift one of his legs.

"I'm glad you're awake," she said in the same soft voice from before. "I was worried."

Her accent was English and though nervous, she didn't appear afraid of being alone with a strange man.

Cairn examined her as best he could through the painful throbbing in his head. She was beautiful with full lips and mysterious, cat-like blue eyes. Her raven-black hair hung loose about her shoulders and he could see the deep waves left by the braids he remembered her wearing.

With her unfashionably dark skin and exotic features she reminded Cairn of a gypsy girl he had seen long ago that trespassed on his lands. The girl regarded Cairn frankly and without fear, just like the woman before him.

"Where am I?" Cairn rasped through a parched throat.

The woman held a mug of honeyed tea to his lips after a long spell of dry coughs wracked his frame. He could feel the warmth of her body through the thick woolen gown the wretched northern weather forced its inhabitants to wear.

"A few miles from the border," she replied. "What is your name?"

Cairn didn't answer. He was still in England, still within reach of Lord Gundy's malevolent hand. That made this beautiful woman his enemy.

"My name is Verena," she said to encourage him. "I found you on the road not far from here."

"I was attacked."

He remembered the two men arguing over him. They unseated him, took the horse and left Cairn for dead. They must have been bandits, for Lord Gundy's men would have returned him to Langthorne.

"I surmised as much. Don't worry. You are safe now."

Cairn could feel himself being pulled back into the dark unconsciousness where the pain in his body no longer tormented him. There would be time enough for the cold political reality to return. Outside a dangerous storm brewed, waiting for Cairn to emerge, but inside the tiny cottage he was reluctant to shatter the tenuous peace. When he was strong enough to travel Cairn would tell her the truth. But not yet.

When she was sure the McPherson slept, Verena quietly rose from her seat. She almost felt sorry for the man. The last few weeks had not been kind to him. Until recently he had lived a privileged life traveling around France with his brother Andreu and making a name for himself in many tournaments. Then with the sudden death of his father, Cairn was summoned home to take control of a clan he barely knew.

The ever-resourceful Gundy was quick to take advantage of Cairn's inexperience. She didn't know how Cairn was lured to England, but he was a fool to trust a man like Gundy. He wouldn't sleep so peacefully if the laird knew what awaited him.

The old hunting lodge was located in a secluded region of the forests surrounding Langthorne. Hadran believed it was the perfect spot to hide their Scottish prisoner while Verena began her work. Owen remained hidden in the woods nearby to discourage the locals from stumbling onto their operation. He would be quick to Verena's defense should the Scot become uncontrollable. She didn't fear the laird, but she was grateful to have Owen silently watching to make sure everything was all right.

Using her body to block the cool wind so it didn't disturb her prisoner, Verena cracked open the door to the cottage. She saw Owen's hulking shape emerge from the shadows of the trees like a child's nightmare. She nodded to him silently before turning back to the cottage. The Scot had awoken and was recovering well.

They could only watch and wait.

Chapter 4

"We have him," Hadran announced in Gundy's private chambers.

For years he had worked as Lord Gundy's shadow, silently trailing him and leaving a gruesome path in his wake. Here in Gundy's chambers Hadran felt important. He had a private audience with the Lord of Langthorne. Though the rich surroundings might intimidate one with Hadran's humble roots, the old spy knew it was the man and not the gold which held the power. The furs, silks and tapestries were paid for by the sweat and blood of peasants just like him. Those people would never own the riches their labors paid for; Gundy was shrewd and miserly enough to see to that.

"How can you be sure?" Gundy asked.

Hadran stared into the man's cold grey eyes and mentally sighed. He was familiar enough with the lord to know the question was rhetorical. After years of service Hadran and his crew had not once failed in an assignment. Nevertheless he answered the question.

"A chestnut mare with two white forelegs, a red woolen tunic with black embroidery, one knife wound just below the right rib ..." answered Hadran in an ever-patient voice, ticking the list off his fingers. "And several bruises."

"I trust he survived the ordeal?" Gundy asked without a trace of remorse. The wounds were much worse than planned, however Hadran knew his lord and prided himself on being prepared for anything. That was why he had Verena and Owen ready with enough medicines to treat a battlefield and a warm cottage nearby where the Scottish laird could recover.

"Barely. Our schedule will have to be adjusted."

"That is unacceptable!"

Gundy reached for his goblet and refilled it for the third time.

As the years passed the old lord started to feel his age and had lost the edge that had made him one of the most feared men in the land. He still possessed a razor sharp wit and his network of spies and assassins, but the old warrior's muscles had long ago turned soft. The once-tanned flesh was ruddy with too much ale. Gundy was becoming aware of his mortality, a feeling Hadran understood only too well, but he didn't sympathize with the lord. Where age had made Hadran cautious, it turned Gundy reckless. The imprisonment of the McPherson laird was bolder than anything Gundy had done in his younger days. He seemed desperate to prove he still retained the strength of his youth. Hadran prayed his spies wouldn't suffer for Gundy's arrogance.

"He is no use to you dead, milord. And I assure you that will happen if we rush."

"How much longer must I wait?" He was irritated with the delay, but willing to follow his servant's direction. Hadran was relieved the lord was not too drunk to listen to reason.

"That depends on the Scot. Once in his homeland my operative should have little trouble locating the treasure."

"So? What is the problem?"

"His recovery time will be severely impeded because of the wounds inflicted by your guards."

Hadran allowed his voice to creep as close to reproachful as he dared. He saw one of Lord Gundy's bushy eyebrows rise in acknowledgement of the rebuke and decided to return to a more docile tone.

"However," he continued. "This will give my operative more time to gain his trust."

"You expect one person to succeed where my men couldn't?"

Hadran knew he was not completely trusted by Lord Gundy. His spies had never failed, but Gundy knew how much he relied on Hadran for information. He also realized that in addition to collecting information on the heads of state, Hadran's spies knew a great deal of Gundy's shady secrets—and that knowledge made him extremely uncomfortable.

"We are all your men." Hadran oozed confidence and trust. "But I have discovered there is a different, more subtle persuasion that is often more effective than torture and war."

"And what might this be?"

Hadran could see the calculating gleam in his eyes. It was better if Gundy didn't know the details of the assignment. That way the old lord was not tempted to meddle. He thought carefully before answering.

"Simply that every son of Adam is in search of his father's missing rib."

"A woman!" Gundy said. "Silly creatures. The Scot will never suspect a thing. I always wondered how you attracted such comely spies. That Verena is especially fine. Perhaps when this is over I will reward her with something other than gold."

"Perhaps," said Hadran noncommittally. He knew his young ward was beautiful, that was why he chose her for this assignment. He was also aware of his lord's reputation with wenches and so far he had been able to keep Gundy's lascivious eye from her. Gundy believed he had the right to bed any woman on his land whether she wished it or not. Hadran would spare Verena that if possible.

"What if he is immune to her persuasion?"

"From my reports Cairn McPherson is no sodomite, but I have taken that into consideration."

"I don't want to know," said Gundy in disgust. Hadran smiled at the squeamish lord. If the McPherson preferred a more masculine form of love Hadran would find someone more to the Scot's tastes, but he preferred to work with Verena. The girl had an easy way about her that gained people's trust. Hadran had already spent several days training her for this assignment. "When shall I hear from you again?"

"I must confer with my agents but I will return in a few days and let you know when we may proceed with the second part of the plan."

Lord Gundy nodded and turned his attention back to his wine. Interpreting that as a signal to depart, Hadran bowed and left the room.

Chapter 5

Cairn McPherson smiled for the first time in weeks as he relaxed into the thick blankets. It seemed ages since he was truly warm, cocooned in a soft bed with delicious smells floating past him. It was the smells that roused him, wholesome food quite unlike the sumptuous meals he had feasted on with his brother in France. His stomach growled loudly at the thought of fresh rye bread smothered in butter and honey and a hearty stew made with local herbs and vegetables—peasant food, his stepmother would call it, but now it was all Cairn desired. He felt rested and better than he had in ages. And he was hungry.

Opening his eyes, Cairn tried to discover the origin of the smells and found the Englishwoman preparing something in a small cauldron hanging in the fireplace. Her back was to him letting Cairn study her as she went about her task. Masses of curls spilled down her back escaping the braids she had fashioned. He knew many fine ladies of court added false hair to lengthen and thicken theirs, but this woman needed no such assistance. She yanked a lock behind her ear in frustration as it fell dangerously close to the stew pot.

She had rolled up the thick woolen sleeves of her gown to work and Cairn gazed thoughtfully at her slender wrists. Her hands were strong and confident, but not overly so like peasants that worked the fields. She was young, but past the first blush of youth. She was old enough and beautiful enough to be a wife, but Cairn had seen no one but her in the lucid moments of his fever. He surmised she must be a servant of some grand household, probably Gundy's though he couldn't imagine a servant of Gundy's showing kindness to a stranger.

Sensing his gaze the woman looked up from her stew and nervously rolled down the sleeves of her gown. Her modesty affirmed she was from a noble household. She had no doubt seen every inch of Cairn's body yet feared showing her wrists. Was she afraid of him?

"How do you feel?"

"Much better," he replied, and then grimaced. Cairn's mouth felt stuffed with wool, but his head had ceased its pounding and the painful throbbing of his wounds had subsided to a dull ache. He felt like he was waking from a long illness; weak, but well rested and confident of his body's ability to heal. "Thank you for helping me ... Verena."

She smiled briefly and shyly looked away.

"Any Christian would have done the same."

"I'm not so certain." Cairn remembered the vastly different treatment he received from other 'Christian' hands. "You saw my wounds."

He referred to the knife cut left by the over-zealous Langthorne guard.

"I had to clean them."

"Why did you help me?"

Verena sighed, fiddling with her hair. She turned her back on him and began rummaging near the fire. For a moment it seemed she wouldn't answer and when she did her voice was low and sounded hollow.

"My husband was a woodsman," she answered with her attention still on the fire. "Last winter he was attacked by bandits in these woods. It took two days to find him and by then ... When I saw you I knew I must do something."

So, she was a widow. Somehow this woman seemed too innocent to have known such sorrow.

"I am sorry for your loss."

"'Twas not your fault."

Verena placed a cool hand on his brow the way Cairn's real mother had done when he was a babe. Unexpectedly Cairn felt a wave of nostalgia at her tenderness. That illness must have rattled his brain. All his life he was taught to hate the English, but she seemed somehow different. She made him feel comfortable and Cairn didn't trust the speed by which she put him at ease. Despite her ignorance Verena was his enemy. He knew nothing about her save her allegiance to Gundy and that was enough. Cairn would do well to be rid of this woman as soon as possible.

"Is something amiss?" she asked, sensing his pensive mood.

"What of the bandits? They cannot be far away."

"I saw no one on the road. Perhaps they chose to flee Langthorne after the attack."

"Perhaps."

"Your fever has broken. You are a very fast healer."

Cairn shrugged off the praise. He had merely lain in bed sweating and delirious.

"How long have I been here?"

Had his men waited at the border as Cairn ordered, or were they now making their way to the castle, fearful for Cairn's safety? With his brother Andreu in charge Cairn wasn't so sure. His older half brother was fiercely protective and stubborn. Cairn had a difficult time ordering him to stay behind with most of the men while he continued to Langthorne with a smaller force. Andreu had demanded to journey with his brother, but some intuitive voice made Cairn refuse. Andreu might be hurt, but Cairn was glad he listened to that voice.

"Almost three days," she replied. "I am sure your family misses you terribly."

She was probing for information, but Cairn didn't answer. He wouldn't lie to this woman, nor would he risk his life by telling her the truth.

"You are here alone?" he asked instead.

She turned away, the shy maid once again. Verena was hiding something and Cairn's pulse quickened, wondering if she meant to betray him to Gundy.

"Not for long," she replied vaguely. Verena gestured to the pot hanging above the fire. "I have made some stew. Are you hungry?"

"Where are your companions?"

His hand reached out suddenly to grab Verena's wrist and felt a shock at the satin texture of her skin. Cairn's hand nearly swallowed her tiny wrist. He could feel her pulse fluttering in alarm. At first she stood stiffly in his hold, frozen by shock. Then she began struggling against him to be free.

"Let me go!"

Cairn released her. If Gundy knew his location, Cairn would either be dead or back in the Langthorne prison, but that didn't curb his unease. He ignored the seductive brush of her hand through his fingers as she pulled away.

"I didn't mean to startle you, but I am curious. How did you bring me here alone?"

"I am stronger than I look. My grandfather shall meet me soon and will take me to live with him in Norham."

Why did her grandfather choose to meet Verena in this secluded cottage rather than in Langthorne? Cairn would have questioned Verena further, but she bent forward to fill a small wooden bowl and graced him with a spectacular view of her shapely backside.

"Are you hungry?"

Cairn was famished and the stew smelled delicious, but he hesitated as something occurred to him.

"You put something in the tea."

"Aye, Valerian and hops. You were thrashing about terribly during your fever so I thought it best if you slept."

Verena had the grace to blush as she ladled stew into a wooden bowl. Valerian was common enough, but England was enveloped in a fierce debate over the worthiness of the new imported hops. Traditional breweries fought viciously for the original gruit ale which was a mixture of several herbs and even tried to have hops outlawed.

Cairn liked the old gruit beer for its variety which could contain any mixture of juniper berries, caraway, nutmeg, cinnamon, anise, sage, rosemary and many other herbs. His stepbrother Andreu was convinced hopped beer would win the debate and encouraged him to plant a field of the stuff. It was interesting that this woman was of a like mind.

"Did I hurt you?"

"It matters naught. You were fevered."

"Still, I apologize."

He sought to make amends, but Verena remembered his strength when he held her wrist and approached him warily. No doubt she intended to dump the steaming soup on him should Cairn reach for her again. When he didn't stir she carefully brought the soup to her lips to blow on before feeding to him. Cairn turned his head away.

"I can feed myself," he declared.

It required all of Cairn's concentration to lift the small bowl to his mouth. To his chagrin Cairn's hands shook, spilling soup onto the blankets. He swallowed the contents quickly before handing Verena the bowl.

She was a spectacular cook, doing wonders with only a few ingredients. It was a shame he couldn't bring her back to Scotland. The overly seasoned food his stepmother loved gave Cairn indigestion.

"Is this your cottage?" he asked looking around. There was nothing strange about the inside of the place except for the curious lack of personal items. There was only one cloak hanging beside the door. Two sets of boots were placed in a corner. The cottage was clean and well-cared for, but spartan.

"This is an old hunting lodge," Verena replied. "Few know of it." Would Lord Gundy remember it? Cairn felt vulnerable in this place without his sword and armor. Verena said he lay there for several days, but the danger might not have passed. Cairn wouldn't feel secure until he left England far behind.

"You know if it."

"My husband often brought me here."

Cairn studied the woman in silence. The cynical part of him didn't want to believe her. His rescue was too easy; this woman was too beautiful, too perfect. And he certainly didn't like the idea of her in a cozy lover's tryst with anyone—even her deceased husband.

"I will leave tomorrow," he announced.

Cairn knew he would be a fool to trust an Englishwoman. If she knew the truth she would immediately turn him over to Gundy. Tomorrow he would sort everything out. For now Cairn needed to rest and recover his strength.

•

Verena silently watched Cairn until she was sure he slept. Then she gathered her cloak and stepped out into the frigid air. It seemed winter would come early this year. For many that would be both a blessing and a curse. Winter ensured peace the way no overlord could. Across the land men would be more preoccupied with keeping themselves warm and fed than fighting battles. Yet it would also strain resources and tempers as people were forced to stretch their reserved grain through the cold months.

All of Scotland suffered after King James IV's unsuccessful invasion of England in support of the pretender to the throne Perkin Warbek. Cairn's clan, the McPhersons, suffered more than most. While Cairn was squired in France with his brother Andreu, his father lay ill for years. Hadran's sources couldn't say why Cairn refused to return to his homeland during those years. Now it was too late. The mysterious illness had claimed Cairn's father forcing him to return to a home he barely knew to take control of a land decimated by warfare and famine.

The peasants were always the first to suffer during any conflict. What would happen to the common people once her assignment was complete?

Verena waved for Owen to follow as she walked to the edge of the clearing. She knew he was watching for the first sign of commotion, ever vigilant, the way Hadran taught him.

"How fares the inquisition?"

He materialized as if by magic beside her and not for the first time Verena whispered thanks that he was part of her team.

"Excellent. The Scot has been remarkably forthcoming with information considering what he went through in Gundy's dungeon."

"He merely needed the proper persuasion. Has he confirmed his identity?"

"He does not completely trust me. Not yet."

"Be careful."

Owen gently grasped Verena's chin in his hand. For a moment it seemed he would kiss her and she froze. She stood trapped in his light embrace not knowing whether to pull away or toward him so she did neither. Thankfully Owen stepped back suddenly, releasing her.

"I don't want anything to happen to you."

She tried to smile, but was flustered by the brief contact. She knew something was changing in her relationship with Owen. He was transforming from her friend and protector into something else. But Verena was not sure she was ready to face that change.

"What could possibly happen with you watching over me?" she asked lightly, turning to return to the cottage. Verena didn't let herself wonder why she would rather return to its small confines than remain outdoors with her longtime friend.

"Verena," Owen softly called after her. She paused just before emerging from the woods and turned back to him. There was something in Owen's gaze that she couldn't define, an uncertainty or desire or perhaps both. Whatever it was, it made her nervous. For years Hadran had groomed Verena to be the perfect spy. She always knew precisely what to say and do, but now with her longtime friend she was unsure.

"Men like the McPherson are kind and chivalrous when the mood strikes them or when they need something, but never forget he is a lord. He does not care for the likes of us. No pretty face is going to change that."

"I know exactly what he is."

Verena shivered as a chill wind swept through the forest. She didn't envy Owen's position out in the cold. There was a little stable next to the cottage where Owen slept, but that was less than ideal.

She thought of Hadran running back and forth between them and Lord Gundy, delivering orders and knew Owen was right. Nobles didn't care about their servants as long as their selfish desires were met. She must remember that as she dealt with Cairn.

Chapter 6

Verena sat on her pallet before the fire, staring into the flames and thinking of Owen's words. Did he truly believe she needed a reminder of the ruthlessness of noblemen? Her job was to seek out the worst in people so Gundy could use it to his advantage. She had little respect or sympathy for any of them. It was true Cairn had kind eyes but that wouldn't erase years of neglecting his home. She shook her head. Why was she thinking of his eyes?

Reaching for her comb, Verena pulled it forcefully through her long, thick hair. She had plans of her own that didn't involve entanglements with noblemen. She didn't intend to be Gundy's slave forever. She knew it would be difficult and dangerous to leave, but Verena was confident she would think of something when the time came.

For years she had faithfully saved her earnings and already had a goodly sum. Soon she would have enough to settle anywhere she wanted. It would be heartbreaking to leave her adopted family of spies. She would have to settle far away where Gundy couldn't find her. There was little doubt the English lord would try to ensure his dangerous secrets were never revealed.

Some niggling unease made Verena turn her head to find the Scotsman's eyes open and riveted on her. She quickly revised her earlier opinion of him. Cairn's eyes weren't merely kind; they were compelling, sparkling with an unnerving intensity. What did he see when he looked at her? Did he see the trustworthy woman she pretended to be, or could he see her deception and cunning?

"I like your hair," he said softly.

The warmth of his voice washed over her, making her shiver as if she had been caressed.

"'Tis unseemly for a widow," she replied demurely, though she made a mental note to wear her hair down as much as possible in his company. "Are you feeling better this morning?"

"I am much better, thank you."

"You must be hungry."

"Not yet. Talk to me for a while."

Despite his words Verena stood up and began putting her pallet away.

"I can cook and talk at the same time," she said, avoiding his peculiar gaze. "Of what would you like to speak?"

"You."

"There isn't much to tell."

"Somehow I doubt that. A woman alone, particularly one as lovely as you, is unusual."

Hadran helped her cultivate a persona, but Verena hesitated. A young maid traveling alone would be wary of confiding in a stranger.

"I know nothing about you," she pointed out. "Not even your name."

She let Cairn consider her words while she stoked the fire and set a cauldron of water to boil over it.

"Cairn McPherson," he said, watching her reaction. She visibly tensed and spun around, though inwardly she rejoiced. Cairn confided in her! Verena hoped she acted properly appalled upon discovering she was trapped in a cottage with the enemy.

"You are a Scot," she said, backing away until her skirts brushed the hearth.

"I won't hurt you." He chuckled. "I couldn't if I wanted to."

"Why are you here?"

"Because I am a fool who believed another man's offer of peace."

She could see the intense fury in his eyes. Gundy had taken a considerable risk by letting Cairn escape. If Hadran's team couldn't complete the assignment, Cairn would be back for revenge. What if he discovered the truth about her? Owen was posted outside the cottage should anything go wrong, but once in Scotland there was little he could do for her.

"I didn't know the depths of Gundy's treachery and will not be fooled again."

"My departure from Langthorne was also less than auspicious," Verena admitted, letting one perfect tear fall down her smooth cheek.

Servants were always at the mercy of their master. From his silence Cairn must have inferred what evil deeds Gundy attempted on a young, unprotected woman to make her flee his castle.

"Gundy is a monster," he growled through clenched teeth.

Verena almost smiled. Cairn did believe her story.

"He is a noble," she corrected. "I am nothing to him."

"Not all nobles are the same."

"Let us eat. It is too early to speak of rage."

This time his hands were steady as he griped the bowl without spilling a drop. His strength was returning with speed, Lord Gundy would be happy to know. It meant they would soon be continuing to Scotland.

"You seem much stronger this evening."

"I feel stronger," Cairn replied as he emptied his second bowl. "Thank you for sharing your food with me."

"'Tis not much," Verena lied. In truth the man ate almost as much as Owen. Verena was pleased. Hadran insisted a healthy appetite was a sign of good health. "I was taught long ago how to stretch a meal."

"By your parents?"

Verena shook her head.

"My grandfather raised me."

"He sounds like a practical man."

"He is."

Verena took the empty bowl from Cairn's hands. She had told him a little of her fabricated history. That would suffice for now. Hadran had instructed her how to tease a man's interest, offering a bit of information at a time. To satisfy his curiosity Cairn would be more likely to divulge information about himself.

Truthfully she didn't seek to learn anything from him. If Cairn knew the location of the treasure her assignment would be considerably different. Since he didn't, all Verena needed from Cairn was a way into his castle. Once there she would find the treasure on her own.

"Would you like some bread?"

Cutting a thick slice of black bread Verena lightly toasted it before the fire. She liberally smeared it with a generous drizzling of honey. Cairn McPherson's affection for sweets was as legendary as his prowess on the battlefield so she was sure to bring the best honey she could find on this assignment.

As she prepared the bread Verena could feel the McPherson's eyes upon her. She wasn't a fool and could easily interpret Cairn's thoughts, but he seemed determined to treat her with respect. He never mentioned his desires, but she knew they were there. It gave her a heady sense of power to know he wanted her.

Chapter 7

Frigid late autumn air blew through the forest, finding its way through the old stable's ancient, crumbling walls. Once it had been a handsome building, regularly housing the fine steeds of Langthorne lords during hunting trips, but as the conflict escalated along the north English border Lord Gundy abandoned the isolated lodge making it the perfect location for Hadran to launch Gundy's plan.

The once-pristine stalls now stank of damp, moldy wood. Piles of rotting hay carried traces of ancient manure. Uncountable spiders lived among the filth, covering nearly every surface with thick white webs. Owen had kept busy hunting in the surrounding area and several carcasses were scattered around the stable to prove his skill. In one corner a space had been cleared for Owen to camp. It was a small victory of order against the decaying structure.

It was late in the afternoon when Verena was finally able to sneak out of the cottage without being detected. Hadran had just returned from Langthorne castle and was anxious to hear of her progress. They stood close together in the clean area next to Owen's pallet, careful not to touch the walls or hay.

The failing daylight cast eerie shadows on the walls, but the three conspirators dared not light a candle. The burning smell, the light, or their voices could easily carry back to their sleeping prisoner. If Cairn McPherson suspected Verena met with the other men their plan would be ruined.

"He told me his name," Verena announced in a whisper.

"Then he is starting to trust you," Hadran said.

"He trusts me enough to tell me his name."

"The McPherson is an intelligent man," said Hadran. "It takes cunning and skill to gain his reputation on a battlefield. You are a beautiful woman, Verena, and the Scot's illness has weakened him, but it is only a matter of time before he begins to question his good fortune, if he does not already. Do not press him too hard."

"I agree." Owen flicked a large spider from his shoulder then crushed it beneath his boot. "We would know this rescue was too easy."

"Make no sexual overtures," Hadran advised. "Not yet. He is attracted because he is a man, but if you appear too interested he will immediately suspect you. Be friendly, but distant and very wary."

"I know what I am doing."

Verena didn't mean to sound petulant, but she had been on countless assignments for Gundy. She knew how to seem intriguing, innocent and trustworthy. Six months ago she had talked her way into the French Queen Anne's private chambers to purloin intimate letters from her lover. The two men's concern was entirely unfounded.

"Aye, girl," said Hadran, playfully tugging Verena's long braid where it lay on her shoulder. It was his gruff, awkward way of showing affection. "If that Scot is not your devoted slave in a fortnight I'll be shocked, but that doesn't mean I won't worry for my best agent."

"I don't know about your best," Owen said grudgingly. He swung a punch at her shoulder. She twisted away, deftly blocking and trapping his fist with one hand and countering with a sharp punch to his gut.

She remembered when they first met long ago. She had been nothing but a nuisance then, an orphan Hadran picked up off the street because he said she had potential. Owen seemed so much older and wiser to Verena even though he was only five years her senior. She looked up to him like a brother.

"Aye," she exclaimed triumphantly as Owen pretended to gasp for breath. "The best! Besides, once Gundy's soldiers are finished with him, the Scot will think I am his only friend."

"I don't know why you won't let me do that," grumbled Owen, referring to the next stage of their plan. "I hate working with Gundy's soldiers."

"As do I," agreed Hadran. "But I will not needlessly risk you or my other agents. You are too valuable to me. I need you to watch Verena in Scotland and I cannot risk the McPherson recognizing you later."

"Gundy's men have been trained for this," said Verena. "They know what to do."

"The Scot's wounds were excessive," protested Owen. "Gundy knew we needed him and yet to allow his men to do that …"

"They were excessive," Hadran broke in with a slight shrug of his shoulders. "But that can't be helped now. He seems to be recovering fine. It was necessary to create a sense of urgency so Verena could act."

"Every day we risk our lives to make Gundy a few pounds richer and he doesn't care enough to follow a simple plan. We made him into what he is today and what do we get? We are as trapped as the peasants in the fields, just better fed. If these soldiers fail …"

"Then Gundy will find great enjoyment in punishing them for their stupidity," snapped Hadran. He was growing weary of Owen's complaints. "They have enough to fear from their lord that they will follow directions. When will the Scot be ready for travel? I need not tell you Gundy is becoming restless."

"Gundy is always restless," said Verena with a laugh. "We can start for Scotland on the morrow provided Gundy's men aren't too enthusiastic in their roles again. He is barely healed enough for light travel. We cannot risk seriously injuring him before I am safely in Scotland."

"I will remind them to be careful. Jon is watching the main road and informed me that a large detachment of men is heading south from the McPherson stronghold." Hadran referred to their youngest operative, a spirited youth from Paris. "They are no doubt the Scottish reinforcements. You should rendezvous with them at the split willow by sunset. That is before the road forks to the east so the Scot will not become suspicious of you traveling so far north with him."

"It will be harder to reach you once you are with the other Scots," Owen cautioned. "But no matter the danger, if you need me, I will come."

"I know, Owen."

Verena spared her friend a smile before turning back to their leader. Owen would come for her, but he was one man who learned to fight in the back alleys and muddy streets of London. Would he be enough to save her should the McPherson learn her true identity? She would rely on herself first and her powers of persuasion. She would be trapped in Scotland with Cairn McPherson and his knights, but she had been in far worse situations. She had no intention of needing Owen's help.

"If everything goes according to plan the McPherson will have no choice but to take you to Scotland."

"Nothing ever goes according to plan," laughed Verena. "But I am adaptable. One way or another I shall enter Scotland and find this mythological treasure."

"It might seem like a myth, but the treasure exists," Hadran insisted. "Somewhere up there is a fortune so secret not even the current laird knows its location. You will find it, Verena, and bring it to Gundy."

"I will not fail."

•

Cairn watched Verena reenter the cabin through half-closed eyes. She said she left to relieve herself, but there was a strange inflection in her voice. She couldn't have betrayed him so far from Langthorne, but the nagging feeling persisted that all was not as it seemed. She was too beautiful, too kind, too selfless and too sexy.

Verena thoughtfully used her body to block the gust of wind from outside, but Cairn could still feel the biting cold. She must be freezing after wandering about in that weather. It was a shame she didn't choose to warm herself in his bed. Sensing Cairn's eyes on her, she softly whispered his name.

"Are you asleep?"

Her voice was low and sleepy reminding him of cozy fires, mulled wine and slow, erotic love.

Cairn squeezed his eyes shut and didn't respond. There was no invitation. It was only his imagination which dared him to touch the creamy expanse of shoulder exposed when she rolled over in sleep.

She was so shy and fearful and at the same time courageous. It made her seem both innocent and alluring. As the fire burned low, bringing a chill to the air, Cairn longed to bury himself in her warmth. That heated response for his enemy, an English woman, made Cairn wary.

After a moment she turned away. She fell asleep soon after, curled into a ball with one hand tucked into her stomach and the other hidden beneath her head. Cairn's stayed awake long into the night, thinking of home and the raven-haired enigma who saved him.

Chapter 8

Verena awoke to the sounds of battle. She heard a loud crash as bodies slammed into each other and the clang of steel meeting steel. Owen was stationed outside protecting her from harm. Was he now fighting for her? Had someone found their hiding place?

Before she was fully conscious her hand went to the knife hidden beneath her pillow and she leapt to her feet.

"S'wounds!" Came an astonished cry.

Verena turned to the noise instinctively to gauge the threat. She blinked rapidly to clear her hazy mind. The sounds of battle were still there, but she was suddenly aware that she had made a colossal mistake.

"'Tis only a storm," said a bemused Cairn. "We are safe."

Mortified, she realized the explosions outside were not the ring of metal and gallop of horse's hooves. Instead they were the cacophony of thunder and lightning of an early winter storm.

Glancing down at herself in mortification, she discovered the light from the dying fire clearly illuminated her shape through her worn chemise. She quickly dropped to her pallet, covering herself with a blanket.

"Thank you," she said shyly. She was not usually so modest—courtesy of growing up with Owen and Hadran, but that upbringing didn't prepare her for the warmth of Cairn's gaze burning through her underwear. When Cairn looked at her like that Verena felt as if she wore nothing at all. She decided she must still be disoriented from waking so suddenly.

"Who is Owen?" Cairn asked, breaking into her thoughts.

She wanted to kick herself. All of her preparation for this assignment, and perhaps her life, would be for naught if she accidentally said the wrong name in her sleep.

"Did I call his name?"

"Aye, before you woke up. Who is he?"

"Owen is my brother, but I have not seen him in many years."

"You didn't mention other relatives."

Verena shrugged, using the motion to more fully cover herself with the blanket. A lie was quickly forming in her mind.

"'Twas not important," she replied. "He is much older and was sent to another of Gundy's holdings as a soldier. I don't know why I dreamt of him."

Cairn nodded, but Verena wasn't sure her answer satisfied him.

"Where did you get the knife?"

"Owen gave it to me years ago."

That was the truth. Owen made several daggers identical to the one he always carried. It was a simple tool, designed for cutting meat or bread. It was also the key to carrying secret messages between Hadran's agents. The handle of each knife was exactly the same width which meant innocuous scraps of parchment, fabric, or animal hides could be wrapped around them revealing vertical patterns of letters written on the material. It was one of many ways the spies communicated and guaranteed that only someone with possession of their knives and the knowledge to use them could read the notes.

"Did he also teach you how to use it?"

"Aye, before he left," she replied, looking him in the eye. There was nothing suspicious about an older brother teaching his younger, pretty sister how to use a knife, particularly if she worked in Lord Gundy's castle. But were her motions too precise, too practiced or smooth?

"I would like to dress," she announced to halt his probing questions. "Could you please turn around?"

Cairn did so, albeit hesitantly. She could sense many more questions forming in his mind. Yesterday he seemed content to accept her aid, but as his recovery progressed Cairn became more inquisitive.

"How do you feel?"

"Much better. I should be able to leave soon."

Much sooner than was wise if Lord Gundy had his way. Verena

couldn't forget she was on a schedule. Her role was one small piece of Gundy's much larger plan. It had only been a few days since Owen knocked Cairn from his horse and most of that time he spent in delirious fever. Cairn needed much more time to recover before he could safely travel, but she couldn't wait. She needed him well and on the road now.

Using what Hadran taught her of herbs and medicine Verena used every poultice, draught, diet, and even astrology to help him. She fed him hearty, savory foods that he told her would balance Cairn's four humours. All people, Hadran insisted, were susceptible to illness when the four bodily fluids of blood, yellow bile, black bile and phlegm were not in balance. Cairn had lost enough blood during his capture so she didn't to bleed him again, but there were plenty of bitter draughts to calm the other fluids.

She glanced longingly at the door as she changed his bandages, wondering when the storm would abate. She hated being trapped indoors for long periods of time, especially when on an assignment.

"I know how you feel."

She realized he had followed her gaze to the door.

"I would also rather be outside."

She forced a smile; a little unnerved that Cairn had read her so easily.

"Do you miss Scotland?"

"A bit." His features softened as he thought of his home. "In truth I spent most of my life in France where I fostered with my brother. I do miss the adventures of youth, exploring the peat bogs and throwing myself down hillsides covered in heather until my skin itched abominably. Scotland has an untamed beauty that is unlike any other land."

"It sounds lovely,"

"Aye, but it is also hard. I am lucky to be in the fertile lowlands, but our harvests are nothing like my brother's in sun-kissed France."

The furious storm ended as suddenly as it began. Verena left the cottage on the pretext of relieving herself, but soon returned, brandishing a tree branch as if it would bite her.

"This is terrible!" she cried, handing the branch to Cairn. He took it and examined the sticky mixture glued to it.

"Lime," he said with a frown. "Where did you find this?"

"Not far away. It looks like it was placed there recently."

"Whoever left this could still be in the area."

Many hunters used sticky lime to coat tree branches and then covered them with seeds and other things to attract birds. When they landed on the branches, the lime stuck to their feet making it impossible for the birds to fly away. This discovery meant someone was hunting in this section of the woods, and Verena and Cairn were dangerously close to being discovered.

"I must leave."

"I know."

"Thank you for all you have done for me. I have no doubt that if not for you I would have died."

"My actions were not so heroic. You would also be hard pressed to leave a wounded stranger in the road, regardless of the circumstances."

"After what that bastard did to me, I am not certain."

Verena paused, allowing her eyes to widen slightly at his anger. She knew how difficult it must be for Cairn. Gundy's betrayal and the loss of his traveling companions was the last in a long line of heartache. In his position she would have called Gundy much worse than a bastard, but the woman she was pretending to be was softer than that.

"I don't like it when you speak so. It reminds me of who and what we are."

She turned away to leave the cottage and was not surprised to hear Cairn's footsteps behind. She knew her words were provocative. Walking away at that moment was a tease. A man like Cairn couldn't resist a reply.

"You are not my enemy," he said in a voice that washed over her like warm honey. "Not after what you have done for me. I am furious at Gundy, but that need not change what lies between us."

She could sense Cairn approaching from behind, but didn't turn around. Every muscle was tense, anticipating his next move, wondering if he would finally dare to touch her. When he did she felt the shock of his fingertips where he lightly grasped her arms. Slowly he pulled her backward into his embrace. She could feel the warmth of his hands through her thick woolen sleeves and the heat radiating from his chest.

She turned in his arms to look questioningly into Cairn's eyes, reading the confusion there. Hadran insisted a man in Cairn's position would be desperate for comfort. He probably hadn't had a woman in weeks, but Cairn was too intelligent to blindly accept his good fortune. She could see the battle being fought in his mind between caution and desire.

He hesitated. Was this happening too fast? He wanted her, but did his feelings go beyond mere lust? In the back of her mind she could hear Hadran's instructions. She must not appear too eager for the laird's embrace. Verena must behave with the proper meekness and fear expected of a woman in her position, but it was hard to think with the Scotsman's amber eyes boring into hers.

It was too fast. A woman in her position wouldn't throw herself at a stranger, no matter how handsome. The woman she was pretending to be would act more cautiously.

She allowed the lime-lined tree branch to fall through her fingers and crash noisily on the ground. They both froze and then she pulled away. She nervously smoothed her clothing as if that brief contact disheveled her. When she finally glanced up, Cairn was watching her with an inscrutable expression.

He wanted her, but Cairn showed a patient restraint that made her suddenly uncomfortable. She was used to gruff men like Owen, Lord Gundy and Hadran. They believed it was their right to take what they wanted. Verena knew how to handle them, but Cairn's patience was not what she expected.

She forced herself to think of Owen's earlier warning. Knights loved to play at chivalry, but she must never forget that all nobles were the same. Despite the tender warmth in his gaze Cairn was a selfish, spoiled lord, exactly like her employer.

"I shall take you to the northern road," Verena offered to break the tense silence. "I know of an old deer trail through the forest that will take you to the crossroads. Few know of it and fewer could find it if they did."

"That is too dangerous."

Too dangerous for her. Something stirred at the thought of him trying to protect her. She shrugged off the feeling.

"I was born here and know this forest well," she replied with forced gaiety. "I have nothing to fear."

"Then you shall seek your grandfather?"

"Aye. We should leave soon, while the weather is clear."

Chapter 9

The sky was oppressively gray as Verena and Cairn made their way through the forest. They knew this was only a brief respite from the storm and hoped it didn't find them on the road. Cairn seemed subdued since they left the relative safety of the cottage, frequently scanning the trees as if he could sense Owen's eyes upon them.

Making a show of examining their trail, she silently signaled into the trees and was happy to hear Owen's immediate response in the form of a bird's shrill cry.

"All is ready," he called to her. Gundy's men were prepared. Owen would follow covertly behind in case she needed help. Verena signaled again with a scratch of her nose and tug on her woolen sleeve. She understood.

While she nursed Cairn to health Owen had marked a trail for them to follow, one that would keep them off the road until they reached the spot where Gundy's men waited. The signs were known only to Hadran's spies. The Scot's untrained eye would think she was leading him from memory. She had only to find the next symbol. There it was, two identical rocks piled upon each other against a tree.

"I have not spent much time in these woods since my husband died," she lied as she deliberately passed the marker. Her backtracking would slow them down, but it would also confuse the Scot in case he noticed the real signs.

"What are you looking for?"

"An oak with a split trunk."

"Is that it?" Cairn asked, pointing in the direction they had come.

"I think so. Aye."

Despite Cairn's injuries they were making swift progress through the woods. He carried a stout branch as a walking stick, no doubt planning to use it as a club should the need arise. It must feel strange for a man like Cairn to be without a weapon. Verena would feel the same without her knives.

A twig snapped behind them and she suddenly found herself thrown against a tree with the Scot's large hand pressed against her mouth.

"Shh!" he hissed. Verena doubted she could take a breath with his body so intimately pressed against hers. She recognized Cairn's protective stance and the way he instinctively shielded her with his body. Hadran would definitely see that as a good sign.

He peered into the direction of the noise as if he could sense their pursuers closing in. She knew it was too soon for the second phase of Hadran's plan and silently chided Owen for following too closely.

After what seemed like an eternity she felt Cairn's body relax and he removed his hand from her mouth. His eyes met hers and she was suddenly aware of a different tension in his gaze. Their eyes communicated a physical awareness that she didn't have to pretend. Every muscle in her body was tense, aware of the heat from Cairn's body sinking into hers.

Cairn let his fingers gently stroke the side of her jaw. His thumb caressed the plumpness of her lower lip. The Scot's frame, which had sought to protect her from harm, now became her prison, pressing her against the rough bark of the tree. As if pulled by a marionette's string her head lifted and her eyes drifted shut.

It was shocking that she could be so bombarded with sensations with the touch of his lips. The massaging pressure was both soothing and tormenting. He caressed her lips with his and without thinking she opened for him.

Cairn groaned with the first gentle brush of her tongue so Verena boldly did it again. She no longer felt the hard bark of the tree against her back; instead she clung to Cairn. Her arms twined around his neck, her fingers tangled in Cairn's silky hair. She forgot about Owen, Hadran and their supposed danger and found herself caught in a new kind of jeopardy. She stopped acting, stopped worrying about what others thought or how she should behave. Verena existed only for his kiss and the sweet sensations Cairn aroused.

Suddenly a bird's angry call sounded, jerking her out of her sensual haze. She wrenched her head away and shuddered as Cairn continued a trail of kisses to the sensitive spot below her ear.

"We cannot do this!"

As her sanity returned she became aware of Cairn's hand resting possessively on her bottom, his other dangerously close to her breast. If he flexed his fingers he would brush against those aching mounds.

Cairn paused, hearing the desperation in her voice. After a tense moment he let her go, but the warmth from his hands lingered like a brand.

"You are right. This is neither the time nor the place for such things."

She nervously studied the ground as if it held all the mysteries of the universe. She was angry with herself for so quickly forgetting their audience and mortified that it was Owen's signal which brought her back. She glanced up at Cairn's words and saw that he was steadily watching her. Did that mean he planned to continue the kiss later?

"I don't like this," Cairn continued when she remained silent. "The forest is too quiet."

Not a single animal disturbed the stillness. The eerie silence made her skin crawl. She knew they were nearing the clearing where Gundy's men waited and unconsciously her body tensed in expectation of the attack.

"Is something wrong?"

As he spoke, Cairn's words seemed to release the forest from its silent spell. Verena heard the familiar twang of a bowstring before she was roughly pushed to the ground by Cairn as an arrow sailed over their heads.

"Rock!" he commanded as another arrow slammed into the tree above them. Without needing clarification she began crawling toward the shelter of a large boulder.

"What happened? Who are these men?" she panted when they were safely hidden behind the boulder. She could see the barely disguised rage boiling within Cairn. He was ready to fight, but unarmed and unarmored Cairn must realize his chances against the bowmen.

"Gundy's men must have found me. I am sorry for this. I didn't want to endanger you."

Despite their situation she couldn't suppress a tiny smile. Cairn feared for her safety. The road to Scotland should be crawling with Gundy's men and if the maid Verena pretended to be was captured with him, things would be very bad for her.

"Can you see them?"

"No. They are hidden behind some trees. I need to draw them out."

"I have an idea."

She knew exactly what to do; she had gone over the plan several times with Hadran and Owen.

"What are you doing?" asked Cairn as he watched her hike up her skirts to reveal the white underdress. She tore off a short strip from the bottom and tied it to a stick then waved the simple flag above her head.

"Don't come out until the right moment."

"What?" he exclaimed, roughly grabbing her arm. "Don't be daft."

"Unhand me," she hissed, incensed that he called Hadran's plan daft. It was certainly ambitious and took a lot for granted, but the old man swore the plan would succeed and she trusted his judgment much more than the Scot's. "Trust me."

Hesitantly Cairn released her arm, but the doubt in his eyes didn't abate. She chose to ignore the cynic beside her.

"Please don't shoot!" she yelled, letting a fearful edge creep into her voice.

"Are you unarmed?" called the archer.

"Aye!"

The knowledge that she was facing strangers from Langthorne was daunting. These men were loyal to Gundy, but Hadran's troupe was loyal to each other first. Verena had no idea what to expect from these men.

"Come out slowly and let me see your hands."

As she rose she was once again stopped by Cairn's heavy hand gripping her arm.

"Don't!" he whispered urgently to her.

She wished she didn't have to.

"It's alright," she replied, taking a deep breath to calm her nerves. "They will not harm me."

Sliding out of his grip Verena stood and turned to face their attackers.

"Where is the man?" the archer demanded.

"He is hurt. I think he is dying."

At those words two men stepped into the clearing. They were young soldiers, probably no more than nineteen years old. Unfortunately their faces showed no recognition of her. Hadran no doubt told the soldiers the Scot would be traveling along this path and mayhap that he was traveling with a woman, but he didn't tell them the woman was working for Gundy. It was perhaps better that way in case the soldiers were captured by Cairn's men; however it would place her in more danger. The soldiers didn't see her as an ally and would feel no qualms about dispatching her should she cause trouble ... as the plan dictated she must.

"Please don't hurt me!" she exclaimed dramatically, taking a step backward and to the side. Her fearful words seemed to bolster the young men's confidence and one of them took a threatening step toward her. His companion followed more slowly.

"What is a pretty maid like you doing with that barbarian?"

"Barbarian? What do you mean?"

She continued to move backward, positioning the two men so their backs faced Cairn's hiding spot.

"He is a murdering Scot," replied the first, gaining more confidence in his role. His lecherous gaze slowly roamed over her disheveled body. "But don't worry, you are safe with us."

Her eyes widened comically at his words. Where did Gundy find such a youth? Only an idiot would completely disregard Cairn without visual confirmation of his demise. In addition to not knowing she was his ally, the man obviously didn't know the true nature of this trap. If he suspected Cairn was not injured and merely lay in wait the young soldier would be more cautious.

•

"Did he hurt you?" asked the other man. He seemed to be the nicer and wiser of the two. Though he followed his friend, he glanced repeatedly at the boulder where Cairn hid. Verena had to do something to catch his attention. She nodded, pointing to an invisible bruise on her bosom.

"Let me see that," said the first.

She obligingly lowered the bodice of her gown a tantalizing half inch. Her ploy worked and the other man forgot all about Cairn. She wanted to roll her eyes. How could men allow themselves to be sidetracked so easily? With chagrin Verena remembered she had been no different a few moments ago when Cairn kissed her.

She attempted to step backward again and was suddenly grabbed by the foolhardy lad and roughly pulled against him. He ran his callused hand along her forearm and she theatrically shrank from his touch. The young man certainly had the brawn to make up for his lack of brains.

"What are you doing?" she exclaimed loudly, pushing ineffectually against him. "Someone help me!"

"What's wrong?" asked the first soldier. "You weren't fighting the Scot."

On cue Cairn stepped from behind the boulder clutching his tree limb. Since the soldiers' attention was focused on Verena they never saw the branch that connected to the second man's skull with a loud and sickening crack.

Suddenly aware of the danger the first man roughly shoved her away and turned to face Cairn who unfortunately had been thrown off-balance by the force of his swing. Verena swore under her breath. She knew he wasn't ready for battle after his ordeal in Langthorne. Nevertheless he recovered quickly, letting the force of the blow gracefully glide into another swing.

The first soldier unsheathed a long knife and she jumped on him. She hooked his ankle and tackled him to the ground. She used her all of her body weight to pin him, but was not heavy enough to hold him for long. He buckled to dislodge her as she tried to wrestle the knife from his grip.

In the second before he broke free Verena was able to position the knife so that the blade pointed up. Taking a deep breath she fell on it, jerking as if the man pulled her down.

The soldier froze, staring at her in shock. She could see the horror on his face as he felt her warm blood on his chest. Despite his foolish bravado, the archer was painfully young. He pushed away from her, but just as he managed to break free Cairn's tree branch slammed into his head. He fell unconscious to the frozen ground.

"Are you alright?" Cairn asked. He stood above her clutching his side where a dark red spot stained his tunic. Cairn must have pulled his stitches during the fight.

"I don't think so," she answered gesturing to the wound on her shoulder. Cairn noisily sucked in his breath as he saw the blood rapidly soaking the front of her dress.

"You little idiot! He could have killed you."

Cairn tore one lavishly embroidered sleeve from his tunic and used it to staunch the blood. He then ripped off his other sleeve and used it to tie a crude bandage on top.

"You are welcome," Verena said.

According to Hadran's plan an arrow was supposed to lightly graze her right arm, injuring her and forcing Cairn to take Verena to Scotland. Unfortunately because of Cairn's quick reflexes or poor shooting she was forced into more extreme measures.

"You should have run when he released you."

"I was trying to help."

Cairn swore, adding more pressure to her wound. The pain was enough to bring tears to her eyes. Though Hadran often said tears were one of the greatest weapons a woman could use against a man, she stubbornly turned away, reluctant to have Cairn see her weakness. He should be praising her for her courage, not berating her for stupidity. She might have saved his pathetic life.

"What is this?" he asked, turning her head to face him. "Tears?"

She angrily wrenched her head away, using her uninjured arm to wipe the wet from her cheeks.

"It hurts."

With those words all the fight seemed to drain out of Cairn. He gazed at her with such a fearful tenderness she had to look away. He was afraid for her. Cairn feared he wouldn't be able to protect her from his enemies. That was the reason for his gruff behavior.

"We should have parted long ago," he began uncomfortably. "But it was easier to accept your help. I should have known better."

"I chose this," she lied earnestly, placing her hand over his. "I chose to help you. No matter what happens you are not responsible for my actions."

"I cannot protect you here."

"I didn't ask you to," she replied with a touch of humor.

"I think the bleeding has stopped."

Cairn pulled his hand from her wound and looked over her critically, then at their two attackers. He had to take her to Scotland now. The staged attack should have proven she was trustworthy and that it was too dangerous to leave her in England.

"We should leave soon in case they have friends nearby."

She painfully climbed to her feet with Cairn's help. After this she would have several bruises in addition to the knife wound. Though she swayed, Verena held her ground, gritting her teeth until the pain was under control.

Cairn warily watched her in case she decided to swoon.

"I am ready."

She stared at her blood-soaked dress and hoped the words were true.

Chapter 10

"We are close," Verena announced.

They had traveled along the main road since their encounter with Gundy's soldiers, darting quickly into the underbrush when they sensed someone's approach. Soon they would reach the crossroads where she told Cairn they would part ways. According to Hadran a party of Scottish knights led by Cairn's brother Andreu was rapidly approaching. They should have met when accosted by Gundy's men, but either the soldiers acted too quickly or Cairn's men traveled too slowly. Verena sighed. After years of working for Gundy she stopped expecting things to go smoothly.

"Soon," Cairn whispered under his breath.

He increased his pace, eager to be gone from England. She opened her mouth to protest and then thought better of it. She understood his excitement. It would be nice to be free of Gundy's sinister control, but in her experience appearances were often deceiving. Even among the wilds of Scotland neither of them could escape Gundy's reach.

Suddenly they heard angry shouts behind. She whipped about, momentarily forgetting her injury. Their earlier attackers were crashing through the underbrush in hot pursuit, trying to get a clear shot through the trees.

"You didn't kill them?" she exclaimed in shock.

"I suppose you could only expect bloodshed from a bloodthirsty Scot."

"Nay!"

But that was exactly what she expected and was the reason Hadran insisted on using Gundy's disposable soldiers. Owen and Hadran would have slit both men's throats and then calmly divested their bodies of valuables. She had become so used to this procedure that Cairn's mercy struck her as absurd.

"Better their lives than yours," Hadran had often said. 'All threats must be dealt with in the most final way possible.'

Cairn took her hand and dragged her off the road, hoping to lose their pursuers in the dense vegetation. They ran together, each supporting the other, ignoring the blood that dripped from freshly opened wounds and bruises that had only begun to heal.

Forgetting propriety, she hiked her skirts up to her knees, concentrating all of her energy in putting one foot in front of the other. The blows to the head would slow their attackers, but Cairn and Verena were also moving at a sluggish pace. They were too weak to maintain even that brutal speed for long. Cairn was pale from the strain and his breath was ragged. Soon they would be forced to stop with or without meeting Cairn's soldiers.

A tree root seemed to rise up from the ground and trapped her leg before she could swerve away from it. She fell hard onto her injured side with enough force to make her see stars.

"Get up!" Cairn barked, yanking her to her feet.

She was breathless and covered in blood. The pain was intense and she almost told Cairn to leave her be, but she was on her feet again before she could utter the words. She did manage to swear indelicately as she was forced to keep running.

The sound of footsteps rapidly increased behind them and somehow she was able to convince her exhausted body to move. Where were Hadran and Owen? They were supposed to keep Verena out of real danger. The foolish, untried soldiers didn't know she was working for Gundy and would treat her as a criminal. If Owen was watching as he said he would, he should have assisted in some way.

They swerved around a large tree and Cairn shoved her ahead, ordering her to keep running. He then turned to face Gundy's men from his hidden position behind the ancient wood, brandishing the small sword he had stolen from the unconscious soldiers. Though the strain of their journey was evident in his sweat and bloodstained clothes, he was burning with anger, eager to smash someone's head in retaliation for Gundy's crimes.

Exhausted and nearly delirious with pain, she defied his order and stopped, thinking to aid Cairn in some way. If Owen wouldn't protect her, she would have to protect herself. Her favorite knife was held loosely by the blade, ready to throw. Another was hidden in the folds of her skirt. She blinked rapidly to clear her vision and even slapped her cheeks when her exhausted body wouldn't comply fast enough.

Above the roaring in her ears Verena heard the twang of a bowstring being released and then another. Cairn fell to the ground in an instant, draping his heavy body over hers. Her last thought before darkness overtook her was how surprisingly good it felt to be in his protective embrace.

Chapter 11

For a moment the forest was quiet and Cairn took advantage of the stillness to catch his breath. As soon as he heard the twang of a bowstring he pushed her to the ground. He didn't know who shot the arrows, but Cairn managed to glance up as he fell and saw one of them pierce the throat of Gundy's soldier. A second arrow found its mark in his friend's cheek.

"Cairn?" a familiar voice called. He rolled off her and saw his elder brother Andreu and a score of men emerge from the trees.

"Aye. You have no idea how pleased I am to see you."

"Where are the others?" asked a giant of a man named Fergus as he helped Cairn to his feet. His beefy fist gripped the pommel of his unsheathed sword, expecting Lord Gundy's army to attack at any moment.

"Dead. All dead."

"Dead?" Fergus repeated. "How? Gundy invited you in peace. I knew you couldn't trust that murdering English swine!"

"It was an ambush. I and a couple others survived, but they were slain in Gundy's dungeons. I managed to escape."

"And her?" Andreu asked, peering at her sleeping form with interest.

"She's mine." Cairn surprised himself with the possessiveness of his tone. "More explanations will have to wait, as will my revenge. Now we must heal and make preparations."

Fergus opened his mouth to protest, but paused. Though Cairn didn't say more, the colorful bruises and blood-soaked clothing was enough to quiet his men. They were so close to Langthorne. It was maddening that they had to retreat, but Cairn was in no condition to fight and Verena needed medical attention. Revenge would have to wait.

"Let's see those wounds," said Andreu, reaching for his brother. Cairn pulled back stubbornly.

"The woman first."

Andreu raised an eyebrow, but didn't argue. Turning back to the woman Andreu was able to examine her more closely. The lass looked like a beautiful street urchin with her stubborn jaw and frowning mouth. There was a gentle delicacy in her features that spoke of too many missed meals. Her slender fingers were loosely coiled into fists, but when Andreu lifted her into his arms, she curled about him like a trusting child.

Carefully he laid her on the blanket one of the men spread out on the mossy ground. He untied her bodice to reveal the deep wound and saw at once it was recent, perhaps only an hour or so old. Cairn's stepmother would likely throw a fit when she saw the bloodstained sleeves that she had so carefully embroidered.

Andreu cleaned the wound, stitched it shut and bandaged it. Luckily the woman remained unconscious throughout his attentions. He took off his cloak to wrap it about her, smiling as she seemed to disappear in its voluminous folds. She tried to snuggle into its warmth and winced as the movement must have pulled her stitches. Without thinking he reached out to comfort her, but was stopped by Cairn's sharp voice.

"Have you forgotten me, brother?" he asked testily. Andreu immediately turned back to Cairn, intrigued by the show of jealousy.

"You will be fine. Someone has taken excellent care of you."

The bleeding had already stopped and required only fresh bandages.

"We are safe for the moment," said Cairn. "Have those bodies hidden and guards posted. We will leave at first light."

"And her?" Andreu wanted to know.

Verena said Cairn was not responsible for her, but it was infuriating that he couldn't guarantee her safety. Cairn had ordered the woman to run but she chose to stay and fight by his side with that pitiful looking knife. That decision pleased and infuriated Cairn.

He had planned to separate at the crossroads, but now it was too late. Cairn couldn't leave her after she saved his life, not after the injury she sustained because of him, and certainly not after that kiss.

It was disconcerting to realize Cairn had lost himself so completely despite the danger they both faced. He wanted to protect her, yet at the first opportunity Cairn behaved like an untried youth. It was no wonder Verena pulled away so abruptly. She was such a confusing mix of innocent and temptress that Cairn never knew what to expect. To have faced abuse in Langthorne and then find herself pawed by the one man she was beginning to trust must have been more than she could bear.

He had avoided thinking of it before when his mind was solely focused on returning to Scotland. Now that they were out of immediate danger Cairn couldn't forget her perfect lips. They had felt as soft as he imagined and when she opened for him it was like tasting ambrosia. With that first brush of her tongue Cairn knew he would never allow Gundy to reach her again.

"She comes with us."

Chapter 12

It was late that night when Verena awoke, lying on a bed of luxurious furs. It was almost too dark to see, but she could make out the inside of a crude shelter and surmised they had finally met with the Scottish reinforcements. Only nobility could travel so comfortably, with pack horses and mules laden with unnecessary items. As she snuggled into a cocoon of warmth, she didn't begrudge the vice.

Outside the noises from Cairn's party were muted, but still discernible. Each one was so distinct she could imagine someone seeing to the horses, checking supplies, whispering a joke and grunting in amusement. Small sounds that would easily blend into the night, but Hadran had taught her how to listen.

She yawned, blinking tired eyes and contemplated going back to sleep. Her shoulder ached abominably making it difficult to relax. She had sustained injuries before; it was a hazard of her profession, but knowing her wound was superficial didn't lessen the pain.

A movement caught her eye and she glanced up, ashamed to find she was not alone inside the shelter. At first, she assumed the shape a few feet away to be merely a pile of clothes or blankets, but as her eyes focused she could make out a sliver of moonlight highlighting Cairn's cheek and his sparkling eyes, which were open and focused on her.

She gasped at the intrusion. Her cheeks flamed in the darkness. Though he seemed relaxed, she could feel the tension as their eyes met. The beat of her heart increased to a furious pound. Cairn's gaze dropped to her lips and she had to force herself not to nervously lick them.

Did he think of their kiss? Verena remembered how perfectly she fit in his embrace. She remembered the warmth of his skin, his smell and the intoxicating play of their tongues and lips. His lovemaking would be magical.

That thought was like ice across her fevered skin. She had no business imagining his lovemaking. Cairn was a means to getting the treasure. Nothing more. Verena abruptly wrenched her gaze from Cairn's, turning away to block out the sight of him, but even with her eyes averted she could feel Cairn's magnetic presence.

It was just a kiss, her mind argued, but she knew it was so much more. With that kiss she found herself dangerously drawn to the man she was supposed to betray. Her effectiveness as a spy depended upon her ability to rationalize and remain unattached. Even physical desire could jeopardize the mission.

Cairn was certainly not the spoiled noble she expected. He tried to protect her though they were virtual strangers, and despite the sensual tension between them, Cairn had behaved with remarkable restraint. What would be the result of the unspoken promise that lay between them? That question plagued her imagination until she forced her exhausted mind to sleep.

Cairn stayed awake for some time thinking of their predicament. Remembering that passionate kiss was enough to have him throbbing in expectation. Verena was beautiful and Cairn hadn't bedded a woman in a long time, but he couldn't afford to be distracted by a comely lass. There were more pressing concerns than bed sport.

This would be a difficult winter for the McPherson clan. Cairn knew a treaty with Lord Gundy was risky, but couldn't afford to ignore his threat during these hard times. The raiding across their border had to stop so his people could focus on rebuilding.

Though the Scottish and English armies never met during Perkin Warbeck's unsuccessful maneuvering, border lands like Langthorne were ravaged as Scotland sided with Warbeck and England sided with King Henry VII. A truce could only benefit them, but Lord Gundy had shown he was not interested in peace or the wellbeing of his tenants. He wanted the glory of war and his own revenge.

The McPhersons lay next to a viper poised and ready to strike. Lord Gundy saw the clan at its most vulnerable and decided to take advantage. The raids wouldn't cease, they would increase, forcing men away from the fields to defend their homes. Cairn's victories on the tournament field didn't seem like adequate preparation for running an estate, but he understood war.

Verena tossed in her sleep, throwing the covers off her upper body and exposing her bandaged shoulder. Andreu had loosened her bodice in order to operate and had not tied it back. Now it gaped open to reveal a creamy expanse of flesh. If she took a deep breath her bodice would fall, revealing the tips of her nipples to Cairn's hungry gaze.

Resolutely Cairn threw off his covers, donned his boots and cloak and stepped outside. He knew he would get no rest this evening.

He approached Fergus who stood guard over their camp and nodded in greeting. He was a McPherson and not one of the men Cairn brought from France, with an infectious grin and burly, uncouth manners that had quickly won Cairn's affection. He had hesitated to bring Fergus into England with his earlier party, thinking the man's distrust for anything English would hinder negotiations. Fergus lived his entire life bordering Gundy's estate and had railed forcefully against trusting him.

"My lord," Fergus began, reading the direction of Cairn's thoughts. "I know why you went to Langthorne. Despite what I said before, if I was in your place I would have done the same."

Cairn looked at Fergus in surprise. He wasn't expecting equanimity from the gruff soldier.

"'Twas not your decision to make, it was mine. And I chose wrongly."

"Nay, you didn't," Fergus insisted. "Gundy was the one that broke his promise. To attack you like that after he offered peace ... even for an Englishman that was wrong."

Cairn chuckled dryly in the darkness.

"Even for an Englishman."

He turned and walked farther into the woods. Half-formed plans rose in his mind and were quickly discarded. Winter was fast approaching and instead of helping his clan prepare Cairn languished in a dungeon. He would have to work day and night to recover the lost time.

Suddenly Cairn paused as some unseen threat caused the hair on the back of his neck to rise. He felt he was being watched by malignant eyes. It could be a wolf or other forest predator, or perhaps the hunter whose lime trap Verena had found. The two young archers were dead, but there must be other soldiers searching these woods.

The thick clouds shifted overhead, allowing a small ray of moonlight to filter through the trees and Cairn finally saw his watcher. It was a bear of a man dressed in muted colors that blended perfectly into the darkness. His arms and face had been liberally smeared with dirt. The only features that stood out were his peculiar eyes that resembled live coals against the dross of his background. So well did he blend in to his surroundings that Cairn blinked, wondering if he were truly a man at all, or some vengeful spirit sent to plague him.

He must be from Langthorne, though he wore no livery. Nor did he carry a tool to distinguish himself as a hunter or woodsman. The man shifted his weight slightly and Cairn tensed, recognizing the man's fighting stance and intent. This was no hunter.

"To arms!"

Instantly Cairn's men sprang up clutching their weapons and itching for a fight. They ran to their lord looking about for signs of a threat, but the forest man had vanished.

"A man is watching us," Cairn explained. "He disappeared through those trees."

Instantly they spread out, combing the forest for any sign of disturbance.

"What is it?" Verena asked, groggily climbing out of the shelter. She looked adorably tousled with her unbound hair, unlaced dress and bootless feet. The knife was once again clutched in her small hand. Cairn noticed more than a few of his men casting curious glances at her over their shoulders as they left in search of the man.

"Stay inside!" he barked a little harsher than he intended.

She blinked at Cairn's tone and opened her mouth to argue, but after casting a worried glance at the giant Scotsmen surrounding her, she demurely returned to the tent. Verena had gotten over her initial fear of Cairn, but he was weakened from his ordeal and she had spent days nursing him to health. She had no such relationship with his men.

"Fergus," Cairn called before he went off with the others. "Guard the woman. Keep her here."

"Aye, milord."

"What exactly are we looking for?" asked Andreu after they scoured the forest for nearly an hour. Aside from a few recent footprints they had failed to find any sign of someone in the trees.

"A man. His clothes and everything about him were made for concealment so I think he has been watching for some time. He was alone, but unafraid so there might be others nearby."

"I don't like this," said Andreu. "It feels like a trap."

"I agree. We have a few more hours of night and I suggest we use them. The faster we leave England the better."

With those words the anticipation of a fight turned to wariness. Each man cast uneasy glances at the forest expecting an army of English soldiers to appear.

Verena had stayed in the tent but Cairn could see her wide, terrified eyes watching from the entrance. She was wise enough not to try to run with Fergus hovering about like a grumpy bear, nor did she scream, cry or speak. The lass merely watched and waited.

Cairn started toward her and gestured for his brother to do the same. Verena noticed the approach of the large Frenchman first and took several steps backward in fear. A Norse ancestor had turned his stepbrother into a formidable giant.

"Verena, this is my brother Andreu."

She looked from one man to the other and frowned, not seeing any resemblance. Though both men were large and muscular of frame the similarities ended there. Where Cairn's jaw was square and strongly cut, Andreu's was more delicate, his overall features more refined and classically handsome to Cairn's ruggedness.

Hadran had told her Cairn's brother was not related by blood; rather he was the son of Cairn's stepmother from her first husband. When the lads were fostered together they became fast friends.

"Milord," she mumbled. She wished he wouldn't stare at her so, as if Verena was some curious new beast they happened upon. She forced herself to meet his inquiring gaze.

"It seems this adventure has yielded many surprises," he said with surprising gallantry, taking her hand to place a light kiss on her knuckles. "I look forward to hearing about them—and you."

"How is your shoulder?" Cairn interrupted.

"Awful. I expect it to hurt for some time, but there is a skilled healer in my grandfather's village."

Cairn glanced significantly at his brother and taking the hint Andreu left to finish saddling his mount. It was time to tell Verena the truth.

"I want you to join me and my clan in Scotland."

Verena gulped, almost giddy with excitement. This was what she had been waiting for. Owen had his doubts, but Hadran knew Cairn would take her back to Scotland and the old man was always right.

A true Englishwoman would be terrified to find herself surrounded by Scottish warriors. Returning with them to Scotland would be unthinkable. So Verena allowed her eyes to go huge with fright, staring at Cairn as if he meant to ravage her.

"I ... I cannot," she stammered. "My grandfather—"

"I promise you shall safely reach him, but I cannot risk your capture now. I will keep you safe in my homeland until I can escort you to your family."

After the days they had shared together she knew Cairn would do his best to protect her. It was strange to be the recipient of such esteem. Of course Owen would protect her too, but that was different somehow. That knowledge didn't cause a warm tingling of excitement in her belly.

"You said we would part at the crossroads. You said you would let me go."

"Gundy's men still comb this forest and they have probably seen us together. I must take you to Scotland."

"I won't tell them anything."

"If Gundy wants you to talk, you will talk. What do you think will happen once he knows what you have done? I will not allow you to be captured and I will not risk more men on foolishness."

"My freedom is not foolishness!"

Verena turned to run, but before she could take more than a step Cairn's heavy arms encircled her, lifting her off her feet. She made a show of struggling against him so he believed she was in earnest. His heavy hand clamped firmly over her mouth so she couldn't scream. Soon her hands and feet were bound with rope; a rag was stuffed into her mouth.

Andreu appeared and carried her to a small stallion where she was dumped unceremoniously in front of Cairn in the saddle. The animal sidestepped nervously when Verena was placed on his back, uncomfortable with her foreign, struggling weight.

"Easy Drago."

The animal was truly the dragon Cairn named him with a fiery temper to match. It was a beautiful creature—strong, healthy, well cared for and much nicer than anything Verena had ridden. His brown velvet coat was broken by patches of white on his face and forelocks. With one hand Cairn stroked the animal's neck. The other arm encircled her like a band of iron.

"If you continue to struggle he will throw us both. Someday perhaps you will understand the necessity of my actions."

How could a voice be so gentle and yet so stern? Cairn sounded calm and reasonable. His voice had not changed from the soothing tone he used on the horse, but there was an unmistakable command in his words and she dared not disobey. It was enough that she had suffered a knife wound for this mission, she wouldn't unnecessarily risk her neck being thrown by a horse. She stopped struggling, but didn't relax into his embrace.

"We should hurry," Cairn said to his men. "We are not out of danger yet."

"Oui," agreed Andreu. "I feel these trees have eyes."

Was it Owen that unnerved the soldiers? He knew better than to let himself be seen, but there was an unrestrained wildness about him that encouraged Owen to show off. What was the point of their elaborate masquerades if their deeds went unknown? he often asked. Once they stole the French Queen Anne's precious love letters from an admirer and Owen insisted on leaving a bloody dagger where the letters were hidden. He had laughed about the incident for months, certain the gruesome sight must have thrown the Queen into a panic. She could easily imagine him leaving a similar clue to taunt the Scotsmen.

How would Owen watch over her inside Cairn's castle? Would he seek employment in the village? Or perhaps Owen would camp in the nearby woods. What if something went wrong and he couldn't reach her? It might be days before it was safe for them to meet again.

She forced herself to relax. Cairn had been remarkably kind during the last few days. She had no reason to believe he would suddenly change in Scotland. Besides, Verena knew she was the greatest threat to her mission.

She remembered their kiss in the woods and waking up to find Cairn intently staring at her. It was strange to realize Verena was attracted to the man she was sent to betray. If Hadran knew Verena was having such feelings he would be understandably worried. He might even pull her from the assignment. No matter what Verena couldn't allow her attraction to cloud her judgment, nor could she give Owen or Hadran any reason to doubt her.

Chapter 13

Verena blinked tired eyes at the unexpected sunrise. She thought to only close her eyes for a moment and instead found she had slept through most of the journey. They had long ago crossed the border into Scotland and their horses' slower pace rocked her into an easy sleep. Cairn was exhausted after a sleepless night and their adventure in the woods, yet he held himself proudly erect in the saddle, scanning their surroundings for danger.

The morning sky was multiple shades of grey broken by brief patches where the sun poked through thick clouds. They had left the forest behind and approached a small, rundown village. Beyond that she could see a large, foreboding castle rising from the ground. There was a certain charm to the barren terrain, but the icy wind slicing through her garments was anything but cozy.

She straightened self-consciously, embarrassed to find her arms had crept around Cairn like a vine, unconsciously greedy for his warmth. Sometime during the night Cairn had released her restraints and wrapped his cloak around them both. A strong wind swept over their party and though she shivered, she firmly pushed the cloak away. She must act as one recently kidnapped, with fear, anger and distrust of the big warriors.

"This is your home?" she asked unnecessarily. Her words were harsh and dismissive.

There was an air of poverty and neglect in the village. Across Scotland people were suffering under the inept leadership of their king, famine and plague. Cairn's father had been ill for many years and the McPhersons had suffered more than most without a strong leader to guide them through the troubled times.

What had driven Cairn away for so many years? Was Cairn

disappointed with his new life? The land was so different from Southern France where he spent his youth. Did he look at Scotland's rugged beauty with scorn?

"Aye, though in truth I have not spent much time here since childhood. I was fostered in France with Andreu. Then we went on campaign together."

"What shall become of me here?"

"Be at ease. No harm shall come to you in Scotland."

"You must release me. I will be with my family by nightfall and no one would know I helped you."

"I fear the worst is yet to come from Langthorne. I cannot allow you to travel the border unescorted and I cannot spare the men to safely see you home. You must be patient."

"My fate is not your concern. I absolve you of all responsibility. Please let me go."

"I told you I cannot," Cairn snapped. The brittle edge of his voice warned her not to test his patience or she might find herself gagged again. He was under tremendous pressure with the sudden death of his father, taking over the clan, Gundy's betrayal, their desperate flight and a sleepless night.

"Do you think Lord Gundy will attack you?" she asked hesitantly.

"Gundy imprisoned me for a reason. Yet he gained nothing from the endeavor. I fear he will try again for whatever he is after. I must be prepared."

"What do you think he desires from you?"

"I do not know. Perhaps he sought revenge for years of raiding across our border. Mayhap he is merely mad. How well did you know him?"

"Not very well. I was chambermaid to his late wife. It was not a love match."

"Only a saint could love that jackal," broke in Andreu. "I heard his wife came from France. Is that true?

"Indeed. Milady Fleurie de Moy was arranged to marry Lord Gundy during the signing of the Peace of Etaples ten years ago."

Andreu immediately let out a rapid string of French profanity at how a Norman must suffer unhappy matrimony to an English cur.

"Milady taught me some French before she passed," Verena said innocently. "But I do not understand all of your words."

"Never mind that," said Andreu. "What my brother said is the truth. You have nothing to fear while you are in Scotland."

"Why are those trees so close to the castle?" Verena asked to change the subject. "The forests around Langthorne are cleared for at least a mile in all directions."

"That ancient forest is said to be protected by spirits," Cairn replied. "Despite the cold no one dares cut wood from those trees. My grandfather, the Old Lord, was buried there in a mound in honor of our Norse ancestors. You'll find my clan is extremely superstitious and most agree that a forest full of vengeful spirits is more fearsome than corporeal enemies."

"A burial mound? I have never heard of such a thing."

"It is not a Christian practice. The church excommunicated him for his wild, stubborn ways, but instead of repenting my grandfather decided to benefit from his reputation. None dared meet him on a battlefield for fear that their souls as well as their lives would be taken."

In preparing for this assignment she had heard many tales of the Old Lord that were as fantastic as they were improbable. According to legend he murdered his wife for putting too much garlic in his food, could kill a man with a single look and picked his teeth with the bones of children. She didn't believe most of that foolishness and judging from Cairn's dismissive tone neither did he. Yet there was a wicked pleasure in repeating the frightening tales.

"We also talk of your grandfather in Langthorne. Were the stories true?"

"No one knows. My grandfather didn't confide in his family or the priest and took his secrets to the grave. The clan was suffering under a terrible famine and he conjured a vast treasure to save us. My clan may be pious, but they know better than to question such good fortune."

"So the treasure does exist!"

Cairn let out a dry laugh.

"I do not know where the Old Lord found the money. He probably sold off some family trinkets. These stories are made up only to frighten children."

"But if it were true …"

"If the McPhersons had a treasure things would be different, but I'll not sell my soul to obtain it."

According to legend the Old Lord made a pact with the devil and was granted the wealth and power to save his clan, but some people like Lord Gundy suspected a different explanation. Centuries ago the Romans established a silver mine on land now belonging to the McPhersons. The mine had long since yielded its last treasures, but every few years a bit of silver appeared to save the people from disaster. It didn't take a genius to realize some of the Roman treasure must still remain hidden.

She didn't know why Cairn was not told its location. Perhaps his father didn't have a chance to tell him before he died. That was perfect for Lord Gundy. Without that money the McPhersons were easy prey to his plans.

Several villagers appeared to watch their procession through the muddy streets. Fergus and a few soldiers nodded in greeting, but the division between the Scots and Cairn's French soldiers was glaringly obvious. They were shy around their new lord and unsure how to greet him. The conspicuous absence of his original party spoke volumes about the success of Cairn's mission in England.

She straightened in the saddle feeling the curious eyes of the villagers fall on her. Before their frank regard Verena felt like a curiosity on display. She would have to be on her best behavior to win their trust.

In order for her plan to succeed she had to carefully question some of the villagers on the whereabouts of the treasure. Though uncomfortable being ogled by so many people, Verena forced herself to think positively. At least the castle folk would have heard of their arrival by now. If she was lucky perhaps an enterprising soul was already heating water for a bath.

They soon left the village and began a steep climb up the side of a mountain toward a large castle. It was bigger than Langthorne, but not as ostentatious, built much earlier when castles were prized more for function than beauty. The stones were darkened with age, but stood proudly against the barren landscape as if daring the world to try and move them. Behind the castle was the so-called magical forest where his grandfather, the Old Lord, was buried. She couldn't wait to explore it.

"This is it," said Cairn. There was a peculiar tightness in his voice. After his trials in Langthorne Verena thought he would be excited to come home, but Cairn's home was among the sun-kissed forests of Southern France with his brother Andreu. This place meant only responsibility.

"It is … big," Verena hedged, not knowing how else to describe the massive stone structure.

"Aye. I hope in time you will come to like it. My stepmother, Ivone, is the lady of the castle. You will meet her soon."

Their horses increased their tired gait as they approached the castle, eager to be inside their warm stables. She caught their excitement. She was also looking forward to a comfortable bed and hot meal.

As they entered the castle she appreciatively took note of its defenses. The thick curtain wall was footed at an angle to counter undermining and deflect battering rams. Not a single window graced the outer wall, but the top of the battlements were dotted with evenly spaced embrasures or open spaces for archers to fire and then retreat behind stone merlons. Soldiers stood at stiff attention atop the allure, the walking space along the top of the curtain wall.

Past the gates their party had to go through a stone passage known as a barbican, designed to narrow an invading army into its tiny confines. Small openings were cut into the stone around them where archers waited with deadly bows. The most inept archer couldn't miss at such range and yet was protected by the thick walls of stone surrounding him. Above their heads a long slit was cut into the stone through which boiling water or oil could be poured.

It was hard to repress the shiver of fear that slid up her spine seeing that. She suddenly understood why Gundy was hesitant to launch a full invasion. Even undermanned and underfunded the McPherson castle would be nearly impossible to take. Gundy's only chance would be a long siege, but a foreign army in Scotland was a less than ideal situation.

Verena breathed a sigh of relief as they passed through the barbican and into a large courtyard. A group awaited them at the entrance to the keep, including a lady unlike any she had seen before. She was tall for a woman and strikingly beautiful, but what stood out the most was the quiet dignity with which she held herself. She was regal and stood aloof from those around her. Her clothing and manner suggested she was a lady of substance and she surmised this was Ivone, Cairn's stepmother and lady of the castle.

Cairn dismounted and helped Verena out of the saddle. Stable boys instantly appeared to lead their weary horses away.

"Lady Ivone," said Cairn as he bowed before her. He bent to kiss the lady's proffered hand.

"My son," replied the woman in a voice both sweet and commanding.

Cairn rose stiffly and then stepped aside so his brother could greet the lady. Andreu was also strangely formal and Verena wondered at their sincerity. They greeted each other more like strangers than family. Verena recalled that Cairn rarely visited Scotland after he was squired. Was this woman the reason for his estrangement?

"Mother," said Andreu. "It is good to see you."

"And you, my son," replied Lady Ivone. "I hope you will be staying longer this time."

"I will stay as long as possible," said Andreu. "You are looking well, mother. The Scottish air agrees with you."

Ivone waved dismissively at her son's praise.

"You know I cannot abide this frigid country," she replied, turning her piercing gaze on Verena. "Who is this?"

Cairn cleared his throat and gestured for Verena to approach. "Lady Ivone," he replied. "It is my honor to present Verena of Langthorne. Verena, this is Ivone de la Marche, my stepmother."

After an introduction like that Verena had no choice but to sink into a deep curtsy. Why did Cairn use such an elegant introduction on a low-born woman like her? Perhaps he felt it was important that Lady Ivone didn't know her humble origins.

"My Lady," Verena said, rising to her feet. She forced herself to put on a pleasantly bland expression as the woman inspected her from head to toe. She wished she had the chance to bathe or comb her hair before their arrival. Her too-tight gown was soaked with dried blood and mud and she could feel tendrils of hair escaping from her plaits to drift in the light breeze. She forced herself not to pat them down lest the gesture be taken for a sign of nervousness. Though she didn't flinch beneath the woman's uncompromising stare, she had the uncomfortable feeling that she was being judged and found lacking.

Finally Lady Ivone nodded.

"Verena of Langthorne," she began curiously, examining her plain attire. "I'm sure there is a very interesting story about that."

"Which I will be happy to speak of tonight," finished Cairn loudly for the benefit of the onlookers. "For now let us rest and refresh ourselves. We have had a hard journey."

"Very well," replied Ivone, turning her attention back to the brothers. "You must be tired after your adventure. I had your usual rooms prepared and water is being heated for baths. If you will excuse me, I will escort our guest to her rooms in the northwest tower."

The strange choice of words immediately caught her attention. Why did she announce to everyone where she would sleep? Despite Cairn's gracious introduction the lady must have reservations about her character. If she judged correctly Lady Ivone would put her as far away from her sons as possible.

After a long walk through the castle they finally stopped in front of an arched doorway. Verena's earlier guess about their location was correct. They were far from the common rooms in a section that looked barely used. She would dare anyone to make improper assumptions about her relationship with Cairn now.

Her quick glance about the room was reassuring. These were no servant's quarters. This room was obviously intended for a person of means. The furnishings weren't as gaudy as some of the noble suites she had seen. This was the kind of room one gave a beloved cousin rather than visiting royalty. She thought it was perfect.

"If you require assistance," continued Ivone, gesturing to the silent maid that had entered behind them. "Roselyn will help you."

"Thank you," Verena replied gratefully. She never wore clothes she couldn't get out of alone, but servants were notorious gossips and she needed to gather some information on this family.

As she left, Lady Ivone's skirts brushed against the large hearth causing a poker to fall to the floor. Roselyn jumped and quickly crossed herself.

"Is something amiss?" Verena asked.

"Oh, 'tis nothing to concern you, milady. The noise merely startled me."

"You seemed about to jump out of your skin."

"I suppose I did, milady. I probably shouldn't be telling you this, but you seem like the sensible sort and I'm sure it won't frighten you at all. It's just that these rooms haven't been used since the Old Lord passed away."

"I see," Verena replied with interest. "His rooms were close to mine?"

"Aye, almost directly beneath you. I don't put much faith in children's tales, but some of the other servants are fanciful."

"I don't believe in fairy tales either," Verena said. "And I think this room is lovely. I'm sure I'll get along splendidly here."

The young woman smiled, showing a large gap between her teeth.

"Shall I have a bath prepared?"

"Please do," she replied, startled by the request. Hadran continually stressed the importance of bathing. People who often had to sneak about in the dark couldn't leave dirt stains and smells behind, but she knew many others didn't share her needs. In the winter when fuel was scarce and a winter chill could easily become a life-threatening disease, many thought it wiser to avoid water. Verena was glad the McPherson household thought more like Hadran. With thick rugs beneath her feet, tapestries lining the walls to keep out drafts and a roaring fire in the hearth, she was not afraid of a cold.

"I'll be back in a moment."

Roselyn scurried out of the room, eager to relate the news of Verena's arrival to her friends in the kitchen. She was glad to finally be alone and have time to think about their strange arrival. What was she to make of the brothers' sober reunion with Lady Ivone? It was more formal than any homecoming she had witnessed.

There was a void between Cairn and his people that developed when he was squired so far away. Perhaps it had something to do with Lady Ivone's imposing figure. She had seen the way she stood apart from the common people and surmised the lady did little to bridge the gap between herself and the rest of the clan. She was disappointed that Cairn seemed to be following his stepmother's example.

Was it because of social status? Gundy didn't encourage familiarity with his people and ruled with fear and intimidation. Why then was she bothered by Cairn's behavior? Her heart sank with the realization that after one kiss she had begun to think of him differently. She was beginning to forget that Cairn was a selfish noble just like Lord Gundy. She would do well to remember the truth as her assignment continued.

She would have to work hard to gain both Lady Ivone's trust and the trust of the commoners. She had to be above reproach and indispensable to the household, able to move freely through the castle and countryside in order to find the treasure.

Chapter 14

Verena was looking around the bed for good hiding places when she heard a soft knock on the door. Soon Owen would deliver the various tools she would need to thoroughly search the castle and she needed a place to hide them from the cleaning staff.

She hastily smoothed back the covers and sat on the bed before the door opened. Roselyn had returned, ushering in a hall full of servants with hot water, soap, towels and a tub. This young woman definitely had the trust and respect of the servants, judging from their eager assistance. Their arrival must have sent the household into chaos, yet Roselyn diverted all these people from their duties to assist her, using hearths to heat bath water rather than the evening meal. That influence could come in handy during her search for the treasure.

An exquisite gown of pale gold velvet with wide sleeves trimmed with rich brown sable was draped on Roselyn's arm.

"This is a present for you," Roselyn said, holding the gown up for her inspection.

"From Lady Ivone?"

"Nay, from his lordship."

Cairn sent her the lovely dress? He was a noble, laird of a Scottish clan. He didn't need to send gifts to a low-born woman like her. Perhaps the dress was his way of thanking Verena for saving his life —or an apology for kidnapping her.

"I have never seen anything so beautiful."

Roselyn turned to shoo the gawking servants out of the room before helping her undress. Last time Verena had been in Roselyn's place, posing as a lady's maid for Anne of Brittany, the queen of France. Roselyn's ministrations were nearly as skilled as the Queen's fine ladies.

"Lady Ivone saw to my training," Roselyn said when Verena remarked upon it. "She says a well-trained staff is more impressive than fine tapestries and silver. Cairn's mother didn't stand much upon ceremony, but her ladyship insists upon it."

"Lord Gundy feels the same way," Verena replied. "There were so many rules to remember and God help us if we made a mistake in front of him or one of his guests."

"Sorry mum. We have heard of Gundy's reputation. He sounds like a difficult man. Lady Ivone may be exacting, but Lord Angus, Cairn's father was a dear, God rest his soul. He never beat us for our mistakes."

"In truth, I do not miss Gundy's authority."

She sank gratefully into the steaming water, relishing the foreign luxury. Usually she made do with whatever icy stream was nearby. Hadran was obsessive about cleanliness, insisting that it was necessary for their profession, but she had never enjoyed her work with such decadence.

This wasn't a barrel requisitioned for bathing. She sat in an oval tub built specifically for the task, contoured to allow her to stretch out comfortably and lined with linen cloth. A plank was set across the top where Roselyn placed small trinkets that she might enjoy while in the bath: a small splatter of food to nibble on, a hand mirror, a goblet of mulled wine and various scented soaps to choose from, painstakingly carved into flowers and animals. She chose a little bird scented with lavender.

She sighed as Roselyn's magic fingers began to work out the knots coiled in her shoulders and the accumulated dirt from her hair.

"Milady," said Roselyn in surprise, referring to the tension in her taunt back muscles. "It seems you've had quite a journey."

You have no idea, thought Verena.

"I look forward to hearing laird Cairn's tale this evening," continued the maid.

She pursed her lips as she remembered Cairn's promise to tell of his travels. How would he explain her presence? Would she be portrayed as a damsel in distress? There was always the possibility that he had seen through her clever ruse and would publicly denounce her before his clan, but that seemed unlikely. If he didn't believe her Cairn would have said something long ago. Besides, it was hard to worry about such things with Roselyn's fingers rubbing away the tension from the journey.

"It is so strange to be here," Verena replied. She knew she should take advantage of this moment to learn more about the clan. "I have heard stories about this place all my life."

"Nothing good, no doubt," surmised Roselyn as she began working on her tangled hair.

"Some good and some bad. I've heard legends of Cairn's grandfather; about his knowledge of the dark arts and how he conjured the lost Roman silver."

Roselyn snorted, obviously familiar with the tale.

"Unfortunately he never passed on the secret," she replied, then hastily crossed herself in case she offended some lingering spirit. "My da says anyone that believes such tales is foolish, but even he won't set foot in the Old Lord's woods or his chambers –they've been shut up since he passed."

"The chambers below mine?" Verena inquired with affected nonchalance. "I suppose if I wanted to make sure no one found my treasure, making up curses would serve to keep most people away."

"I never thought of it like that before. The stories certainly kept me away."

"Wouldn't it be nice if the treasure really did exist?"

"Lord knows we could use it," muttered Roselyn.

"What do you mean?"

Roselyn mumbled something unintelligible, hesitant to discuss her clan's financial troubles with a stranger. Instead she moved on to a less troublesome subject and asked about supper. That small prod was enough to set Roselyn gossiping about the wonderful delicacies that were being prepared as well as the likes and dislikes of the people in attendance. It wasn't long before she knew the names and descriptions of half the clan.

As the water began to cool she started to fidget. The bath was nice, but she wasn't used to being idle for long and she was growing restless. She was grateful when Roselyn finally rinsed her hair with sweet-smelling water.

Rising from the tub, she was wrapped in the softest cloth she had ever felt. It was pure decadence on Ivone's part to supply her with something so fine. A yard of the stuff would feed her for a season. Perhaps she could swipe a bit of it to take with her as a souvenir.

"Who is it?" she asked in answer to the loud knock on the door. Instead of answering the intruder pushed the door open to reveal a freshly bathed Cairn.

Verena gasped, clutching the cloth about her as if it were no bigger than a handkerchief. The thin fabric felt hopelessly inadequate to cover her heated flesh. She felt naked, and under Cairn's powerful gaze she might as well have been.

The short beard which both irritated and enticed her during their kiss had been shaved off revealing his stubborn chin. Without his beard he looked younger, boyish and more approachable. If she kissed him again would the magic be the same?

The sound of Roselyn politely clearing her throat brought her back to reality. Verena hastily looked away while Cairn's shoulders visibly straightened.

"I have come to escort you downstairs."

Of course. She had completely lost track of time listening to Roselyn's friendly chatter and her stomach took the opportunity to remind her how long it had been since she'd had a proper meal.

"I'll be ready in a moment," she replied.

"I'll wait outside."

Roselyn glanced speculatively at Verena once the door closed, no doubt wondering at their obvious sexual chemistry.

"Did you know lord Cairn before he went to France?" Verena asked as Roselyn laced her into the beautiful gown. She needed something to distract her from Cairn's wolfish smile.

"Not very well. My laird wasn't encouraged to associate with the village children, but he was always kind to me."

"When we rode through the village the people seemed reserved around their lord."

"The others don't know him yet. They are afraid he will be like la ..."

Roselyn stopped, bringing her hands to her mouth as she realized what she was about to say.

"Lady Ivone?" Verena supplied the name. Roselyn shrugged her shoulders noncommittally. The luxuries she had been provided with were in stark contrast to the McPherson's state of affairs. There was only one person who could be responsible for such irresponsible spending: the woman who controlled the clan while Cairn lived in France. Did he know what his stepmother was doing with the clan's finances?

"They don't know him yet," Roselyn repeated, finishing off the laces with a dainty bow.

Chapter 15

Outside Cairn was leaning against the opposite wall, but he stood up as soon as the door began to open. First Roselyn walked through with a tiny, knowing smile in Cairn's direction. He ignored her; Cairn's whole attention was focused on Verena.

She stood behind the maid, gazing at Cairn with eyes filled with uncertainty and excitement. She hoped he saw the shy maiden she tried to portray, the desirable woman, and trustworthy friend. There was fire in his eyes, but she wanted more than his sexual desire.

"Good evening," she said, stepping forward to offer her hand. Cairn took it and brought her fingers to his lips. It was a small caress, but she felt her pulse race at the sensual touch.

"Good evening," Cairn replied. "You look beautiful."

Her mass of thick hair had been brushed until it shone like ebony and plaited into a circlet atop her head. The gown Verena wore was an inch too short, but that would keep the hem clean of the floor rushes. Roselyn tightly laced the bodice, lifting her breasts so they appeared larger and fuller. It was one of the strange and random tricks Verena had learned from Hadran, but was not surprised that Roselyn knew it too. She smiled as she saw the effect it had on Cairn.

The smile Cairn gave her in return was anything but shy. There was something distinctly predatory in the way he was looking at her now. Belatedly she wondered why she never noticed his dimples before.

"Thank you, milord, for the use of the gown."

"It is yours."

"Again I thank you."

Cairn's dimples deepened and Verena had the wild desire to kiss those two spots.

"Shall we go down?" he asked offering his arm. The words were hesitant as if he would much rather return her to the bedroom and undo all of Roselyn's hard work. She had a brief vision of his strong fingers gently tugging the strings of her bodice. She mentally shook herself, forcing those wayward thoughts from her mind. She needed to focus on her assignment and not the virile man beside her.

The great hall sounded more like a battlefield than a feast. The sounds of falling dishes, heated arguments, babies crying and dogs barking was deafening as they crossed the bailey. But everyone, even the dogs, quieted as Cairn and Verena entered the hall arm in arm.

Most probably thought she was Cairn's new leman, but the gown told a different story. She learned from Roselyn that it had once belonged to Cairn's mother. He must regard her highly to have given her such a gift. As Cairn strode purposely toward the head table Verena could see the clan's puzzlement increasing. Andreu entered the hall soon after and sat on Cairn's left, leaving an empty space next to her for Lady Ivone.

Once they were seated the feast resumed, but this time the conversations were muted with men and women whispering their speculations about Cairn's mysterious lady. She put a mask of serenity firmly on her face and tried not to fidget. For one used to skulking in the shadows she was uncomfortable being watched by so many people.

Cairn was extremely attentive, wasting no opportunity to offer Verena the best piece of meat or cheese. Despite the somber mood of the gathering she found herself enjoying Cairn's company. That is, until his fingers accidently brushed against hers while offering her a piece of sweet bread. Her cheeks flamed as she caught the knowing glint in his eye. Cairn had not forgotten their kiss in the woods and it seemed he would repeat it very soon.

Halfway through the meal Lady Ivone appeared. She walked proudly to the head table, not acknowledging the clansmen in any way, only pausing briefly when she noticed the empty seat beside Verena. Cairn had positioned her between the two clan leaders leaving no doubt as to his regard.

Verena gazed around the room noting the expressions of the clansmen as they watched Ivone's entrance. Many of them looked like they had been caught between mouthfuls and would much rather continue their suppers in peace. They were respectful, but didn't show much affection for the lady.

Once Ivone was seated the strained meal resumed. The clan seemed nervous around Cairn's mother and Verena perfectly understood the sentiment. There was something uncomfortable about having a lady of her caliber seated beside her, like inviting a judge to her table. Cairn and Andreu were busy talking about the much more interesting clan affairs, but Ivone gave her no chance to eavesdrop.

"I trust the bedchamber was to your satisfaction?" said Ivone. Verena was unsure if that was a question or statement of fact.

"Oh, yes," she replied with a friendly smile. "The room is lovely. Thank you."

"Wonderful," said Ivone. "I'm delighted to see my son has found use for those old rags. They were cluttering the storerooms."

"It was kind of him to loan the gown to me."

For the next half hour Verena took charge of the conversation and kept the woman happily chatting about "woman's nonsense" as Hadran would put it. She had honed her skills while serving Anne of Brittany where she had to navigate the web of idle women's gossip.

Ivone had a sharp wit, but was brutally judgmental and could find fault with everything. Nothing in Scotland seemed to compare to the splendor of her original home in France. Verena was relieved when Cairn finally rose to his feet. The minstrel, Harry had been idly strumming his lute, but halted mid-chord.

"Many of you have wondered about the long and dangerous journey I have undertaken," he began. "And how I have returned depleted of men, but gifted with a mysterious new lady."

At Cairn's words all eyes turned uncomfortably on Verena once again. Everyone had eagerly awaited this tale and she strove to take note of every gesture and inflection in his speech to see how well she had fooled the Scot.

"We were lured to Langthorne with promises of peace and trade," he continued bitterly. "But were instead met with treachery."

Cairn went on to tell of the ambush which claimed the lives of half his party and how the rest were dragged, wounded, but still struggling into the depths of Langthorne's dungeons. As Cairn continued he diplomatically skimmed over the graphic details of his confinement, but told how each of his men were killed until only he was left alive. He bribed the guard with promises of silver and was able to steal a horse as he made his escape.

Next he explained how he was attacked by bandits in the woods and left for dead. He closed his eyes on that nightmare, but when he opened them again he found himself in heaven with the most beautiful angel smiling down on him. Here Cairn paused to salute Verena with a bow. Her cheeks burned as she smiled in acknowledgement of his praise. By the end of Cairn's tale there was little doubt everyone would see her as a savior.

Why should Cairn's praise make her uncomfortable? Verena forced herself to smile at the hearty cheers of his clan. If it wasn't for Hadran's plan Cairn might still be rotting in the Langthorne prison, or worse. Besides, she was as much a pawn as Cairn in this mad scheme.

"An amazing tale," Lady Ivone commented as they lowered their goblets for what had to be the third toast in her honor. "My son is quite the storyteller."

"Yes," Verena said absently. "It was very well done."

Lady Ivone left the hall soon afterward, claiming fatigue. Unfortunately the brothers had finished their conversation about the clan's finances and turned their attention to more neutral subjects. All Verena could catch was that their plans had something to do with a trip to France.

"Would you like to retire?" Cairn asked, noticing her barely suppressed yawn.

"I am a little tired, milord," she admitted. "I am surprised by your energy. You must have been awake all night."

"It was not the first time. Nor will it be the last, I expect. I hope my speech didn't bore you."

"No," she said. "It was brilliant. I have never received such a wonderful compliment."

"You deserve it and more for what you have done for me."

"I also want to thank you," Andreu chimed in. "For taking care of my little brother."

Verena saw the look that passed between the two; it was a look of anxiety, but also of love and confidence in each other. No matter what trials came the brothers would face them together. Verena knew Cairn would need such a friend in the coming weeks.

"I think I should retire." The thought of Lord Gundy's plans had chased away her pleasure. She wasn't the savior she pretended to be. The McPhersons would fall because of her and though she told herself she was merely doing her job, it suddenly became harder for her to smile.

"Are you alright?" asked Cairn perceptively.

"Just tired."

Cairn's hand was at her elbow to help her rise, but he didn't move to escort her from the hall. She was surprised when the entire clan rushed to their feet as if she were a grand lady. She forced a smile, nodding to familiar servants as she walked out alone.

Chapter 16

A cheery scene greeted Verena as she opened the door to her chamber. Sometime during the feast Roselyn had snuck away to prepare her room. A fresh pitcher of water lay beside the bed for her evening ablutions along with a goblet of mulled wine. One corner of the bedcovers had been invitingly turned down and a small bouquet of late-blooming flowers lay on one of the overstuffed pillows. The slight bulge of a warming pan could be seen beneath the covers. She could certainly get used to life among the McPhersons.

"I thought you might be exhausted from your long journey and the feast," said Roselyn as Verena entered the room. "So I wanted to have everything ready for you."

"Thank you."

The maid's smile was genuinely kind as she undressed her. Her fingers in her hair were deft and gentle.

"No, thank you," said Roselyn. "Milord's tale was amazing. What you did for him ..."

"It was nothing."

"Nothing?" repeated Roselyn. "It was incredible, like something out of a romantic tale."

Verena didn't respond and Roselyn quieted, correctly assuming that she was not in a mood to talk. Though she feared she was rude to the kind maid, it had been a long day and she was exhausted from the strain of being on display before the entire clan.

"I think I had too much wine," Verena said.

Would Cairn come to her this night? The message in his eyes said he would, but if so, what should Verena do? Would an honorable maiden submit to Cairn's lovemaking? Should she act coy or fearful or seductive?

Verena felt both excitement and apprehension remembering the feel of his arms around her and the press of his lips. Though they had only known each other a short time she had seen to it that the sexual tension built between them until they were both ready to burst; resting her hands just a little too low as they rode together and brushing against him as they walked side by side.

She bid Roselyn good night, but didn't climb into the inviting bed. Instead she wrapped a warm fur around her shoulders sat on a chest under the window to wait.

It was a beautiful night despite the late autumn chill. Outside the land was quiet. The clouds had parted to reveal a sky filled with twinkling stars. Several feet below the menacing darkness of the Old Lord's woods beckoned. Verena knew that before this assignment was over she might have to search its forbidden depths.

The Old Lord had done his best to perpetuate the story of this land's curse, going so far as to be excommunicated for his behavior. Was there truth to the stories, or had he merely wanted to frighten people away from his treasure? The sight of those dark woods was chilling on such a peaceful night. It was unnatural to see trees so close to a castle where they might provide cover for an invading force. The logical part of her mind argued it was all foolishness, but McPherson lairds had believed in the ancient forest's power for generations.

As the minutes crept slowly by Verena realized Cairn wouldn't be visiting her chamber. As laird of the McPherson clan his first responsibility was to his people. Perhaps he had other matters to occupy his mind on the first night of his return. Maybe another woman had enticed the handsome McPherson lord to her bed.

With a sigh she climbed into the large bed. She should not feel disappointed. Verena had gotten all she needed from the laird. In fact it would be better if he never visited her chamber so that she may use the night hours to search the castle. Unfortunately such logic didn't stop the twinge of anxiety from twisting in her stomach. She was so sure he would come to her and she hated being wrong.

It was too late to sneak about the castle this night. She barely remembered the twists and turns of the maze-like structure and didn't want to risk getting lost. She would wait until morning to look around, thinking up a good excuse for her wanderings. Then tomorrow night Verena could do a more thorough search without arousing suspicion.

Chapter 17

It was late that night before Cairn was able to leave the hall. He keenly felt the wariness of his clan and wanted to bridge that with the normalcy of a feast. As their party rode through the village that morning the strangeness of this land struck Cairn like a blow. He had been in Scotland less than a season and felt more like a visitor than laird.

The clan's state of affairs was appalling. Cairn had listened to the shame-faced steward describe the clan's dwindling finances and the reasons behind them. It all led back to Lady Ivone and her greedy mismanagement of funds. She had ruled the clan during his father's long illness and assured Cairn everything was fine. Now it appeared she had been less than truthful. Cairn's first impulse was to demand answers from his stepmother, but Andreu had urged caution.

The clan was already unsure about their future and knew the winter months would be hard. They needed strength and unity in leadership, not an ugly family squabble. Cairn reluctantly agreed, though it galled him that he must show restraint to the one that had bankrupted his clan. Andreu agreed to help find a nice cottage in France for the lady and send her off posthaste.

Those thoughts were stewing in Cairn's mind all afternoon as he washed off the dirt from his journey and prepared for the feast, but when he saw Verena emerge from the bath, clad in that sheer cloth like a greek goddess, all thoughts of the future fled. He wanted her with a hunger he had never experienced before. The kiss in the woods was the briefest taste of heaven that left him forever unsatisfied. It took all of his strength not to dismiss Roselyn right then and carry Verena to the bed, forget the feast and make his apologies to the clan later.

Only one thought kept Cairn from doing just that. He remembered the look in her eyes as she pulled away and her flushed embarrassment. Cairn's shame at having so thoroughly lost himself in passion kept him away. He felt like a youth experiencing love for the first time.

Now more than ever Cairn needed to be in control. He couldn't afford to get swept up in a love affair, but neither could he walk away. He needed to touch and taste her again. His loins throbbed to be inside her. Mounting the stairs Cairn tried to tell himself that his passion was due to the length of time he had been without a woman and the intimacy they had shared while in the Langthorne woods, but those were paltry excuses. He craved the fire of Verena, her passion and laughter. He needed to take her and so sate himself that Cairn was able to completely push her from his mind. At least that was his plan.

She had given up on Cairn visiting her chamber and was asleep, but the sound of her unlocked door creaking open brought her instantly awake.

"Why didn't you bolt the door?" Cairn asked. Verena was silent. He was the laird of this domain. Would a locked door keep him away?

She told herself this was just another assignment; Cairn was like any other man. In his castle Verena was under his control and Cairn could take her whether she wished it or not. But in her heart she knew better. Cairn was different. He wanted her, but he would never force her.

"I know you have suffered," he continued, taking another step forward. Cairn was close enough to touch her now. Her senses were overwhelmed with his presence, his clean smell and heat, the sound of his voice. "If you do not want this, tell me now and I will not bother you. You are safe here and have no obligations to me or anyone else."

Verena squeezed her eyes shut wishing those words were true. Suddenly Gundy's angry face rose in her mind. Even here Verena could feel his influence. She saw Hadran and Owen in her mind's eye. Regardless of Cairn's words she felt her obligations like chains around her throat. They had always been there, but for some reason when she was around Cairn, they became heavier to bear.

She opened her eyes again. A shaft of moonlight filtered in through the window and she was able to study Cairn in its pale light. She knew he desired her, but Cairn said he would walk away if she asked him to.

"You kidnapped me."

"You know why. Are you afraid of me?"

"I think I should be."

"Why?"

With one hand he reached out to gently caress her cheek. His fingers traced the line of her bottom lip.

"You are a lord," she pointed out, not having to contrive the catch in her throat. "You can do whatever you want with me."

Cairn leaned forward to capture her lips in a kiss. It was soft and gentle unlike the one in the woods. He teased her with his restraint. She could feel the passion in him but Cairn kept it firmly in check, determined to go slowly.

The sensual play of his lips and brush of his tongue were not enough for her. She wanted more. Verena expected to feel the storm of passion from before, but Cairn savored her, tasting as if she were a fine wine. His lips drifted across her face and her drew in a shaky breath as he kissed the sensitive spot below her ear.

"I can take you," he whispered against her throat, making her tremble. "I can have you anywhere I want for as long as I want, but I cannot command your trust."

With those words Cairn released her and turned to leave. She couldn't gather her thoughts enough to respond. She was shaken, left raw and aching with desire. How could he reduce her to this? She was the seductress, Hadran's star pupil taught by the master manipulator. He was supposed to be panting for her.

"Bolt the door," Cairn called over his shoulder as he left the room. She reconciled herself with the knowledge that he sounded as shaken as she felt.

Chapter 18

"You are certainly in a touchy mood this morning," Andreu pointed out as he and Cairn sparred on one of the large, muddy practice fields inside the bailey. "I wonder if it has something to do with the extra bags under your eyes."

"I am merely concerned with the clan's state of affairs."

Andreu swung a snap just as Verena walked by the field. Cairn, temporarily distracted, was knocked backward a pace.

"Keep that up," Andreu warned. "And I'll have you chained to your bed—where you should be after what Gundy did to you. You can see to the clan's affairs from there."

"I'll not have Ivone and her females carrying on over me as if I were an invalid."

Andreu chuckled at the image of his brother cosseted by the ladies of the castle. Perhaps they would entertain him with idle conversation and unending verses of French poetry while waiting for his bruises to heal. It was no wonder he insisted on working as if he were healthy. Cairn retaliated with a combination that left Andreu's shield arm trembling with the strain of blocking it.

"Have you spoken to the steward today?"

Cairn stepped back, signaling their match was at an end.

"Unfortunately," he replied with disgust. "More bad news and dire predictions. There is so much to do I don't know where to begin."

"I will leave most of my men here to assist you."

"Good morning," Verena called from the side of the practice field.

"Good morning," chorused the brothers.

Verena was wearing another dress belonging to Cairn's mother.

Early that morning Cairn had sent a trunk of her things to her chamber, glad to see her in something other than her original ill-fitting rags. She had chosen a dark brown wool gown with velvet sleeves and a thin band of gold trim around the bodice that emphasized the understated elegance of the ensemble. Unlike Esperanza his mother didn't feel the need to flash her wealth with gaudy baubles and bright colors. She had possessed a quiet dignity that was evident no matter what she wore. It was startling to realize Verena was like her in many ways.

"Did you sleep well?" asked Andreu, noting the dark circles under her eyes. She looked like she hadn't slept at all.

"It must be the strangeness of my new surroundings," she lied. In truth she had lain awake most of the night thinking of Cairn's puzzling behavior. He should not have been able to walk away from her. Perhaps if she had acted more brazen he would have succumbed, but that might make her persona less credible. For hours she had thought of how to make sure that embarrassing episode never happened again while planning the best place to begin her search for the treasure.

"You will feel much better tonight," Cairn softly promised.

There was no mistaking the sensual intent in that statement. It was strange that her feelings mattered to a noble, but they did. Tonight Cairn would give her a second chance and she knew if she rejected him again, he would leave her alone.

He clearly wanted her, but Cairn was willing to walk away if Verena wasn't ready. She could see the tension in him, the strain of masking his injuries so he could fully dedicate himself to his responsibilities. The clan needed to prepare for Gundy's next attack so Cairn was on the practice field with them despite his recent wounds. She had never thought to meet a lord capable of a selfless act, but Cairn seemed to be full of surprises. She wondered what it would be like to make love to someone like that.

They would make love soon. She would see to that. Hadran was right; the Scottish laird craved tenderness, though he would never admit that to himself. He often said that people were too simple. They thought a person or experience would make them happy, but Verena had learned to look deeper. That was how she was able to mold herself into the perfect woman for Cairn. By the time she was through with him the Scot would understand that one night in her bed was not enough. She would ease his stress and bring him peace, but also tease his senses so that Cairn felt he could never get enough.

Make him feel like a man, Hadran advised. It was part of her job, but she found herself looking forward to doing just that.

"Roselyn is taking me to the village," she announced, anxious to change the subject.

"The servant?" Andreu asked in surprise.

"Yes, the servant."

Did the brothers share Lady Ivone's dislike of the lower classes? Andreu's question brought to mind several conversations Verena had with Owen. How many times had he told her the nobility had little affection for those deemed beneath them?

"She promised to show me the town and chapel."

"You should have told me," Cairn replied. "I will have one of my men escort you."

"I'm sure your men have much to do before winter," she replied. "I wouldn't take them away from their duties for a walk to the village and back. We will not go far and Roselyn will ensure I do not get lost."

She gave Cairn her most innocent look. That last bit was to prove she had no intention of running away and couldn't with Roselyn's escort. He had kidnapped Verena the day before, but she wanted him to feel she had put that behind her. It was crucial to her assignment that she be allowed to explore the land unchallenged. Verena hoped Cairn wouldn't try to stifle her movements.

"Very well," said Cairn after a thoughtful pause. "But be careful. And do not go past the village."

"Of course," Verena said immediately. She spotted Roselyn coming toward her with a basket and waved. "Good day."

The only person she needed for this task was Roselyn. The woman was best friends with or related to half the clan. An introduction from her would do much to integrate her with the villagers—especially the generation old enough to be around during the time of Cairn's grandfather. Plus with the villagers' distrust of nobility having an armed escort would certainly not make them comfortable with her.

"This is my mum, Henny," introduced Roselyn a few moments later. Verena stood in the doorway of a small cottage. The room was divided with a cloth hanging from the rafters separating the living area from the common space where six people stepped agilely between a loom, spinning wheel, chest, table, several stools and a tabby cat sprawled unconcernedly in the middle of the floor. "And this is my da, Peter, and sisters, Megan, Meg, Rosie and Rose."

She smiled as she greeted Roselyn's family. All of the sisters had Roselyn's bright curls and infectious grin, which they inherited from their mother.

"They say my da was drunk when he named us," she explained conspiratorially. "So we got whatever names he could think of at the time: my grandmum's name was Megan and there was a rosebush beside her home."

"It's nice to meet all of you," said Verena, enjoying the informality of the small cottage. Despite the outside chill, inside all was peaceful and warm. A peat fire burned inside the hearth and the aroma of savory stew mingled invitingly with the smells of various herbs drying in bundles hanging from the ceiling.

"Listen to you!" Roselyn's mother exclaimed, Henny in alarm. "Always running your mouth. And then you wonder why you can't find a husband."

"I can't find a husband because this town is two meters long!" cried Roselyn. "Maybe if you let me visit aunt Ester in Sheepsdale."

"Not that again," Peter interrupted. "You aren't going to visit that crazy old bat and that's final."

"But Da ..." chorused the sisters.

"Don't you call my sister crazy!" Henny warned, yielding a cooking spoon like a deadly weapon. "Next you'll be blaming this infernal frost on my family too."

"I don't see why not," Peter replied. "There's no telling what your mother did up at the castle with the Old Lord."

"She was just a chambermaid," shouted Henny. She glanced pointedly in Verena's direction and Peter, taking the hint, cleared his throat nervously and began cleaning his nails.

"It's all right," Verena said to break the awkward silence. "I've heard about the Old Lord. I think the stories are fascinating, though I'm not sure I believe them."

"Finally a woman with sense!" Peter said, ignoring the matching scowls on the faces of his wife and daughters. "I don't put much stock in horror stories either, but it is always fun to tease them about it."

"It's no laughing matter," warned Henny, crossing herself. "I don't know what the Old Lord did, or if he was as bad as everyone said he was. All I know is that when we were in trouble he found a way."

Verena tried to question her, but Henny was reluctant to speak of that time. Years ago the McPhersons struggled under warfare, a harsh winter and plague, but just as the clan faced ruin, the Old Lord produced a miracle. Piles of silver appeared, paying for much-needed food, clothing and medicine.

He saved the clan, but there were those that spoke of the matter in hushed voices, believing the miracle was not the work of divine intervention, but another, darker influence. Verena could understand Henny's reluctance. As a pious woman she was caught between loyalties to the clan and the church. It was much easier not to question it, not to have the burden of guilt on her mind, always wondering if she owed her survival to a wicked agreement.

They talked of other things, of sewing and recipes and babies. Peter suffered through it with barely a grumble, used to being the only man in a house full of women. Though Verena knew she would get no more information from them, as the hours passed she found herself reluctant to leave. Despite the poverty of their circumstances a bond existed between them which she could only admire. The relationship she had with her adopted family of spies was more practical than emotional. For the first time since she could remember she found herself longing for a real family.

"We should be leaving," said Roselyn, taking advantage of a lull in the conversation. "We have much to do today and the hour grows late."

Verena rose slowly from her stool. She watched from the doorway as Roselyn kissed her mother and father goodbye. She told herself she had nothing to envy. Roselyn's family had neither her resilience nor skills. They were the kind of people who would till the same dismal fields for generations and yet every year hope for something different. Owen would scornfully call them hopeless.

"I am sorry we stayed so long," Roselyn apologized, misinterpreting Verena's pensive mood. "My sisters and I don't know when to stop talking."

"Don't be silly. It is the cold that has me so grim."

"Welcome to Scotland!" Roselyn cheerfully replied.

Chapter 19

Next the women visited the small village church to attend evening prayers and meet the priest. Verena wasn't surprised to find the tiny chapel nearly overflowing with people praying for a gentler winter. They respectfully made room for her and Roselyn. From their awed looks she surmised many of them had heard Cairn's story the night before. They treated her like a curiosity and though uncomfortable it was better than scorn for her English heritage.

The priest was a thin older man named Father Simon. Despite his small stature he was a gifted orator and possessed a powerful voice. He kept the congregation enthralled with his sonorous tones. Father Simon spoke of redemption of past sins and of hope for the future—subjects the McPhersons were sorely in need of.

He was old, perhaps old enough to be the confessor of Cairn's grandfather. They approached him after the service for an introduction.

"You look like you haven't been to confession in a while," said Father Simon with little preamble.

Verena smiled nervously and promised to come back soon. It would take hours to confess the sins of her shady past and she knew better than to trust anyone, even a priest, with the truth. Instead she would tell him the story Hadran concocted for her, perhaps embellished with a few more maidenly virtues. Though a part of her felt guilty for lying to a priest, that was a small sin compared to the others she had committed.

There was no time to question the priest about his knowledge of the Old Lord, but she now had an excuse for wandering about the village alone. Verena could say she was visiting Father Simon or Roselyn's family.

The women made two other stops that day—one to greet a clanswoman named Abby and her adorable new babe and one more to see the blacksmith about new hinges for a castle door. Thanks to Roselyn's friendly introductions much of the curiosity surrounding Verena began to fade. On their return to the castle several villagers waved cheerfully as they walked through the muddy streets. She decided she was well on her way to becoming ingratiated with the community.

"That was brilliant the way you handled Old Thomas," exclaimed Roselyn as they made their way back to the keep. Thomas was one of the McPherson clan elders. He was firmly set in his beliefs about Langthorne and anyone from there. To make matters worse he had lost a grandson during Cairn's recent travels. Thomas had no intention of being courteous to Verena, even if she did save his laird's life.

Encouraged by the reception she had received from the other villagers, she worked to conquer the old man's prejudice. The others had overcome their distaste of her background and she was confident Thomas would too. Hadran told her often enough that there were many ways to get around a person; she just had to discover some common ground.

Inspiration struck as she saw the old carpet, frayed from years of use, covering the floor of his cottage. Though shabby and faded, it had once been a thing of beauty and looked incongruous in a peasant's cottage. It must have come from the castle.

The dour old man's expression instantly brightened when she asked of it. He explained it had been a gift from the old lord to Thomas' father for years of service. From his confident look Verena knew this man took great pride in serving his laird.

Verena exploited that, telling Thomas his grandson had died bravely in service. Indeed, he sacrificed himself for Cairn. No elegy could have been more inspirational, not even the one Cairn had given Verena the night before. By the time she was finished old Thomas had tears streaming down his cheeks thinking of the glory of his family.

Somehow she had preserved his grandson's memory—a man she had never met—and connected with a man that was certainly old enough to know about the treasure. Verena couldn't help but think how proud Hadran would be of her progress.

Late that afternoon the ladies entered the castle through the large kitchen located just beside it. They had both built up ferocious appetites during the long day and hoped to sneak off with something before the evening meal. Roselyn made a half-hearted protest that it wasn't proper for a lady to be wandering about in the servant's areas, but she brushed that aside. She knew plenty of ladies who took very active roles in running their households, including cooking, cleaning and the often-dangerous chore of brewing, but it was obvious when she entered the kitchen that Ivone and her resident ladies didn't share this belief.

The pandemonium of food preparation was immediately halted as the servants became aware of Verena and Roselyn hovering just inside the door. She had made too much progress in the village to become shy now. Resolutely she squared her shoulders and strolled into the kitchen as if it were the most natural thing in the world.

"That smells delicious," she said to the rotund matron she assumed was the head cook. "Is that rosemary?"

The woman nodded her head nervously, but was obviously pleased by the compliment.

"It's one of my favorite herbs, especially made into marmalade with honey."

The cook broke into a full grin as she accurately guessed her recipe. Verena returned the smile, remembering with nostalgia the glorious summer she had spent posing as a servant to the French Lord Charles de Ravenna's head cook. Verena had gained at least 10 pounds that summer picking up the delicious leavings from his table and made off with his prized spice cabinet.

"Lady Verena," said Roselyn, enjoying her position as her guide. "Allow me to introduce you to Mistress Gertrude."

"I am delighted to make your acquaintance," she said respectfully. She knew from experience that it was always a good idea to make friends with the kitchen folk.

The leftovers from the previous night's feast had been picked over by the castle staff, but Mistress Gertrude insisted on making something fresh for Verena and Roselyn. The ladies munched happily on the simple meal, sitting at one of the large kitchen tables and comparing recipes.

She found Gertrude to be a very able cook with the simple tools she was given, but strangely hostile to experimentation.

"Our haggis is better than anything some fancy French chef could throw together," she proudly argued with a hint of bitterness. Verena surmised she had disputed that point with Ivone on more than one occasion.

She nodded her head in agreement; nonetheless she found Gertrude listening raptly as Verena hypothesized a way to cheaply double the recipe's yield. Thanks to that summer in France she knew how to stretch a meal and the simple tricks she explained to Gertrude instantly endeared her to the cook.

"Gertrude is never that nice to me," whispered Roselyn as they made their way up the castle steps.

"'Tis merely a matter of how people are approached," she replied, echoing one of Hadran's favorite sayings. "That old, fancy rug looked conspicuous in Thomas' cottage so I asked him about it. And as the head cook Gertrude would obviously be interested in discussing food so I used that to establish a connection between us."

"That sounds so methodical," said Roselyn, looking at Verena in surprise. She inwardly winced, wondering if she had said too much. Perhaps an innocent, young maid wouldn't be so socially savvy.

"But it makes sense. You wouldn't speak to Lady Ivone about your father's indigestion."

Roselyn giggled, picturing that conversation.

"There is a great deal I wouldn't dare discuss with her," she replied, conspiratorially.

Lady Ivone was twice a widow and the former ruler of the McPherson clan. She held herself apart from them, perhaps to reinforce her cloak of nobility. She was used to a certain amount of power and now with the death of her second husband she was forced to concede that power to her stepson. How did she feel about the change? As ruler of the clan Ivone would have been privy to her husband's secrets. Perhaps she should question her about the treasure.

Throughout the day she had identified three individuals who might know something of the Old Lord's treasure: Lady Ivone, Father Simon and Thomas. Until Verena was assured of their trust she would go slowly with the questioning to not arouse their suspicion.

First Verena would conduct a detailed search of the castle with special attention on the Old Lord's chambers. When Cairn's grandfather died his son shut up that wing of the castle. It seemed like the most promising place to begin her search.

"I'm glad his lordship brought you with him," said Roselyn impulsively.

Verena gave a bland smile before entering her chamber, surprised by the girl's esteem. Roselyn wouldn't feel the same when her work was done.

Chapter 20

The door creaked open and Verena's hand reflexively reached for her hidden knife. She had long ago retired for the night, exhausted from the day's exercise, but came instantly awake at the sound of her late night intruder.

"Milord?" she mumbled in the dark.

"You didn't bolt the door," Cairn replied as he stalked toward the bed.

She knew he would come tonight, but could no more lock him out than stop her anxious heart from pounding in her chest. She waited in breathless anticipation as he slowly began to undress.

"Tell me to stop."

Verena dumbly shook her head. Cairn's hand had reached below the blankets to caress her calf, working its sensual way up her leg.

"Tell me to leave."

"No."

"Why?"

His hand had reached the top of her inner thigh and paused there, waiting for her response.

"Because ... because I want you, Cairn McPherson. It has nothing to do with fear or obligation. You are stronger and braver than any man I have ever known and I know I would have your protection regardless of my actions tonight."

Cairn smiled in the moonlight and for a moment the worry lines disappeared from his brow. His eyes communicated the hunger she had seen in the woods, but this time she returned his gaze with confidence. She reached up to trace the dimple on his cheek, running her fingers slowly over his chin, nose and lips. Before she could pull away Cairn's hand cupped her chin, lifting her for a gentle kiss.

She gasped as Cairn began to gently massage her breasts. She cried out in pleasure as he used his thumb and forefinger to tease her nipples. There was no pretense or coyness in her response. All thoughts of Langthorne, Hadran and Owen were forgotten as she reveled in Cairn's skillful touch.

He released one hand to slide across her stomach and touch the vee between her legs. She felt like a flower opening itself to his expert caress. As his fingers stroked her Cairn released her fragrant dew into the air.

In the midst of pleasure Hadran's training came unbidden to her mind. Verena was supposed to be seducing Cairn, not the other way around. She reached for him, but her fingers were inexplicably clumsy. It was hard to concentrate with Cairn working his magic on her nether regions.

"Relax," he said softly, pleased by her reaction.

She sucked in a sharp breath watching Cairn reposition himself. His head was dropping lower, kissing a fiery trail across her bosom, down her stomach and lower. Surely he wouldn't …? But Cairn's mouth didn't hesitate. She was puzzled by his tender attention. Where was the selfish noble? Where was the haughty upper-class disdain?

He was gentle at first, teasing Verena with a release that hovered just beyond her reach. But he soon grew bolder and more vigorous until the workings of his mouth were a sweet torture. She was calling his name, moaning and panting beneath the light of the full moon.

She buckled wildly, unaware of the sounds coming from her. She needed more, but didn't know if it was possible to go higher than the heights of passion she was currently soaring. She was soon to find out that she could. Cairn lifted her knees and dipped his head again. Waves of passion rolled over her coaxed by the expert dance of Cairn's tongue and lips.

Without removing his mouth Cairn began to massage her with his hand, penetrating and caressing her with his fingers and tongue. She clutched the covers, arching her back and pleading for another release. When it finally came her entire body vibrated, unconsciously tightening around Cairn's fingers and holding him hostage within her.

She collapsed onto the bed, sweating despite the early winter chill and panting, at a loss to explain the wonderful passion he had awakened within her. She had never before so completely lost control of herself. As she lay in the afterglow of her orgasm she couldn't help but feel unnerved. No one had ever affected her the way Cairn did.

"What's wrong? I hope you don't regret ..."

"No," Verena broke in uncomfortably. "It was wonderful."

She looked up to find Cairn watching her intently. Though a light smile played upon his lips she could see the tension still in his body and was aware that though she had gained release, Cairn was still waiting.

"Good," he said in a self-satisfied tone. "You deserve wonderful."

Before Verena could say another word he rose up to cover her body with his. She protested weakly, not knowing if she was ready for another rush of passion, but soon found her body had a mind of its own. It was eager to feel Cairn's body pressed close to hers.

His hands on her breasts brought her back to the height of passion she had experienced moments before. When he plunged his fingers between her legs she was wet and ready for him. Cairn positioned himself between her legs and slowly entered her. It was shocking to be filled so completely. He stretched her insides in a most peculiar way, but she relished the sensation.

Cairn paused for a moment upon entering and held himself tensely above her. He looked up in surprise when he didn't move, wondering if she had done something wrong. But the look on Cairn's face took her breath away. He was waiting for her, giving her a chance to get used to him before continuing. She smiled, pulling Cairn's head down to place a tender kiss on his lips. Together they began to move.

They were perfect for each other, each sensing the other's need and responding without instruction. There was a strange symmetry of motion as if they had made love a thousand times. She didn't know it was possible to be so aware of another person, his breathing and each sound he made. Cairn followed the clues of Verena's reactions to bring her closer to bliss.

He began slowly, teasing Verena with his languid strokes, but soon Cairn increased his pace until they were both buckling wildly with mindless passion. It wasn't enough. She could feel her body hungering for that wonderful climax she had felt before and knew he felt the same urgency. This time when Cairn brought her there, he followed her into that blessed oblivion. He collapsed on top of her with a guttural roar, panting and replete.

They stayed motionless for a long time, both hesitant to speak and break the peaceful afterglow. Without thinking she brought her hand up to brush a lock of hair from his brow.

It was several hours later before Cairn left her, when the first rays of dawn crept across her room. His motions were sluggish, as reluctant to leave as she was to see him go. Cairn looked happy now. There was contentment in his eyes that she had put there.

"Tonight?"

Cairn hadn't made any grand declarations of love, but he wanted her again. Perhaps all men weren't as fickle as Hadran claimed.

"Tonight," she confirmed. Though the day would find her up to her neck in Gundy's dirty work, the evening was hers and Cairn's.

Chapter 21

Since Cairn's return the castle ladies had retreated to the solar, claiming it as a "woman's sanctuary" where few outsiders dared to enter. For a woman raised with mostly men Verena knew pitifully little about the sort of activities that went on in such a room. She assumed there was weaving, sewing and gossip, but none of that seemed particularly attractive.

She paused outside to take a fortifying breath. She knew how valuable Lady Ivone could be to her search. According to Roselyn she too had searched for the McPherson treasure and found nothing. If anything the lady could tell her where not to look.

As soon as she knocked a hush fell over the room. Lady Ivone sat comfortably in a large chair surrounded by her ladies like a queen among her courtiers. Trailing across her lap was an exquisite piece of embroidery that she had probably worked on for the past year. She imagined it someday hanging on the castle walls as a testament to her sedentary life.

The lady stopped in mid-sentence, extolling the virtues of carrying a vial of arsenic tied about the neck as a safeguard against the plague, and turned her sharp eyes on her.

"Good morning, Lady Ivone," Verena said respectfully. "Ladies."

Ivone nodded in acknowledgement as if she were greeting a foreign ambassador. She was painfully aware that she had not been invited to sit and decided to see if flattery would work on the impressive woman.

"That is exquisite!" she exclaimed, coming forward to examine Ivone's embroidery. It truly was a thing of beauty with vividly colored silk threads dancing across her lap in a vibrant masterpiece of animals and artistic flowers. "I have never seen anything like it. Is that a couched stitch?"

Lady Ivone nodded self-assuredly, but she could tell she was delighted by the praise.

"It is a variant of the Bayeux stitch," she explained. "Developed by my father, Olivier de la Marche. You might have heard of our embroidery workshop near Auvergne?"

Verena shook her head like the simple peasant she was supposed to be, though she was well acquainted with Auvergne work. The Duc de Ravenna had commissioned several pieces from there which were unfortunately too distinctive to steal. If she studied there Lady Ivone had the right to be proud.

"It is beautiful."

Ivone smiled and motioned for her to take a seat near her. The other ladies moved aside grudgingly, unsure how to respond to this interloper.

"Have you brought a project?" asked Ivone, glancing at the small basket she carried.

"Just a bit of mending," she replied, holding up the gown she had purposely torn before coming to the solar.

Hadran believed skill with a needle ranked close to skill with a knife. He made her practice needlework endlessly until she could remove the valuable metalwork, silk threads and beads from a garment without damaging it.

She took her time making her stitches small and even under Lady Ivone's watchful eye. She then turned the seams inside out to finish them with a flat French seam guaranteed not to unravel as the garment was worn and washed in the future. When she finished Lady Ivone quietly examined the garment and then suggested she add a row of embroidery to the sleeves.

As a rule she never embellished her clothing for fear it would be too recognizable, but if Lady Ivone wanted a demonstration of her skills she was happy to oblige. She borrowed some green wool thread and set to work.

"Curse this infernal thread!" exclaimed a rotund lady named Bidonne. Her embroidery had become hopelessly tangled and by the time she painstakingly removed the knot the spun wool thread had stretched too thin to use. She was forced to cut it short (wasting a large chunk of it) and begin again.

"If you kept your threads shorter," admonished Lady Ivone. "You wouldn't have that problem."

Bidonne lowered her head to hide the embarrassed flush of her cheeks and she quickly stepped in to fill the uncomfortable silence.

"This green is so vibrant," she exclaimed. "I have never seen the like."

"Yes," replied Ivone in a lecturing tone. "The Scottish stock for all its coarseness holds dyes remarkably well. I only use Leominister and Herefordshire wool for my projects, which are outrageously expensive, but worth every penny. Please don't tell my boys I prefer English wool to theirs!"

The ladies tittered as if Ivone had said something amusing. What would Cairn think of Ivone's extravagant spending?

"The best wool, of course," continued Ivone. "Comes from the Spanish merinos. My mother gave me a bushel as a wedding present. It came all the way from the Royal Escurial flocks."

Ivone saucily displayed a slender leg covered in fine woolen hose. Even Verena couldn't help smiling at the display.

"I've heard," said Bidonne, dropping her voice to a conspiratorial whisper. "Smuggling merinos is a crime punishable by death!"

"It's true," confirmed Ivone. "What I wouldn't give for a talented smuggler right now!"

Verena glanced up at those words, but Ivone was focused on her work, applying rich, multi-colored shading to a leaf. There was no way Lady Ivone could know about her early escapade, smuggling a merino ewe out of Spain. Unfortunately the valuable newborn didn't survive its first winter in Langthorne.

"I'm sure Scotland has its own treasures," she replied.

"Like the Old Lord's treasure?" Bidonne scoffed dismissively. "That is a myth like everything else of value in this awful land."

"We didn't think so at first," pointed out a dour matron named Marie.

"Did you search for the treasure?" she forced her fingers to move steadily over her work as if the answer barely interested her.

"Did we?" replied Bidonne. "We searched every room in this drafty, old castle and half the countryside. If there was a treasure the old man took the secret to his grave."

She nodded without looking up from her work. For the rest

of the morning she skillfully questioned the ladies until she knew exactly where, when and how they searched for the treasure.

Ivone had concentrated her search in the abandoned chambers that used to belong to her father-in-law. From their descriptions She knew they had been less than thorough, looking in only the most obvious places like behind furniture and storage rooms. To them if the treasure was not in plain sight it didn't exist. Verena would have to conduct a more detailed search of the Old Lord's chambers.

Chapter 22

Cairn paced the floor as he mulled over his steward's disturbing news. They met in the chambers he had appropriated as his own since the true master suite was housed in the closed section of the castle where his grandfather had lived. Although large, Cairn's chamber was not big enough to bring comfort to his restless feet.

"We cannot fight Gundy," repeated the steward. "We don't even have the funds to replace your armor—and shouldn't do that until after the next harvest."

Cairn growled in frustration. Things were never this bad while his father, Angus, was alive. During his father's long illness, the truth of their finances was hidden from him. Cairn should have been here years ago, learning to take over the clan, but Lady Ivone had struggled to maintain an illusion of wealth. Even now any visitor might see only the fine tapestries and never notice the haggard faces of the peasantry.

Perhaps it was pride that had kept Cairn's father from divulging the truth of their downward-spiraling finances. He had made an effort to rouse himself out of bed during each of Cairn's visits, masking his pain from his son. His pride when Cairn showed him the spoils of a newly conquered battlefield or tournament suggested everything was right with the world.

Lord Angus had foreseen the coming strife between Scotland and England and sent his only son away to be squired in France. He wanted to spare his son the dangers of a border war. Now in the aftermath of a bloody upheaval Scotland was trying desperately to heal and Cairn found himself the unexpected and unprepared savior of his people.

•

Earlier when Cairn questioned Lady Ivone about the bewildering state of affairs, she had cried tears of genuine sorrow, claiming Angus forbade her from revealing the truth. He didn't want to spoil Cairn's adolescence with such troubles. Now, when faced with ruin Cairn saw the accusing looks of his clansmen. Regardless of his ignorance Cairn didn't blame them for believing they had been abandoned. He hoped it wasn't too late to make things right.

"What can we do?" asked Cairn wearily. "How do we get through this?"

"Most of the animals will have to be slaughtered as they will not survive the winter. Our wool might fetch higher prices abroad, but I'm not sure we can wait that long. We need every grain from our harvest and more which means we will have to buy seed for planting. I think it is time to ask your brother for aid—and pray."

Cairn winced as he realized the truth of the steward's words. He hated begging even to his brother. Andreu had his own troubles in France, but he wouldn't allow Cairn's people to starve. The McPherson clan was lucky to have such a friend.

"Your grandfather had a knack for materializing wealth the moment it was needed."

Cairn raised an eyebrow. That was the first positive remark he had heard about the Old Lord. Most only whispered about him in fearful tones.

"Yes. It is a shame I haven't his talent for attracting lucrative familiars."

"Those are just stories. Even your stepmother searched for the treasure after he died."

"I would think Lady Ivone would have more sense than that," replied Cairn dismissively.

"Many people still believe in the treasure. I know we could use some of it right now."

Cairn turned to look at the man in surprise. Surely he didn't believe the stories. It was ludicrous to even contemplate evil spirits and haunted silver, but finding the treasure would certainly solve many of his problems.

"Lady Ivone searched for it?"

"Aye, milord," replied the steward. "It was one of the first things she did when your father became ill. She soon gave up though. No one can stand to be in the Old Lord's wing for long."

Did Ivone have reason to believe the treasure was real? Cairn didn't believe in the supernatural, but if there was a chance the treasure did exist he owed it to his people to look.

"I'll need the keys to that wing."

Chapter 23

Verena hated castles ever since she was caught in a siege two years ago. They were large and spooky and usually haunted. Once inside it was often difficult to escape. She much preferred the outdoors where she could disappear in an instant and forage off the land.

Unfortunately the only things to forage in the Old Lord's wing were cobwebs and spiders. The rats didn't seem to mind. She could hear them scurrying about in the dark, burrowing nests into long-forgotten furniture. The scrape of rodent claws surrounded her, staying just outside the reach of her tiny light.

If only Lady Ivone had given her more practical information. No matter what Bidonne said it was hard to imagine such delicate ladies venturing down here. She found several forgotten storerooms that hadn't been opened in ages, filled with rotting furniture and other useless artifacts she couldn't begin to name.

Several doors were locked and since she had not yet gotten her lock picking set from Owen nor stolen the steward's keys, she moved on. Today she merely wanted to familiarize herself with the castle layout and make a list of the materials she would need for a more thorough search.

It was easy to imagine the Old Lord walking through these passages. Many rooms looked like they hadn't been disturbed in decades. She could feel his presence as if the Old Lord were watching from the darkness. She heard a footstep behind her and spun around, but the passage was empty.

"Is someone there?" she called. The only answer was the ominous scratch of rodent claws.

The next door was unlocked and Verena pushed it aside. She had to lean into it with her entire body to coax the rusted hinges to move. They did so grudgingly with a loud groan she was sure could be heard as far away as the village. She would have to obtain a small vial of oil for the hinges on her next visit.

She stepped into the room, ignoring the thick cobwebs that trailed like silken fingers along her skin. This room was mostly empty except for unidentifiable refuse piled on the floor. Verena turned back the way she came. It was another dead end.

She wasn't expecting the treasure to be lying on the floor—not after so many had searched this place. The Old Lord's suite should give her insights into his character and suggest where else she might look.

She frowned as she reached the end of the passage and came across yet another locked door. This one was in much better shape, made from an expensive imported wood. Iron spikes were located along the wall where luxurious tapestries once graced the corridor and sconces were left on either side of the door for torches. This room was located at the farthest corner from the castle entrance in its strongest and most defensible wall. Her instincts told her something valuable was behind this door. It was a shame she would have to wait until Owen contacted her to find out what was there. Stealing the steward's keys was expedient, but dangerous. It would be foolish to needlessly put herself at risk while there were many other places to search. She would look elsewhere and return with the proper tools.

"Why are you here?" asked an imperious voice behind her.

Verena jumped, screeching as if Satan himself had materialized in the corridor. Her candle clattered on the floor, plunging her into darkness as she reached for her knife.

"Damn it, woman!" Cairn exclaimed, clutching his ears as her screams echoed off the walls. "Calm down. 'Tis I, Cairn."

She disguised her instinctual fighting crouch by fumbling about on the ground for her candle, ignoring the disgusting debris lining the floor. Her fingers brushed against something warm and furry and she quickly snatched her hand back.

"I ... I'm sorry milord," she said in her most timid voice. "You startled me."

"Why are you here?"

Cairn unshielded his candle and Verena immediately wiped dirty fingers on her woolen gown, holding back a shudder.

Why was he down here? Cairn certainly had not been following her all afternoon. He must have his own reasons for wandering about the Old Lord's chambers. Perhaps he had discovered new information on the whereabouts of the treasure.

"You will think I am silly," she replied, touching her wick to Cairn's to relight it. "I have heard so much about your grandfather and I am sleeping directly above his old chambers. I suppose I was curious."

"You should not wander about alone in the dark."

"I am not afraid."

"Perhaps you should be."

There was something in his tone, a slight inflection in Cairn's speech that let her know he didn't refer to the Old Lord's wing. The sensual rumble of his voice made her palms sweat despite the damp of the corridor.

Cairn's huge frame blocked the only exit. He stepped forward to close the distance between them and her breathing came faster. She felt the strange magnetic pull that bound them and unconsciously swayed toward him. One hand came up to cup her chin, gently brushing the nape of her neck. Her eyes drifted shut, enjoying the soft pressure of his massage.

Last night they were wild in their lovemaking, reveling in the ecstasy of coming together. Now she wanted Cairn with renewed passion, as if it had been months and not hours since they made love.

His lips were coming closer, descending a tantalizing inch at a time, but before they touched Cairn yelped and snatched his hand back as if he had been burned.

"There are spiders in your hair!"

She squealed and began furiously brushing herself off. Getting dirty was an unfortunate consequence of her clandestine activities, but she didn't relish the thought of vermin crawling over her.

"Good afternoon," said a voice behind them.

Andreu suddenly appeared from the shadows, watching them with interest. For a moment he seemed like an unholy specter emerging from the gloom and she fought another scream. Though she managed a smile, her heart was hammering in her chest.

"Milords, are you searching for the treasure?" she asked, noticing the large bunch of keys hanging from Cairn's belt.

Andreu shrugged.

"It seems like a popular activity."

"May I stay with you?" she asked in her best damsel-in-distress voice. "After the last scare the thought of returning alone is frightening."

"Of course," replied Cairn. "Would you like to go back now?"

"I am fine as long as I'm with you."

The look Cairn gave her in response turned her knees to jelly. If Andreu was not there Cairn would be kissing her—regardless of the spiders. He unlocked the large, wooden door. It opened grudgingly, hesitant to give up its dark secrets.

They stepped through the portal and she felt an immediate chill go up her spine. The room was inexplicably colder than the hallway, causing their breath to fog before their eyes. Cairn held his candle up to peer into the darkness and the flame made eerie hissing sounds as it came in contact with the cobwebs falling from the ceiling. Their flickering light illuminated what used to be the Old Lord's bedchamber.

Cairn's grandfather had an affinity for red, judging from the predominant color of the tapestries and blankets, which spread like a bloodstain across the bed. The light from their candles cast a rosy hue on the thick, dusty fur before the fireplace. Though it was too dark to be sure, she thought it might be arctic bear, perhaps a gift from their Norse relatives.

A young man she assumed was Cairn's grandfather watched from a large tapestry that dominated an entire wall. In the background was a landscape of the McPherson castle and lands while dark clouds hovered in the sky above him. At his feet a strange child stood, peeking mischievously from behind his legs. It looked like an aged cherub with piercing black eyes and bright red hair that might also have been a cap.

"Is this Auvergne work?"

"Yes," replied Andreu. "Our families have been connected for years."

"And that must be his familiar."

Verena referred to the strange child by the Old Lord's feet. She was surprised the tapestry hadn't been taken down to protect it from the creatures that inhabited the Old Lord's chambers. The rodents that destroyed the contents in the other rooms seemed to have a curious reverence for this chamber and left the Old Lord's belongings untouched.

"I have no idea what that is."

"There is nothing here," said Andreu, brushing the cobwebs from his fingers in disgust.

She pursed her lips in thought. There was something here. She could feel it, but she couldn't adequately search with Cairn and his brother hovering about.

Out of the corner of her eye she saw Cairn pause to gaze at the tapestry. The resemblance was eerie. Even Cairn seemed a bit nervous as he brought his fingers up to trace his face. Had he ever seen his grandfather's picture?

Glancing down Verena noticed the eyes of the peculiar creature resting at the Old Lord's feet seemed to be fixed on Cairn, studying him with a look that sparkled through the cloth. The tapestry was so life-like she half expected the thing to walk out of the portrait.

A heavy hand descended on her shoulder making Verena shriek and breaking the hypnotic moment.

"I am sorry," said Andreu, quickly removing his hand. "I didn't mean to startle you. Are you ready to leave?"

She nodded, drawing a shaky breath. She was not looking forward to returning here alone, but she knew she must come back. There was something in this room that tugged at her mind. She had a hunch that something was hidden just out of sight waiting for her to discover it. If Owen didn't appear soon with her tools, Verena would have to improvise on her next search.

Chapter 24

A memorial service was held the next day for Cairn's lost comrades. Though Father Simon gave a beautiful sermon, the glaring absence of bodies cast an eerie pall over the ceremony. The families were robbed of the chance to properly bury their dead.

Verena scanned the crowd, mentally reviewing the many people she had met since coming to Scotland. There were so many odd things that warranted investigation. The crotchety old Thomas stood proudly in the cold air, crying silent tears for his lost grandson. This was a man that upheld the clan's honor with conceit. He even refused to sell the valuable rug given to his father by the Old Lord. Despite its origins most would have sold Thomas' rug if faced with hunger.

Father Simon's easy camaraderie with the clan was also suspect. He was trustworthy and non-judgmental, the kind of man who invited secrets. Perhaps someone had told him of the treasure or asked him to hide it, but if so, why hadn't he revealed that secret to his new laird?

Verena stood to one side of the cemetery with Cairn and his family wearing a luxurious fur-lined cloak that once belonged to Cairn's mother. Standing next to Lady Ivone Verena felt like an invisible wall separated her from the rest of the clan. There were times she seemed so silly, gossiping about expensive treats her clan could ill afford. Yet other times she felt the woman's gaze fastened on her in a calculating way. Were her mannerisms pretense? Surely if Ivone had the silver she would have spent it long ago. It was hard to dismiss the suspicion that Ivone was hiding something.

When the lady sat in the great hall her presence infected the entire clan with unease. The McPhersons had been careful not to say disparaging remarks about her, but she knew Ivone was not loved by the clan.

After the funeral the nobles quickly returned to the castle, anxious to get out of the freezing cold, but she stayed behind to pay her respects to the families. She was pleasantly surprised when Cairn stayed with her. He had spent many hours training with his men, but she doubted he was close to their families. Though shy around their new laird, the villagers appreciated the gesture of kindness.

"Shall I escort you, milady?" asked a gravelly voice near her side.

She turned to see old Thomas's spindly form beside her. He was still reserved around the elegant newcomer, but not as hostile as the day before. She decided to take advantage of his unexpectedly social mood.

"Thank you."

She threaded her arm through his and slowed her steps to match his shuffling ones.

"It isn't right for a lady to be wandering the lands without an escort."

"Surely there is no danger here."

"It's about what's proper," he replied stiffly. She couldn't tell if the words were bitter or accusing. Once he had been the laird's chief steward, but now he was forced to live out his retirement in a cottage far from the castle. Did he envy her position or condemn her for it?

"It is nice to be treated like a lady, but I would rather us be friends. Surely there is no need for formality between us."

She wanted Thomas to believe there was a vast difference between Verena and Cairn's stepmother. He eyed her suspiciously, but his next words confirmed her earnest words had worked.

"Hmm … That is what you say now, but time will tell. You should have seen Lady Ivone when she first arrived. Her baggage train stretched for half a mile. The others were so happy to see it. They thought with all that stuff we would be the richest clan in Scotland."

"But you didn't trust her. What happened?"

"I didn't trust her for a minute. Her fancy things are still in the castle, but for some people there is never enough."

Thomas shook his head at the mysteries of the nobility.

"I've noticed," she hedged, not wanting to sound too direct. "The clan seems reserved around her."

"Of course they are! When Lady Ivone arrived she tried to model us after the French nobility. What good are fancy ways when crops are failing?"

"It is strange. The McPhersons had so much wealth when the Old Lord died and then when Lady Ivone arrived it disappeared. Do you suppose she spent it all?"

"I hope the Old Lord had the sense to hide it from her, but he isn't around to ask."

Chapter 25

The pale sunlight hesitantly peeking through the clouds gave Verena the perfect excuse to search the surrounding countryside. She borrowed a basket from the kitchen, offering to collect some late-season herbs for the cook.

To avoid prying eyes she began her search far away from the village. She headed deep into the woods searching for an abandoned cave, a well, or the entrance to the old silver mines. Unfortunately, after several hours all she had to show for her work was a muddy gown and growling stomach. She reached down to collect some wild rosemary and decided to try again tomorrow.

Instinct made her glance up then, catching sight of the large man watching intently from the shadow of a nearby tree. His face was hidden by the dense underbrush, as was most of his body. How long had he stood behind the tree silently watching her? If not for the unsettling awareness of danger, she might not have noticed him at all. She covertly reached for the knife hidden in her boot. Though it wouldn't stop an attacker his size, the small weapon would certainly slow him down.

"I like mine better," said the man, drawing an ordinary-looking knife from his belt. It was a crude and undistinguished piece of wood and metal, but she had seen it too often to mistake it or its owner. It was the exact duplicate of the one she lightly clasped, ready to throw.

With an expert flick of the wrist the man hurled it at her, planting the knife less than an inch from her foot.

"You must be bored," said she levelly. She gracefully rose to her feet, wrenching the blade from the soggy ground. "Owen."

He stepped from behind the tree finally revealing his face to her. It seemed like ages since she had seen Owen. He had grown a beard and now wore a dirty grey tunic and cap instead of the brown one from previous winters.

"It's good to see you, Verena," he replied, giving her fine new clothes an assessing and appreciative glance. "Scotland agrees with you."

She shrugged at the compliment, waiting for him to get to the point. Owen wouldn't seek her out, placing her cover at risk, unless he had something important to report.

"Is there somewhere you can hide this?"

"Aye."

She didn't need to open the small bundle to know what was inside. Her lock picking set, throwing knives and all the other necessary devices of her trade left behind in Langthorne were neatly packed and transported by Owen.

Only he would understand how naked she felt without her things. The contents were more than the tools of her trade. They represented a lifetime of clandestine work. Each item was specifically made for her, costing more than half a year's work. With her tools Verena felt invincible.

"Do not bother searching out here," said Owen. "I'll do that. Concentrate on the castle."

Being outside the drafty and possibly haunted stone walls was wonderful. She had enjoyed roaming the countryside without having to worry about the proper thing to say or do, but they had to work efficiently. Her wishes hardly mattered with so much at stake.

"You should hurry," he cautioned. "Lord Gundy grows impatient."

Verena gave him a sour look. Lord Gundy was always impatient. That was why Hadran handled him. He had much more finesse than his younger associates.

"He knows the McPherson is preparing for war and wants us to make sure that doesn't happen."

Though she had been preoccupied with searching for the treasure she could see the preparations being made by the McPhersons. Animals were slaughtered to extend the winter stores; arrows were being made by the hundreds while every man old enough to hold a sword was drafted to learn something of combat.

It was oddly touching to see the busy activity. Villagers with no skill in combat were now forced by necessity to defend their homeland. Though she didn't know all of Gundy's plans she knew they might soon have to use their new skills.

"What does he expect us to do?" she asked, but she already suspected the answer. The McPhersons were a stubborn lot. Verena had seen the tight bonds connecting the families and knew they would fight with their last breath to save their homes. With Andreu's help they might have a chance of surviving. Given enough time Cairn might also be able to convince his neighboring clans to join the fight. No wonder Gundy was anxious for Verena to find the treasure. He needed the silver to finance his invasion, but if he waited too long the McPhersons would be ready for him. The only way for Gundy's plan to succeed was to cut off the head of the McPherson clan, namely Cairn's head.

"You know," replied Owen quietly. "We can't allow the McPhersons to recover. Secure the treasure first, and then take care of their laird."

Verena nodded. She knew this was coming. As soon as Cairn outlived his usefulness he would be killed in a manner least likely to arouse suspicion. It was the only way to succeed.

"I've heard," continued Owen, "that you've become the McPherson's leman. Don't get too close. We both know how this must end."

"I can still do my job."

Owen reached for Verena and pulled her into his arms. He was rough where Cairn was gentle, hard where Cairn molded perfectly to her body. Owen had done so much for her. He deserved her respect and kindness, yet she was stiff in his embrace, unable to stop comparing him to the man that had held her so tenderly the night before.

"I know. When this is over you and I ..."

"Someone is coming!" she whispered, hastily stepping away. She felt a twinge of guilt at her enthusiasm. It wasn't Owen's fault he didn't feel right. The only reason she allowed the embrace was because he was her friend, but when she felt his rough hands skimming over her hips it took every ounce of willpower not to shove him away.

Perhaps it was familiarity. They had known each other for years and she had grown accustomed to thinking of him as a brother. Maybe that was why the bulge in his hose had seemed so wrong. Verena would have to sort out her puzzling reactions later. Her conspirator disappeared behind a tree moments before Cairn appeared along the forest path.

"Verena," he greeted her warmly. "I heard you were collecting herbs."

Her heart was surely pounding loud enough for Cairn to hear. Though she tried to smile she was horrified by that close encounter. If Cairn had stumbled upon her in Owen's arms no amount of explanation would save her from his wrath. She glanced up at the sky as the pale winter sun passed behind a cloud and felt a shiver of premonition. Soon enough the joy they had shared together would dissipate like that sunlight. Soon Cairn would realize that the maiden he had welcomed into his home was a viper undermining everything he held dear.

"Is something amiss?" she asked in her sweetest tone.

"Nay. There is something I would like to show you."

She followed Cairn along a separate path that led deep into the southeastern woods. Her mind was awhirl after her conversation with Owen. So much of Gundy's plan depended on her success. She must locate the treasure, arrange for it to be transported to Lord Gundy and dispatch Cairn before the English army arrived and she had no idea when that might be. The McPhersons would likely secure the castle as soon as the English appeared in preparation for a siege. If she was not careful she would be locked inside with the clan.

"What would you like to show me?" she asked, to take her mind off the dizzying future. They were heading deep into the Old Lord's woods. Above them the canopy had thickened with foliage, obliterating the sparse sunlight and giving the trees threatening, distorted shadows. A thick, sparkling mist wafted through the trees and she imagined a host of mischievous nymphs hiding in the gloom. The spooky atmosphere made her skin crawl.

"Don't worry," teased Cairn, sensing her unease. "I'll protect you from any demons interested in devouring your soul."

"What of thieves and brigands?"

Cairn pointed to the sword at his side. "Do you think this is for decoration?"

Taking a deep breath, she allowed him to lead her deeper into the woods. They walked along an old trail that was mostly covered with fallen leaves and overgrown bushes. Wherever Cairn was taking her must be special. Was it also important during the Old Lord's time?

"This is it," said Cairn, stopping in front of a massive hill. Verena looked at him curiously. Did Cairn bring her all this way to look at a mound of dirt? The hill was mostly covered in soil except for one side where several small boulders poked through the mud.

"This is my grandfather's grave," Cairn explained, placing one hand reverently on a stone. "As a child I used to come here to think. In the spring I would roll down the hill until my limbs were on fire from the itchy grass. For some reason I always thought this place was safe. When I was here nothing could touch me."

"Did you often run away?"

"Children sometimes need a secret place, or anyplace to hide. My father was always so busy and Lady Ivone ... I needed it even more after she came to live with us."

She could understand why. Ivone didn't seem like the type to dedicate much time to children. If his parents had also tried to keep him away from the village children Cairn must have been a very lonely boy.

"He died before I was born, but sometimes I wonder what it would be like to know him. As a child I imagined the Old Lord letting me keep one of his familiars as a pet. Or I would imagine saving the clan from one of his lingering spells ..."

Cairn didn't continue and she gently slipped her hand into his. She turned to face him, resting her cheek against his heart. Verena didn't know why he brought her to this place, but she was glad to offer him whatever comfort she could. When his mouth sought hers she raised her lips to him eagerly. His fingers gripped her hips, pulling her tight against his groin. She arched against him, curling her fingers into his hair. She wanted him to forget, just for a moment, the loneliness of the past.

Desperate fingers dug into her flesh, pulling her closer. She leaned into him, matching Cairn's passion with her own. In spite of the chilly weather she was on fire from the blazing heat of his kisses. When his wandering mouth was stopped by the rigid Tudor neckline, Cairn ripped it so that her breast spilled into his eager hands.

Verena gasped, pleasantly surprised by the violence of his action. She could repair the gown later. What mattered was the intensity of his need for her. Their eyes met and she saw wildness in Cairn that was frightening and compelling. He needed her. He needed to bury himself deeply within her and allow the madness of their lovemaking to drive away his fears.

Verena was suddenly afraid of such a coupling. She knew she was much too close to this man she intended to destroy, yet her traitorous body craved his touch. Cairn was not the only one that needed to be loved.

He lifted her skirts and thrust one hand between her legs to massage her already throbbing flesh. She cried out as she was filled with the sudden, overwhelming pleasure. Her legs buckled beneath her and Cairn pushed her onto the burial mound.

Through a haze of pleasure she saw Cairn shift his weight as he followed her to the ground. She instinctively drew her knees up in anticipation of his first, beautiful thrust. When it came her entire body shuddered in ecstasy. She arched, uncaring of the mud and leaves sticking to her back and hair. All that existed was Cairn and the feel of him inside her.

As their lovemaking reached its thundering climax she clutched Cairn in her arms, twining her limbs about him as if she would never let him go. Gently Cairn turned her head and gazed at her with a look of tenderness and awe. He kissed her swollen lips and teasingly bit the plump lower one. Her limbs were heavy, completely spent by Cairn's intensity, yet a strange excitement suffused her body. She felt cherished. Cairn softly brushed his lips against her forehead and for the first time in her life she felt loved.

Verena pondered that feeling as they made their slow, leisurely way back to the castle. There were so many things to occupy Cairn's time, but for the moment he was content to walk beside her, holding her hand. It was perhaps silly to feel this way since she had engineered the situation, but knowing Cairn had chosen to spend his precious moments of freedom with her caused her heart to beat a little faster.

This must be how lovers feel. Would she have the same with Owen? Verena shuddered at the thought. It was hard to imagine being so intimate with anyone else. She didn't want to think of the future when she would only have the memory of Cairn to carry her through the empty nights. She resolved right then to stop worrying about the outcome of her actions. She knew her duty to Lord Gundy and wouldn't dare betray him, but that didn't mean she couldn't enjoy these precious moments with Cairn.

Chapter 26

"There you are!" exclaimed Roselyn when Verena re-entered her bedroom. "I have been worried sick. Did you have an accident?"

She glanced down in embarrassment to find she was dragging mud, leaves, straw and other questionable objects, stuck to the hem of her gown. She removed her heavy cloak, displaying the ruined gown underneath.

"I was gathering herbs and fell into some brambles."

"You poor thing!" clucked Roselyn. "I'll fetch some salve for your scrapes and prepare a hot bath for you. You must be chilled to the bone. Would you like some mulled wine?"

"Yes, please."

Roselyn bundled Verena into a luxurious robe of red fur-lined velvet and slippers that had been resting above a warming pan just in case. She then prepared a steaming mug of spiced wine for her to drink while Roselyn prepared the bath. She knew it was a servant's duty to see to her master's comfort, but her service was too thoughtful to be done out of obligation. She seemed to genuinely care for her well-being, perhaps due to the time they spent together in the village.

"Roselyn," she asked, when the maid returned with the bathtub and several buckets of steaming water. "You have kin in Sheepsdale that would house you should things take a turn for the worse. Do the other McPhersons have such ties?"

"Probably," said Roselyn. "Why do you ask?"

"No reason."

"If you are worried about the harvest," she replied. "Don't be. Laird Cairn will never let us starve."

"And Langthorne?"

"I'm not afraid of the English. If Gundy meant to attack us, he would have done it while Lady Ivone ruled the clan. We have our Laird back now."

Lord Gundy was very much aware of the McPhersons' activities. He probably paid more attention to his enemies than his own fief. Though skilled warriors surrounded Lady Ivone, Verena doubted she would be very effective in leading them into battle. Why did Gundy wait for Cairn to return?

She wished she knew more about the plan, but Hadran insisted it was safer this way. If his operatives were captured, there was very little they could confess. Gundy suspected there was a hidden treasure and was planning to invade, but most of the McPhersons had surmised as much. Many had searched for the treasure before she and the clan was constantly on the practice field.

She shook her head in confusion. It wasn't her job to understand Lord Gundy, only to follow his instructions.

"There you go," said Roselyn, as she sat her in front of the fire to brush her drying hair. "You'll be warm again in no time."

Actually, she was warm a long time ago and was now dangerously close to overheating, but she was enjoying the foreign luxury of being coddled too much to complain. She added Roselyn to the long list of things she would miss after she left.

"Thank you for taking such good care of me, Rosie."

"My da used to call me that when I was a little girl," she replied softly. "I'd forgotten the name."

"Should I call you something else?" Verena asked, perturbed by the girl's reaction.

Impulsively Roselyn reached out, enfolding her in a quick embrace. "Nay, it is sweet, just like you," Roselyn whispered against her hair. Verena stood stiffly in the embrace, unused to such affectionate outbursts. First Owen, and now Roselyn. This was turning into a very emotional day.

"I'm sorry," said an embarrassed Roselyn. "That was improper."

"Nay, I wasn't expecting that, but it was ... sweet."

As an assassin and spy, sweet was a word that rarely described her. No doubt Owen would find the description amusing. She still felt a twinge of unease remembering how she had left her comrade. What was he about to say?

"When this is over you and I ..."

Verena decided she didn't want to know the end of that sentence. Eventually she would have to explain that she didn't have the same feelings for Owen. How would he react? He might be hurt, or even angry, but she had never given him cause to hope for anything more than friendship. She wished she could talk to someone about her dilemma. Hadran was always good for strategizing, but he was in Langthorne. she dared not talk to anyone else.

Chapter 27

The door to the Old Lord's chamber eased open with a tiny groan. Verena was glad she had thought to oil the hinges first. It was bad enough to be discovered by Cairn and his brother. If she were caught sneaking about again, people might become suspicious.

Inside the room looked exactly the same as they left it; barely disturbed. She shook her head at the brothers' inexpert search. If Lady Ivone and her maids were also satisfied with such a cursory look, it was no wonder the treasure was still hidden. Now it was time for the real search to begin.

Walking over to the bed, she pulled off the blankets one by one, running her fingers across the dusty fabric in case something was sewn into the hems. She ripped open the pillows at the seams to look inside, before carefully gathering up the spilled down to sew back inside. She looked under the bed, behind the tapestry, behind and under the furniture. She sifted through the ashes in the fireplace, and searched the furniture for hidden compartments. There was nothing out of the ordinary.

The chamber had been shut up after the Old Lord died, leaving it perfectly preserved, as if the castle folk expected him to return any day. His clothing was neatly folded and put away by the last faithful servant. An empty pitcher and goblet rested on a small table beside the bed. She could even see the scuff marks left on the floor where the bathtub had been placed. Like Verena, the Old Lord was fond of bathing in front of the fire.

This was where he spent most of his time. This was the bed where he made love to his wife, and where his son was born. She could feel his presence, as if the Old Lord stood before her, but there was no hint of the treasure.

Unheeding of the cobwebs, she trailed her fingers along the walls. They were excellently constructed and still smooth, despite their age. She pressed gently against each wall. It was hard to be sure, but it felt like the texture had subtly changed beneath her fingers.

Verena used the rag she brought to clear some of the dust and cobwebs away. One small section of the chamber was definitely constructed differently, as if changed after the room had been built. She could barely contain her excitement as she realized she had just stumbled upon a secret passageway.

It was ingeniously built, using the room's architecture to hide the outline of the door. If she had not been feeling for abnormalities, she never would have found it. She pushed against the wall with all her might, but nothing happened. Frowning, she turned to look around the room, searching for a lever or button that would open it. There was nothing.

Verena chewed her lip in frustration. The treasure could be right behind that door. She just had to find a way in. She wished Hadran were with her. He was a genius with solving puzzles. She took a deep breath and closed her eyes, mentally reviewing her search in case she had overlooked anything. Hadran taught her that the answers were usually obvious to the person that was calm enough to see them.

When she opened her eyes again they immediately went to the tapestry. Throughout her search, she had imagined the Old Lord's silken eyes watching her, daring her to find what he had so cleverly hidden. There were so many rumors circling about this strange man. Was he a practitioner of the dark arts? The faintly smiling familiar at his feet seemed to indicate so. He stared haughtily down at her from the past and she couldn't help sticking her tongue out at him.

Behind him, the McPherson banner proudly displayed a red phoenix. She had seen it a hundred times since she came to Scotland. The crest definitely fit the family. Though faced with calamity, they always seemed to rise from the ashes like the mythological bird. Cairn was no doubt praying that knack for survival would continue with him.

She squinted at the tapestry. Was there a message hidden in the cloth, a clue to opening the secret passage? From her lessons with

Hadran, she knew artwork was often filled with symbolism, usually Christian, but after staring at the tapestry for a while, her eyes began to blur. She shook her head tiredly. If there was a message in the cloth she couldn't puzzle it out.

Her eyes went back to the phoenix hovering protectively over the Old Lord, the symbol for victory rising reborn from the ashes. She knew secret passageways were often constructed to allow the nobility to escape during warfare or a siege. It gave the family a chance to survive and fight another day. Like the bird, they could rise from the ashes of defeat.

Ashes ... she walked back to the fireplace. Could she have overlooked something? She had already sifted through the ashes, but now she was looking for something different. She pressed against each of the façade stones, running her dirty fingers across the soot-covered exterior. When nothing happened, she squatted in front of it, reaching inside the dark space to feel along the inside.

Ever so slightly, one of the stones moved. She grinned in excitement and pushed harder. The stone slowly gave way. When the chamber was occupied, a person would have to reach through fire to find this device. She turned back to marvel at the tapestry, and found the Old Lord and his familiar gazing down at her with matching looks of haughty contempt.

"I have to do this," she explained. "I don't have a choice."

The tapestry didn't respond and she forced a laugh at her overworked imagination. Behind her, the passageway had silently sprung open, as if pushed by invisible spirits. Her stomach chose that moment to growl loudly, reminding her it was almost time for supper. If she wasn't back soon, Cairn might search for her and she still needed time to wash the telltale dust from her gown. Nevertheless, the dark passage beckoned her. She found curiosity propelling her feet forward. She had to go through that door.

The darkness inside the narrow passageway seemed much thicker than the outer chamber. The shadows pressed against the meager light of her torch. She decided to leave the door ajar as she explored. It was a risk in case anyone came behind her, but she would prefer that to being trapped in this place.

The passage was so small she had to tuck her skirts up to keep them from dragging along the dirty walls. If the Old Lord was as tall as Cairn, he would have had to duck his head as he walked through.

She walked slowly, unable to see more than a couple of feet before her. With each step she moved farther away from the relative safety of the Old Lord's chamber. Was this passage stable? What if the walls suddenly collapsed? Would anyone think to look for her here?

The tunnel seemed to go on forever, first downhill at a steep angle, then flat, and finally upwards. The icy stones cooled the stale air making her shiver in the darkness. A thick particle of dust lodged in her throat and she sneezed. The sound echoed off the moist walls like an explosion.

Verena came around the next bend and halted. In front of her the passage had caved in, blocking her way. She held her torch up for a better look and quickly revised her opinion. The walls had not caved in; someone had filled in this section of the tunnel with stones carried in from elsewhere. They wanted to block the tunnel without damaging it.

If they had done this a little closer to the Old Lord's chamber, she would have been saved from a long, fruitless trip. Did the Old Lord do this or some nameless caretaker after his death? She didn't relish the thought of coming back with a shovel, but that was exactly what she would have to do.

Far from being discouraged, this new obstacle made her pulse beat with anticipation. Someone had gone to a lot of trouble to keep her from the other side of this tunnel. Something special had to be hidden there. Hadran would be rubbing his hands together in glee at the thought of tackling this mystery.

In the back of her mind she was glad this would give her a few more days to spend with the clan and their enigmatic leader. Just thinking of what they had done that morning made her blush. She wouldn't mind staying a few extra days to finish her search ... and continue her exploration of Cairn's body.

Chapter 28

"You are lucky to have such a loving brother," growled Andreu as he lay shuddering in the tiny cottage next to Cairn. Though a cheery fire blazed nearby, it did little to dispel the icy chill in the air.

"You could have stayed at the castle," snapped Cairn, tired of his brother's grumbling. "I dinna ask you to come along."

"And have you traipsing all over the Scottish countryside alone? Not bloody likely."

"Then stop complaining! Sometimes you are worse than Ivone."

Despite the weather, an amused chuckle forced itself through Andreu's chattering teeth.

The two brothers had ridden to speak with the MacFies, a neighboring clan, about the upcoming war with Langthorne. Cairn thought the clan would be anxious to match themselves against the despised Lord Gundy, but they had enough problems, dealing with crop failure and frost. They wouldn't commit their men to war.

Cairn raged at them, reminding the MacFies of ties forged long ago between their clans. He reminded them of their pride and duty to stand together, but it was no use. The MacFies wanted no part in Cairn's conflict with England. The McPhersons had to fight this war alone.

Their laird had offered the men hospitality for the night, but Cairn stubbornly refused it. Two days had been wasted arguing with the MacFies and Cairn was anxious to return home and make up the lost time.

"I'm sure the farmer is much warmer in the barn," continued Andreu. "Tucked in with his sheep. I thought the poor man would soil his pants when he saw us ride up as we did, covered in mud and mad as the devil."

"We will be gone soon enough."

The two brothers knew they would someday grow up and become lords, but that future had always seemed far away. Andreu had also been abruptly thrust under the yoke of responsibility. It was tough, but Andreu survived just as he knew Cairn would. They had their wits and they had each other.

"These are hard times for everyone. If the MacFies had come to you with a similar request, you would have given them the same answer."

"Perhaps," Cairn replied. It galled him to have to ask for help and being turned away had not improved his mood. "I hate being helpless! And I am too old to share a bed with my brother!"

"Fine," snapped Andreu, poking his brother in one thickly muscled biceps. "I'm sure Fergus' fat is a lot more comfortable than you anyway. The thanks I get for helping my family!"

Cairn grabbed a pillow and pushed it over his head to drown out Andreu's angry muttering. He wished Verena were there. She was unbelievably comfortable with just the right amount of womanly softness. He loved the magical way her breasts filled his hands, the way she responded to his every caress. He could picture her eyes growing unfocused and heavy-lidded as he played with her. If Verena were with him, they would no doubt find ingenious ways to stay warm.

Cairn hadn't wanted to stay with the MacFies, but that wasn't the only reason he left so abruptly. He missed her. He missed the taste of her and the feel of her in his arms. Cairn wanted to barricade them in his bedroom and never come out.

"Stop there, you little thief!" came Fergus' gruff shout from outside. His voice was immediately followed by a loud crash and Fergus' howl of pain.

The two brothers rushed outside with drawn swords. Did marauders think to attack their small band of warriors? They looked about; scanning the area for the glint of metal or bright colors of livery, but the scene that greeted them caused both men to blink in surprise.

Fergus was hopping up and down on one leg, holding his shin and bellowing curses at the top of his lungs, while a lad of about 13 tried to dodge between the newly awakened soldiers. His head was covered by an oversized, dirty cap and mismatched rags disguised his scrawny limbs.

Cairn had seen that frightened, hungry look in the eyes of many peasants who were caught stealing, and felt sorry for the scamp. If he couldn't produce a miracle, the boys of his own clan may soon share his fate. Cairn opened his mouth to call off his men, but before he could speak, the boy dived between Fergus' legs, punching sharply upward with strong, little fists.

Fergus howled again, clutching his groin and crumpling to the ground. Cairn couldn't let the boy go after a stunt like that.

"Catch him."

The other men took up the chase, trying to corral the boy. He was fast and agile, ducking under an old workbench, climbing up and leaping off a large wagon. The lad was remarkably coordinated, as if he was taught his skills by a master. There was a definite strategy to his moves as he dove between the soldiers, expertly positioning the men so they couldn't surround him. The blows that he delivered with his tiny fists were always on target, catching the soldiers in sensitive areas like the groin, the kidneys, and behind the knees. Several times he almost escaped, but someone always managed to cut him off before he could go far.

"Are you going to let this brat best you?" shouted Andreu, obviously enjoying the spectacle.

The lad crouched down and swung his leg in an arc, catching Fergus' ankle and sending him flat on his back in a large puddle of mud. Fergus sat there for a moment, inhaling huge gulps of air, and then an amazing thing happened. The most infectious grin lit Fergus' features. He leaned back his head and laughed until his great belly shook with mirth, and tears were streaming from his eyes.

"Milord, we should have him train us on the practice field," said Fergus, when he could speak again. The others joined in his laughter and the contest soon became a game. The men would laugh uproariously as the lad evaded capture. It was nice to have a moment of fun to ease the stress.

Their mirth came to an abrupt end, however, when the youth finally saw his chance and tried to run past the two brothers. Andrew and Cairn had been calmly watching the spectacle, but when the lad came near, Cairn reached out and caught the boy by the arms.

"That's enough!" said Cairn sternly. "Tell me why you are here."

"He is a thief, milord," spoke up Fergus, when the lad didn't answer. "I caught him sneaking around the barn."

"Search him."

The lad submitted to their rough search, finally realizing there was no escape. They found only a knife hidden on his small frame, but the haunted look didn't leave his eyes.

"Who taught you to fight?" Andreu wanted to know. After a moment, the lad tore his gaze from Cairn's impressive bulk and answered.

"I taught meeself."

Fergus scoffed, ineffectually wiping mud from his wet bottom.

"There aren't many grown men that can best me, and you took on all of us."

"You fight like knights," the boy answered simply.

From the time Cairn was born, he was carefully groomed for knighthood. He had trained extensively in various forms of combat and weaponry until he was legendary on a battlefield. This youth's disdain was perplexing.

"What is wrong with the way we fight?"

The boy bit his lip, clearly unwilling to volunteer anymore information.

"What is your name? Where is your family?"

It was clear there would be no more information from him without resorting to heavy-handed persuasion. The moon peeked hesitantly from behind a cloud bank, illuminating a patchwork of old bruises on his face and neck. This lad had learned to fight by necessity, perhaps for his very life. What kind of parents would allow their child to come to such a state? Did he have parents at all?

He stared defiantly into Cairn's eyes and something softened within him. The boy's passion and fearful determination reminded him of Verena. She had worn a similar expression when they first met in Langthorne.

"Thieves must be punished," announced Cairn evenly. Though his lower lip began to tremble, the boy refused to cower. "You have also injured my men and must atone for your actions. Fergus, make sure he does not run away. I'll deal with him in the morning."

Chapter 29

Verena stepped through the darkened archway leading to the McPherson family crypt. She traveled down a steep, winding staircase at the back of the church, trailing her fingers along the icy stones for balance.

Protective gargoyles had been carved into the corners of the ceiling, but the light from her candle gave them a ghoulish appearance. Above her, Verena could hear the boys from the village singing mass. The music echoing off the high rafters gave the setting an ethereal mood.

She drew her cloak closer about her as she traversed the large room. Around her lay stone effigies of Cairn's deceased family. She stared into the smoothly carved faces, wondering how accurate the artists had been. Did Cairn know the exact location where his body would someday come to rest?

She stared intently at the face of Cairn's father. What manner of man was he? Did Cairn cry at his father's funeral, or had he composed himself with the quiet dignity he showed at the funeral of his clansmen?

She heard the soft thud of feet descending the spiral stairs behind her. Soon Father Simon's voluminous cassock came into view. He smiled at her, not surprised to find her wandering alone in the dark and icy crypt.

"I thought I saw someone enter here," he said brightly. "The echo makes this an excellent place to listen to the holy choir."

She smiled as if that was exactly why she had come down here. In truth, she was hoping to have a few moments alone with Simon, to question him on his relationship with the Old Lord.

"It was heavenly," she agreed.

"Of course I have never experienced it. I am always up there with the choir, but ... Is something troubling you, my child?"

"I wanted to be alone for a while. Coming to Scotland was an abrupt change for me."

Simon nodded, but his eyes sparkled with curiosity.

"I am always available should you need to talk."

"Thank you. Everyone has been so kind, despite my origins, but I am worried about the clan. How will the McPhersons survive this winter?"

"That is not for me to say," replied Father Simon, lifting his eyes heavenward. She knew the doomed clan would need a miracle to survive—a miracle or a fortune in silver.

"I noticed the McPhersons are very pious folk."

"It is not unusual for people to seek comfort with the church during times of strife. Is that not why you are here?"

Verena turned back to look at the face of Cairn's father. She was drawn to touch the stone sculpture, to trace the lines so similar to Cairn's. Where had the treasure gone when the Old Lord died? Why didn't he pass on the secret to Lady Ivone or Cairn?

"He looks so peaceful," she said as she studied the effigy. "I supposed I wanted to absorb some of that peace."

"Angus McPherson was a surprisingly gentle man, despite his genealogy."

"What do you mean?"

"I'm sure you've heard of Cairn's grandfather, the Old Lord? Many still fear that he will rise from the grave."

Father Simon shook his head at the foolishness of peasants.

"Did you know the Old Lord?"

"Aye, but not very well. He had little interest in religion, but in his son I found a surprisingly agile mind. Angus had so many questions about things I had never thought to consider, questions that could be deemed sacrilege by some.

"It couldn't have been easy growing up with the Old Lord as a father. There were so many secrets whispered about what went on in the castle. The Old Lord certainly didn't confide in me. Several times I saw strange bruises on Angus' face and hands, but he bore them stoically—much too stoically for a young man.

"I counseled him as best as I could, but in the end I think he just came for the company. There were times when he looked so sad."

Father Simon shook himself, embarrassed to find he was rambling.

"It has been a long time since anyone asked about Angus," he said in chagrin.

She touched his arm, offering silent comfort to the priest. It was obvious he cared deeply about Angus and it pained him that he was unable to help his friend.

"Surely his wives brought him some comfort," she ventured.

"His first wife, perhaps. That was Cairn's mother. She was a sweet girl with a competent head on her shoulders. You remind me a bit of her actually. I could tell Angus was exceedingly fond of her, but she died in childbirth with their second child and took the babe with her. Poor girl.

"You are smart, lass," continued the priest. "And you must know how the clan feels about Lady Ivone. She never embraced lowland life, even after living with us for years. Women must maintain a sense of propriety, must act with humility, decorum, compassion, obedience and restraint. There are divine laws that must be obeyed for the safety of your immortal souls."

She glanced away, knowing where the conversation was heading. After her speaking with Owen she wouldn't be surprised if the whole clan knew she had become Cairn's leman.

"I do not mean to preach," he continued kindly. "I do enough of that at the pulpit. But I have found that most people know the difference between right and wrong. They just need a little encouragement to set them on the right path. Think about your life and your future. And if you ever need to talk, my door is always open."

Verena thanked the priest as she hastily backed out of the crypt. It was difficult to stay focused on her assignment with the priest's gentle chatter. Just as she reached the stairs she paused and turned back.

"Father," she said curiously. "Why wasn't the Old Lord buried here? Didn't he want to be close to his family?"

Father Simon shrugged as he reached down to brush some dust from Angus' face.

"The Old Lord wasn't close to anyone on this earth. After he was excommunicated he preferred to be buried in a pagan mound like his barbarian cousins to the north."

Chapter 30

Verena's pensive mood followed her back to the castle. Cairn had led a small contingent of men west a few days ago, but hadn't told her where he was going or why. She surmised it was to solicit aid from the neighboring clans, but was perturbed that he hadn't told her the details. Was she so far beneath his notice that he didn't feel the need to inform her, or did Cairn wish to protect her from the reality of his clan's condition?

A village boy running errands for the kitchens informed her that Cairn had returned and was discussing his new armor with the blacksmith. She shook off her doubts and ran to meet him.

"I've found a few places that need work," said Cairn, as he painfully rotated his shoulder. She entered the blacksmith's workshop in time to see the nasty bruise left by the metal uncomfortably rubbing his skin. His favorite suit had been stolen in Langthorne, so Cairn had to make do with an older set.

"I know some herbs that will help," she suggested. "I can make a compress for you."

"I would like that."

Cairn's gaze held Verena's and she felt herself blush all the way to her toes. He had used the soft tone usually reserved for her bedchamber. She wished they were there now. She wanted to rip off his clothes and show Cairn how much she missed him. How had her longing for this man become so desperate? Each time he held her felt new and precious. It must be because their time together was drawing to an end. Cairn was a decent fellow, and a spectacular lover. Of course she would miss him when she left. It was nothing more than that.

"Were the barbarians entertaining?" asked Lady Ivone from the doorway.

"They're Scotsmen," protested Cairn.

"And supposedly your allies," Andreu added.

Gundy would no doubt be pleased to hear Cairn had failed to gain the support of the other clans. Did he have operatives at work in other households making sure this scheme succeeded?

Lady Ivone came forward to see Cairn's injuries, tsking and shaking her head.

"These are from my replacement armor. It needs to be re-fitted."

"If you had a proper squire," she insisted. "This wouldn't have happened. These straps were too tight."

Verena held her tongue as Ivone complained about the incompetence of their servants. She knew the lad that helped Cairn strap on his armor. He was the son of the blacksmith and probably knew more about armor than most knights. She looked quickly at the blacksmith and found his lips compressed into a tight line.

"The straps were fine," Cairn replied. "It is the fit that needs adjustment—which is to be expected with new armor. I should not have worn it so long on its first fitting."

"I want you boys to come to the solar after you've washed the horse filth off and see the new doublets I'm making for you. I scrounged up some silk thread that I'm using to couch a phoenix and ..."

"You can embroider with wool," broke in Cairn. "If you found silk thread, you should have brought it to me."

Lady Ivone scoffed at the idea. "My sons are of noble blood. They deserve to have silk on their garments."

"While people go hungry?"

This was a group preparing itself for a hard winter, but Ivone was unconcerned with their plight. It was no wonder the clan didn't accept her as one of their own.

Even without her preliminary reports, she could see the evidence of crop failure. It was in Gertrude's never-ending quest for cheaper food alternatives, and the lean, stubborn faces of the clan.

Andreu's hand on Cairn's arm checked his anger. Cairn had worked hard to create an image of solidarity. It wouldn't do to have this dispute in front of his clan.

"Do not leap to conclusions," he warned. "You still have a very loving brother with resources of his own. In fact, I think it's time I returned to France. I will be back before you miss me."

...with more men and supplies to last the winter, Verena silently finished. Lord Gundy knew about the McPhersons' close ties to France. He must know Cairn would have his brother's support. That must be why he was growing impatient. Gundy needed the treasure before Andreu returned with reinforcements. She had expected him to leave days ago, but he hesitated. With Gundy expected any day, Andreu was loath to abandon his brother—even to gather more supplies.

Verena shook her head, tired of imagining intrigues. Deciding to withdraw from the family meeting, she left in search of medicines. She stepped outside and made her way to the castle entrance, but soon she heard a commotion ahead.

Jon, the youngest member of Hadran's team, came flying out of the kitchens with a loaf of dark bread clutched in one hand. A furious Fergus chased after him, shouting obscenities and clutching his side. From the stiff way he was running, Jon's fast little fists must have caught Fergus in the kidneys.

An overloaded hay wagon clamored into the courtyard, cutting off Jon's escape. He swerved around it, abruptly changing directions. Jon ran full speed around the stables, looking for a place to hide, and barreled into Verena.

They fell together and Verena, who had fallen on her still-injured shoulder, was momentarily blinded by pain. The boy pummeled her in desperation to get to his feet.

"Jon," whispered Verena through clenched teeth. "It's me."

The boy stilled, finally recognizing the female beneath him.

"I'm sorry! I didn't ..."

"Enough!"

Cairn suddenly appeared, grabbing Jon by the scruff of the neck and lifting him high into the air. He shook him as if Cairn meant to snap Jon's head from his shoulders.

"S'wounds! You will drive me to murder!"

"Truly milord, he didn't see me."

Verena hastily climbed to her feet to prove that she was not injured. Unfortunately she was still disoriented from the fall and had to grab the wall to keep from swooning. Cairn dumped the boy unceremoniously in the mud, but before he could scramble away, Fergus captured him in an iron grip.

"Did he hurt you?"

"Nay. It was an accident, and he already apologized."

"This boy is a demon!" growled Fergus. "I ought to take a switch to his backside."

"What has he done?" she questioned.

"We discovered him last night trying to steal from our camp."

If Gundy was as anxious to find the treasure as Owen claimed, it was not surprising that Jon was called in to assist the other agents. It wasn't like him to be caught spying, but Jon was young and they had all made mistakes in the past.

"The poor thing. Where is your mother?"

Verena made a show of checking the boy for injuries and made a point to reveal each of the bruises left by Owen during their last vigorous training session. Taking the hint, Jon put on his most miserable face, and even made his eyes fill up with tears.

"I don't have a mother."

"Neither do I. Are you hungry?"

Jon hesitated, staring at Verena as if she were an angel sent to deliver him from the scourge of the world. They had used this routine many times in the past and found most people couldn't turn their backs on a reformed orphan, particularly one with Jon's angelic face.

Hesitantly, as if to a wild animal, she reached out her hand and Jon fearfully took it. Verena turned anxious eyes on Cairn and he nodded his approval. Still holding his hand, she led a decidedly sheepish Jon into the kitchens.

"What are you doing here?" she hissed as soon as they were alone.

"Hadran sent me to follow the Scot and see if he allies with the other clans."

"And they caught you?"

"That wasn't my fault! The big one, Fergus, has eyes in the back of his head. I can't scratch without him coming after me. But I showed him!"

"I saw that," she said, affectionately ruffling the boy's shaggy hair. "But now you are trapped here with me and Gundy won't get your report."

Jon visibly paled, imagining Gundy's displeasure. As the architects of his ambitions, the spies knew what happened to those poor souls that displeased their lord. That was why each of them had made a vow to be loyal to each other first. Gundy's agents never failed because they worked hard to ensure their mutual success. No matter what, she would protect Jon.

"Be at ease," she continued thoughtfully. "Owen is nearby and can deliver your report. Today lord Cairn bemoaned the lack of a squire. Perhaps you should develop an interest in armor?"

"I can do that!" replied Jon with a grin. Like Verena, he had a knack for insinuating himself into any situation. Within a week, Jon would probably become the best squire Cairn ever had.

"I could also use your help searching for the treasure. Someone knows where it is hidden and I have identified a few likely suspects. I need you to befriend the clan children and see what they can tell you. Try to have them followed if you can do it without raising suspicion."

"Easy."

Briefly, she described Lady Ivone, old Thomas and Father Simon. She was sure at least one of them knew something about the treasure. In the meantime, she memorized Jon's report to deliver to Owen. Hadran would want to know as soon as possible about this change of plans and she needed Owen to locate some excavation tools so that she may begin clearing the tunnel. There was a lot of work to be done.

Chapter 31

A meeting was taking place in the great Langthorne hall. Five of the most influential North English lords had gathered to discuss what they termed their "Scottish dilemma." They knew all too well the Scots were a testy bunch and wouldn't remain weakened for long.

Above them presided Lord Gundy. As landlord of the main road into the Eastern part of Scotland, he was the self-proclaimed leader of the group.

"Couldn't this wait until spring?" complained Sir Reginald, one of the lesser lords in the assembly. He huddled in front of the fire, still wearing his traveling cloak. If the summons had come from anyone else, with the exception of the king, the nobles might have ignored it and stayed safe and warm at home.

"We cannot let the enemy rest for a moment," insisted Gundy "Or they will rise again."

Some of the nobles visibly flinched at those words. As border lords, they bore most of the damage from the raiding and border wars.

"The Scots are not defeated, merely stunned. We must strike now before they have a chance to recover."

"How do we know the Scots are plotting against us?" asked Lord Oswald. "From what I've heard, the place is a mess with the crop failure and recent plague."

Gundy looked at the assembled lords with pity, not believing their naivete. He had always despised the sniveling Oswald, with his bulbous nose and high, whining voice. His skeletal shape reminded Gundy uncomfortably of the grim reaper.

"I know the Scots are plotting against us. That is why we must act."

"He is right," spoke up Lord Dewey. His lands bordered Langthorne to the southwest, so he was anxious to form an alliance with the venerable Gundy. "I have heard rumors of an unusually large portion of forest being cleared by the MacFie clan."

Reginald snorted as he turned his back to the fire to warm his rear. "No doubt firewood for this blasted winter," he muttered.

"Siege engines," insisted Dewey. "We have all heard of the McPherson activities. They are openly preparing for war! I am with Gundy. Those Scots are plotting against us."

"What exactly would you have us do?" asked the fifth member of their group. All eyes turned to Lord Percy who had nearly been forgotten in his silence. The old man had lost all four of his sons in the recent conflict with Scotland and had no one left to inherit after he died. If anyone had the right to hunger for revenge, it was he.

Gundy rose from his throne-like chair and crossed the room. Gently he took the old man's gnarled hands and pressed them, as if in reverence to a martyr.

"We have all lost so much. We have seen so much suffering. That is why we must ensure it never happens again. We will strike the McPhersons first and once they have fallen, the rest of the lowlands will crumble. That is the only way to keep England safe from those barbarians."

At least that was the rhetoric that would gain Lord Percy's support. Scotland was in disarray with the inept leadership of their king. There were few leaders capable of steering the country through this difficult time. Gundy saw this as the perfect opportunity to carve out a large chunk of the fertile lowlands for himself, but he couldn't do it alone.

"What of the young lord, Cairn McPherson?" asked Sir Reginald with his backside still close to the fire. "He is strong and brave and has gained quite a reputation on the battlefield. Why start with him?"

"My dear lords," Gundy explained. "Cairn McPherson is the Achilles heel that will bring all of Scotland to its knees. We must defeat him first. Do not forget Cairn possesses a brother, the powerful Lord Andreu. If they join forces, we don't have a chance of defeating the lowlands."

"How do you expect to overpower them?" asked Oswald. "The McPherson castle is too defensible for a siege and the French forces are too numerable to defeat in battle. It's not like they will politely line up for you at the executioner's block."

Some of the lords snickered at Oswald's wit and Gundy forced a sickly smile. "They will do just that. Cairn is strong, but he is also young, angry and inexperienced. All he needs is a gentle nudge to place him right where I ... we want him."

Gundy called for more wine to allow his words to sink in. They naturally wanted to hear the details of the plan, realizing Gundy had invested far more in this endeavor than he had shared with his neighbors, but he would say no more. The less they knew the better. He wouldn't risk them meddling too soon in his affairs.

Every time he called the lords Gundy heard more objections and complaints. He wished he could rely solely on Hadran and his team of spies. They had never failed him and never complained about an assignment. Lords were a capricious bunch.

Gundy caught Oswald's shrewd eye and gave an ingratiating smile. That one was too cautious and wouldn't blindly follow Gundy's command. It had taken weeks to convince his neighbor of the necessity of this attack. Thankfully the cunning lord wouldn't bother Gundy for long. In the blaze of war many arrows were known to go astray. One of Hadran's operatives would see to that.

Chapter 32

It was early morning before Verena could sneak away from Cairn's bedchamber. He had been insatiable in his lovemaking, eager to make up for the days they were apart. He had not stopped until he probed each crevice of her body, making her scream as wave after wave of passion rolled over her. She felt limp and pleasantly sore, but she forced her limbs to move. She had work to do.

Leaving Cairn had been much harder than she expected. She was surprised by her desire to linger in his arms and wasn't able to pull herself away until nearly dawn. Jon was curled up in front of the great hall's dying fire with the castle hunting dogs. At first he appeared to be sleeping, but when she gently tapped him, he nearly took her hand off with a swipe of his knife.

"Jesu!" she whispered, jumping away. "Tis I, Verena!"

"I'm sorry, V. That is the second time I attacked you. You must be getting soft."

Before he could blink, she pulled out her own knife and held it to his throat, knocking Jon's small blade away. If he took more than a shallow breath, the sharp metal would pierce his throat, but instead of fear, Jon's eyes danced with excitement. She saw his fingers twitch as he thought of a counterattack.

They often played this game under Hadran's watchful eye. Ambushing each other kept their senses alert and the play gave a welcome release of tension. The competition took the edge off their constant training.

"Still think I am soft? I need your help. Come quickly."

A few minutes later, she pressed the stone in the Old Lord's bedchamber, activating the secret passage. Jon swore in surprise as the door swung open.

"Lord! How did you find that?" he asked, taking the supplies she had collected earlier from Owen. Jon's greedy little eyes scanned the room, searching for valuables to steal.

"It took an obscenely long time. Don't touch anything. Cairn was recently searching for the treasure and would know if something was missing."

"Just my luck!"

Verena lit one of her expensive tapers. She definitely didn't want to carry a smoky torch in this cramped space. She tucked her skirts into her girdle to keep them from dragging on the dusty floor and led the way into the passage.

"Must we walk so slowly?" Jon asked. "If I'm not back soon the kitchen brats will eat all the food."

"'Tis only a little farther." She felt the path tilt upwards under her feet as they neared the end. She reached into her pack of supplies and handed him a chunk of bread and cheese. "Were you able to discover anything about Lady Ivone, Father Simon or Thomas?"

"Aye, a strange lot they are, to be sure! Father Simon is a dear. If you ask me, he couldn't tell a lie to save his soul. He loves this clan and helped raise Cairn from a babe. If he knew about the treasure, he would have said something."

"As I thought. Still, his position gives him a fair amount of autonomy. It was best to be sure."

"Ivone is a terror. At first I thought she was as simple as they come, empty-headed like some other ladies I've seen—no offense. Then she caught me snooping around her bedchamber. I told her I was fetching her used linens, but the way she looked at me, it was as if she could see into my soul. She is cold-hearted and ambitious like Gundy. I don't trust her."

"Did you discover anything?" She decided to ignore his remark about empty-headed ladies.

"Nay. The kitchen brats are afraid to go near her so I'll have to watch Ivone myself."

"Be careful. Of all the McPhersons, she is the one to fear. She tries to appear less intelligent than she is, but I cannot fathom why."

"I know," replied Jon with a dramatic shiver. "That Thomas is definitely hiding something, too. I spent the afternoon chasing him through the forest."

"Did he see you?"

"Of course not! At first I thought he was walking suspiciously, as if he knew he might be followed. He kept changing directions. But then I figured as old as he is, he probably couldn't remember the way. I felt sure he was leading me to the treasure, but instead he took me to a large mud hill."

"The Old Lord's burial mound."

"So the brats told me. Thomas brought a shovel and replaced the dirt that had been washed away by the rains. Do you think the treasure is buried there?"

"It is certainly a possibility, though it seems too obvious. Surely someone would have excavated the Old Lord's grave by now."

"Maybe they are too afraid of his ghost."

"Perhaps. Try to get some rest today. Tonight we'll dig up the Old Lord's grave."

"Have I told you how much I love this job?"

Verena laughed, glad to have Jon beside her. She often wondered how someone so young could handle the more gruesome parts of their assignments, but Jon approached each duty with courage and sarcastic wit. She didn't know anything of his life before Hadran found him wandering the filthy London streets, but she was glad to have him in her group.

When she felt a twinge of guilt that he would never have a normal childhood, she reminded herself that her life had been no different. She didn't know what 'normal' was, but the longer she stayed with the McPhersons, the more she was beginning to understand. Jon had already made himself the leader of the castle boys—much to Fergus' chagrin. They would cheerfully devise ways of terrorizing the gruff soldier. When this was over she would try to find a place where he could forget about the pressures of duty and just enjoy being a child.

The large pile of stones suddenly came into view, blocking their way.

"I suppose this is what the shovels are for," said Jon, inspecting the obstruction. "Someone went to a lot of trouble to keep us from going any farther."

"I am sorry to disappoint them."

Verena grasped one small boulder and with a grunt, lifted it free of the pile. Working the rock free, she had to brace herself against the wall as she felt a wave of dizziness.

"Are you alright?"

"Just tired. There will be plenty of time to rest when this is over."

For someone that was rarely ill, she couldn't understand her body's lethargy. She had worked through the night on much more strenuous assignments and her injured shoulder was nearly healed. Perhaps it was Cairn's lovemaking that was making her so fatigued. She had gotten little sleep since coming to Scotland, but staying away from him was unthinkable.

"I can see!" Jon exclaimed, sticking his head through the hole their excavation had revealed.

"What do you see?"

"Another long passage."

Swearing indelicately, she continued her efforts. Despite his small size, Jon was a strong lad and cleared more than his share of the rubble. They worked together with silent efficiency for what seemed like hours, calling a halt when they could both squeeze through with ease.

"Did you expect this to be easy?" Jon teased, glimpsing her foul mood. She was exhausted and more than willing to continue their search another day. Verena was growing annoyed with this never-ending quest.

"You forget I have been searching for this infernal treasure since I came to Scotland."

"We can't give up now. This is too exciting."

Jon gave her shoulders an encouraging squeeze and ushered her though the passageway. After another long walk, they came to a heavy, wooden door. Verena placed her hands on the rusted, iron handle and pulled, but nothing happened. Thinking the door stuck, she pulled again. Still nothing. Jon added his strength, swearing furiously as he did so, but it was no use. The stubborn door was locked.

"This will only take a moment," he said, kneeling before the lock. "Could you hold the light?"

Verena did so, watching as Jon laid his lock picking tools on the ground with the care of a surgeon. She craned her neck to watch him work, comparing his technique to her own. Jon was absorbed in his task, using his instruments like an extension of his fingers.

He was familiar with this style of lock and knew exactly where the tumblers were, but they were large and heavy. Jon's tools were mostly for smaller locks found on jewelry boxes and chests. He twisted firmly, but gently, praying his tools wouldn't bend or snap in the large keyhole. Finally, Jon grinned in satisfaction when he heard the faint click of the lock spring open.

The door was thick and heavy, with hinges nearly rusted solid. Verena liberally doused them with oil. They pulled with all of their strength and the door gave way grudgingly, an inch at a time.

They found themselves in a small, nearly empty room. A door lay opposite, but it was what lay in front of them that held her attention. A stone sarcophagus stood before them, its lid carved with the effigy of a man she recognized immediately.

"This is the mound," she said in puzzlement. "We are in the Old Lord's burial mound."

"That is impossible! Have we walked that far?"

It certainly felt like it. Verena's entire body ached with the strain of moving rocks, the long walk, and hours of energetic lovemaking. She suspected the large hill hid more than a body, but she didn't expect to find a room this size.

"I don't understand. Where is the treasure? Why would someone go to so much trouble for a dead body?"

The room was completely bare except for the sarcophagus in the center. The floor was made of hard, packed dirt that looked like it had been undisturbed for years.

"Perhaps it is beyond that door," Jon suggested.

This one was also locked and Jon knelt before it and went to work. When it finally opened yet another pile of stones lay in their path. Jon began to poke at them, but she pulled him away. It was the same pile of rocks Thomas had tried to conceal. He was not protecting the treasure; he was safeguarding the Old Lord's body.

She turned to leave, grumpy at having so much of her day wasted on a fool's errand, but something caught her attention. Kneeling beside the Old Lord's stone coffin, she uncovered a small, shiny object glinting in the candlelight. She hooted in excitement as she recognized the tiny Roman coin.

"This wasn't buried," she explained to Jon, who began digging the hard packed earth for treasure. "It was dropped. Someone moved the treasure and must have overlooked this coin."

"It was probably the same person that tried to barricade it," Jon surmised.

"We must discover who moved the treasure. Concentrate most of your efforts on Thomas, but do not overlook other likely suspects. We need to question all of the Old Lord's surviving retainers to find out who may know something."

With the clan's current difficulties, it was only a matter of time before someone searched the Old Lord's grave. The treasure had to be moved to a safer location, but where? Verena had been inside Thomas' tiny cottage and hadn't noticed anything suspicious. Perhaps she needed to take a closer look.

Thomas should have come forward long ago if he knew about the treasure. The circumstances were certainly dire enough. Verena understood why he might have felt compelled to hide the silver from Ivone, but why continue to hide it from his lord?

•

"Where have you been?" Cairn demanded as she reentered the hall. She had washed off most of the filth from the Old Lord's tunnel and hoped to rest before the midday meal. She was surprised to note that nearly half the day had been spent underground with Jon. "No one has seen you for hours."

Verena spun around, catching herself as another wave of dizziness made her head spin. Perhaps it had been too long since her last meal.

"Good day, milord," she replied with false gaiety. "Mary's son, Robert, fell out of a tree so I brought her some salve. The lad is fine, just bruised. Is something amiss?"

"Nay, but I would have you stay closer to the castle. It is not safe to wander the lands unescorted."

"Of course, I ..."

Verena gulped as the meager contents of her stomach threatened to erupt. What was wrong with her? For the past few days she had been unusually fatigued and nauseous. She opened her mouth to speak and was sick all over Cairn's boots.

Chapter 33

Someone was stroking her hair. That was strange. No one ever stroked her hair. She opened her eyes to find she had been carried to her chamber. Cairn was perched on the bed waiting for her to awaken.

"How do you feel?"

A pitcher of cold water was beside her bed and some fennel. Verena gratefully rinsed out her mouth and chewed the herb to freshen her breath.

"I am much better. Thank you for staying with me, but I am sure you have more important things to do."

"Not now."

Verena eyed Cairn suspiciously, startled by the gentleness in his voice. He was always passionate, but this was the first time he tried to woo her with romance. Why now after they made love? She expected Cairn to loose interest as their love affair continued. Instead she found herself counting the minutes until she could be with him again. It was a relief to know he felt the same.

"I will be alright."

"You are always alright," Cairn replied. "But I have never seen you happy."

"I am happy now."

Cairn tightened his arms around her, pulling Verena closer to his heart. She pushed Cairn onto his back, covering his mouth with a lingering kiss. She cared for this man. Verena's heart ached with the certainty that she would directly cause his destruction. She didn't want to hurt him, but she knew she must. She couldn't betray her family of spies.

Verena kissed him to hide the turmoil in her heart. She spread her kisses across Cairn's chest and down his torso, using her lips and tongue to work him into a fever. She traced his nipples with her tongue before gently sucking the dark orbs.

Her head moved lower, across the tight muscles of Cairn's abdomen. She loved the way they contracted under her mouth. She felt his disappointment as she avoided his male organ and instead brushed her lips against his firm upper thigh. Giving Cairn a saucy look, she lowered her head again and kissed his opposite thigh.

"Tease," Cairn ground out through clenched teeth. Another kiss was placed less than an inch above his manhood.

"Did you want something?"

"You know exactly what I want."

Verena could feel the heat radiating from his skin and smell their lovemaking in the air. She felt intoxicated with passion, savoring the salty taste of his sweat.

Finally she took him into her mouth. She heard a sound that was part sigh and part groan, and decided to take her time, letting his reaction guide her. She loved the feel of him in her mouth, the power of knowing she controlled his pleasure. Verena went faster, using her lips and hands to drive him wild.

The muscles of his thighs and abdomen tensed as he came closer to ecstasy. Suddenly she found herself on her back. Cairn lifted her legs and drove himself deeply inside her, tired of the maddening caresses. She gasped at the sudden, intense pleasure, growling and arching her back. She wrapped her legs firmly around Cairn's torso, grinding her hips to his.

Verena tried to go slowly and draw out the intimacy of the moment, but Cairn would have none of that. She nearly drove him insane with her mouth and now Cairn showed her how much he desired her.

It wasn't what she planned, but she couldn't complain. She was mindless with pleasure. When she reached her climax, Cairn was right behind her, letting out a guttural roar as he released his seed deep inside her.

She collapsed with a smile of contentment; their arms were still loosely entwined. It was a long time before Cairn broke the perfect stillness, raising himself on one elbow to gaze at her naked flesh.

"How do you feel?"

"Wonderful."

"Is there something you would like to tell me?"

"About what?" she asked in puzzlement. Had Cairn somehow discovered her secret? Was he now interrogating Jon in the dungeon? Cairn's satisfied smile belied that thought.

"About the child."

Verena froze, sure she had misheard him.

"What child?"

He laughed a deep, rumbling sound and once again drew Verena into his arms.

"You didn't know?" he asked in astonishment. "I forget how innocent you really are. My child, the one you are carrying."

She was pregnant! Hadran had diligently instructed Verena on how to avoid this. She had been so careful, never missing her daily dose of bishop's lace. Verena didn't understand how this could have happened.

What would she do with a child? She certainly wasn't in a position to raise one. Verena's life was inherently dangerous. It was ludicrous to even contemplate it, but that didn't stop the slow rush of joy that enveloped her heart.

Secretly, she had always wanted a real family, it just never seemed possible. She knew what it was like to grow up without parents. If Hadran had not found her, she would certainly be dead. No matter what, she would ensure this baby never experienced that life.

"Don't worry," said Cairn, sensing her growing panic. "All will be well."

If not for Lord Gundy, she might believe him. Already the cunning lord was amassing an army to sweep across the lowlands. The McPhersons would be destroyed and Cairn would be the first to die. Verena had to make sure she was far away before the English armies arrived. Now she had something infinitely valuable to protect.

Chapter 34

Late that evening, when she was sure he slept; Verena slowly extricated herself from Cairn's embrace. She retrieved her dark cloak and tiptoed out of the room. She carefully made her way past the sentries; glad she had taken the time to learn their rotations. She silently moved through the forest, her form concealed by the deep shadows of the trees. Verena softly signaled her presence to Owen, and after a few moments, he stepped from the gloom. They stood before the Old Lord's burial mound with the heat from their breath clouding the air.

"Is the McPherson dead?" Owen asked.

"Nay. I thought I would have more time."

"There is no time. Gundy's men will be here in less than a fortnight."

She felt her body go cold. This assignment was different from the ones of the past. Lord Gundy didn't want something stolen or damning evidence to blackmail a neighbor. He wanted Verena to prepare for an invasion. So many people would die because of her, people that she called friends.

"I need to be removed from this assignment. Jon has integrated himself into the McPherson household and can replace me."

She knew Hadran would be displeased by her failure, but more than her life was at stake. She couldn't risk her unborn babe.

"Are you in trouble? Has your position been compromised?"

"There is … another reason," she admitted hesitantly. "I am with child."

Owen stared at her for a long moment. Verena could see confusion, anger and sadness cross Owen's face as he absorbed her startling words. She had been so focused on the babe; she didn't think how this would affect her friend.

Before she could react, Owen slapped her hard. Verena fell to the ground, momentarily shocked by his aggression. They had practiced together many times, often Owen had given Verena bruises that hurt for days, but he never touched her in anger.

Abruptly Owen changed. He lifted Verena to her feet and wrapped his beefy arms around her in a crushing embrace.

"I am sorry," he said, burying his face in her hair. "I am so sorry for what Gundy has made you become."

"I merely wish to withdraw until after the babe is born," Verena replied, uncomfortably pulling away. She was shocked by Owen's violence and was not ready to be coddled by him. "I have some money saved."

"No. You will return to the castle and find the treasure."

"Jon can search for it. Gundy need never know."

"Jon was a fool to be so easily caught. I need you there."

"But ..."

Why was Owen being so unreasonable? The agents had always looked after each other in the past. Verena remembered several occasions when she covered for Owen while he was drinking, wenching, or fighting instead of working. As long as Gundy got what he wanted, there was never a problem.

"This isn't for Gundy. It is for us."

"I don't understand."

If Owen didn't intend to give the treasure to their lord ... Verena felt goosebumps break out across her skin. She knew what happened to those who tried to steal from Lord Gundy. Verena had often fantasized about running away from this dreadful service. The other agents must have felt the same, but acting on their desires was another thing entirely.

"We have worked our entire lives to make Gundy richer, living in fear of his displeasure. No more! Your babe is the sign. I have been waiting for the perfect time to act and this is it. The next few weeks will be chaotic as Gundy tries to lead an invasion into Scotland. He needs us now, but by the time he realizes how powerful we have become, it will be too late."

"He fears our power. Gundy will never let us go."

"He won't have a choice. He risks too much on this foolish quest. Gundy knows he does not have the full support of his neighbors and plans to murder a few of them during the battle. I doubt anyone would be disappointed if the tragedy befell Gundy instead."

"You will kill him?"

Verena backed away from her friend. She had no love for their master, but turning against Gundy was tantamount to turning against each other. Everyone in their group had been picked up off the streets. What would happen to them without Gundy's patronage?

"What about us? What about Jon and Hadran?"

"You don't need Gundy. Trust in me. With our skills we will have more wealth and power than Gundy could imagine."

"Financed by murder and deception? You don't want to free us from Gundy, you want to replace him. Aren't you tired of this?"

"Never. I will make us great, but I need you by my side. I can't do it without you."

Owen pulled Verena into his arms. He ground his lips to hers, bruising her with his kiss. She tried to pull away, but Owen crushed her body to his. His hot tongue delved between her lips like a burrowing worm.

Had he always been like this, secretly plotting his rise to power, and she was too blind to see? Owen had always been censorious of Lord Gundy. He loudly criticized each of their missions. Why had Verena refused to believe he was capable of open rebellion? Perhaps she didn't want to believe that the man who had worked with her and fought beside her for so many years dreamed of vengeance.

They heard shouts from behind as an enraged man crashed through the trees.

"You were followed!"

Owen roughly pushed Verena away. She saw his instinctive grab for a knife and knew whoever was out there had only moments to live.

"What is this?" Cairn demanded, glaring at Owen with the wrath of his grandfather behind his gaze. Had he overheard their conversation? Cairn paused; his burning eyes racked her bruised and disheveled appearance before hurling himself at Owen.

"No!"

Recklessly she threw herself in his path, unsure whom she was protecting. She knew that one hand was gripping the handle of Owen's favorite dagger, ready to plunge it through Cairn's heart.

But she doubted one knife would stop Cairn in his current rage, despite the skill of its user. He looked ready to take on Gundy's entire army.

"Owen, run!"

"We can finish this," said Owen in puzzlement.

"No! Not like this."

Cairn grabbed Verena, shoving her aside as he saw Owen melt into the shadows. Verena knew it would take Owen a moment to disappear. Nevertheless she reached for Cairn, hoping to slow him and give Owen a little more time.

She was a hellcat. Verena clung to him, willing her body to be heavier. Another man might have knocked her to the ground. She half-expected the blow, but it never came. Even in his rage, Cairn held himself back, unwilling to hurt her.

"Unhand me, woman!"

Verena stopped struggling, hoping she had given Owen enough time. She knew he wouldn't abandon her, regardless of the circumstances. Owen was probably hiding just out of sight, the better to watch these curious proceedings.

Why didn't Cairn strike her? His rigid jaw was clenched; hands were tightly curled into fists. Cairn's eyes burned into Verena like live coals.

"Who was he?"

Cairn roughly grasped her arms. A moment ago she had been a tigress, fighting tooth and nail to keep the men apart. Now she went limp, knowing she couldn't explain her presence in the forest.

"Answer me!"

"Someone from my past."

Verena had never felt more foolish. How could she not know Cairn was awake? How could she not have known he followed her? Not only had she compromised her cover, she had also lost Owen's faith in her abilities.

"Why did you meet him?"

If Cairn asked that he couldn't have heard their conversation about Lord Gundy. Perhaps she could salvage this, but her mind was reeling with the night's events. Verena needed a moment to think of a plausible lie.

Infuriated by her silence, Cairn dragged her toward the castle. Behind his back she gestured urgently to Owen. Don't follow.

Cairn crashed noisily through the underbrush, dragging an unresisting Verena in his wake. Branches slapped painfully against her arms and face, but Cairn didn't slow his brutal pace. A raised tree root caught her foot and Cairn effortlessly caught Verena and set her back on her feet. The whole time his body vibrated with rage.

The castle sentries watched their procession in silence, not knowing if they should offer assistance. One look at Cairn's fierce expression silenced them. Verena recognized a couple of the guards and though kind, they knew better than to interfere in their lord's business.

Cairn threw Verena into her chamber, bolting the door behind them. She instinctively backed away, though she knew that was moot. If Cairn wanted to hurt her, he would have done so already.

"I want answers now!"

Perhaps it was better for Cairn to think he caught her in a tryst. Verena knew the depth of his hatred for Gundy. If he knew she worked for him, things would be much worse.

"Is he the man you ran from in Langthorne?"

"Will you let me go?" she asked softly. "I can run away and never return."

"Nay! Do you think I would abandon you now? You are carrying my child."

Her heart fluttered at Cairn's answer. Was he trying to protect her? Cairn was furious, but he didn't hit her. Owen, the man she had looked up to for years, didn't have such restraint.

"Was I not enough for you?" Cairn demanded, pushing Verena back until she fell on the bed, still rumpled from their lovemaking. "Was I too gentle with you, too weak? If I knew you liked what that English bastard did to you ..."

"Stop! You don't understand!"

"Then explain it to me. Explain how you ran from me into the arms of another."

"He didn't mean to hurt me. He was confused, but he has always protected me in the past."

Cairn stared at Verena as if she were a stranger. She was surprised to realize her lie was dangerously close to the truth. She didn't believe Owen meant to strike her. He was merely stunned by her pregnancy. For years he had been her family and protector.

Now she didn't know what to think.

"You will not leave this chamber."

Cairn turned and left the room. Though the door had no lock, Verena would bet a soldier would soon be guarding the outside. She might be able to fit through the small window, but there was no point in trying to escape now. The McPhersons would be watching for that.

If only Hadran were here! She desperately needed to talk to him and warn him of his most dangerous agent's defection. Now Verena must concentrate all of her efforts on helping Jon locate the treasure and hope Owen contacted her before doing anything foolish.

Though she would do anything to be free of Gundy's yoke, she had no interest in trading him for Owen. Hadran had thus far been able to protect Verena from Gundy's lusts, but who would protect her from Owen? Verena was finally forced to acknowledge that she no longer trusted her friend.

Chapter 35

Jon entered her chamber moments after Cairn departed. He was investigating a dried-out well as a likely hiding place for the treasure when he saw their curious return, and knew something was wrong.

"Does he know?"

"Nay, Cairn believes he interrupted a lover's tryst."

"Poor fellow," replied Jon with a slow shake of his head. "He loved you."

"Why do you say that?"

Verena unconsciously tensed, clenching the covers beneath her hands. She had worked so hard to gain Cairn's trust. Could his feelings run deeper than physical affection? Was that the reason for his restraint?

"I have seen the way he looks at you. He wants much more that what is beneath your skirts. The kitchen brats agree."

"It is no matter. I am restricted to this room so I cannot do much to assist you."

"That's easy," replied Jon. His roving eye skimmed over the embroidered pillows and bedspread, noting the semiprecious stones sewn into the fabric. He was always looking for an opportunity, just as Hadran instructed. "I'll spread a rumor that you've come down with a horrible sickness. The clan will be tripping over themselves to show their support."

"If Cairn doesn't share the details of my incarceration."

"He won't. I know how the laird thinks. He wants everyone to feel at ease and believe they are safe. He'll tell them you are unwell or my name is King Henry."

"I think you are right. He will try to keep this quiet. Stir things up a bit and see how he reacts. While we wait, I want you to take my tools. You'll have more use for them than I at the moment."

Jon's eyes lit up. He was in the process of building what he called 'the perfect collection' of useful items and was intrigued by Verena's tools. Each of Hadran's associates had a personalized set that changed depending on the assignment. Jon's enthusiasm for collecting made Verena cautiously add:

"Do not think of appropriating a single item."

"How you malign me!"

"After what I heard tonight, I'm not sure I trust anyone."

Briefly she described her meeting with Owen, leaving out nothing. Jon was shocked by her pregnancy, Owen's violence and the forceful kiss. Owen was the best of Hadran's agents at fighting, tracking and skulking through the shadows. He could steal anything, reach anyone, and kill anyone. Verena knew Jon was terrified of Owen, but he idolized him too.

"Lord!" said Jon in wonder. "I knew Owen was a devil, but he has always looked out for me."

"He is rough," Verena amended, thinking of his burly, uncouth manners and fierce determination. "But I never thought he would go against family."

"Aye, that's exactly how it is. We all hate Gundy, but without him, what would we be? Do you suppose Owen wants to set himself up as our master?"

"That's what worries me."

A knock sounded at the door and Jon dived under the bed a moment before Roselyn appeared. They had been so engrossed discussing their plans, she hadn't noticed the sunrise lighting the room. Roselyn was used to Verena rising early and now appeared with a tray full of hot tea, sweet breads, cheese and meats to break her fast.

"Good day, Milady," she said brightly, setting out a pitcher of fresh water.

"I do not feel entirely myself today," she admitted, lying weakly against the pillows. She had no intention of dressing with Jon hidden in her bedchamber. "I think I shall sleep a little longer."

"Are you unwell?"

Roselyn was immediately at her side, checking her temperature with the back of her hand.

"I am merely overtired."

"Of course, milady. I can bring you a cup of my mother's special tea. She says it can cure anything."

"Thank you."

Roselyn turned to leave and almost collided with Lady Ivone as she sailed into the room.

"Leave us," she commanded. Roselyn meekly nodded and backed out of the chamber.

The sash of Ivone's exquisitely embroidered dressing gown was open; her hair had not been brushed or styled. Clearly she had been disturbed with news of great import much earlier than she was used to rising.

"Something happened last night between you and my son."

"Milady?"

"Don't play coy with me. I know you work for Lord Gundy."

Verena froze, trying to school her reaction. She knew Ivone was cunning, but never expected her to be so clever.

"You really are quite good at your ... profession. At first I thought you were too simple-minded to be anything other that what you claimed to be. The way you traipse around the countryside, spending time with peasants! Then I began to see your real purpose.

"The peasants aren't your friends, they are your accomplices. You are using them to gather information as you are using my son to gain access to our lands. Tell me, how much is Lord Gundy paying for your services? Do you grant him the same courtesy you do my son?"

"I do not work for Gundy," she replied through clenched teeth. "I hate him."

"I know you work for him. Have you found the treasure yet?"

Verena had no intention of confessing to Ivone, but wanted to see what the lady would do next. How did Ivone know she was after the treasure? Verena could be an assassin, or spying on the McPherson's defenses for the coming invasion. The lady seemed more concerned with the silver than the safety of her clan.

"Milady," called Fergus from the doorway. "Is everything alright?"

They both jerked around to see Fergus hovering in the open doorway. If Hadran trained her, Ivone might have known to bolt the door before an interrogation.

"Of course it is," lied Ivone with a smile. She patted her arm in a show of affection. "I was merely chatting with our guest. Do you have business with Verena?"

"I was hoping she could help me located Jon. The little imp was due in the stables an hour ago."

"Jon?" she asked, blinking in confusion. If Ivone suspected her, she wanted to create as much distance as possible from her associate.

"The brat who crashed into you in the courtyard a few days ago. He seemed to take a fancy to you."

"I am sorry. I haven't seen him since that day."

"Peasants," sniffed Ivone as she left the room. "They are as fickle as they are untrustworthy. No doubt he is halfway across the country with my best serving spoon."

As soon as she left, Roselyn rushed back into the room with a worried frown. She must have found Fergus and solicited his assistance, correctly guessing Lady Ivone was in a less than pleasant mood.

"Is aught amiss?" questioned the maid. "I knew there would be trouble when Lady Ivone appeared in such a state. It was a good thing Fergus was nearby."

"Thank you," she said with an audible sigh of relief. Why was Fergus near her bedchamber? According to Roselyn, this section of the castle was rarely used. Perhaps Cairn instructed him to guard Verena after last night's disastrous incident. "Lady Ivone merely suggested how I might better occupy my time."

Roselyn gave an unladylike snort and muttered a few choice words under her breath.

"Forgive me, milady, but there is nothing wrong with how you spend your time. We appreciate the hard work you do for the clan. You are more of a lady than ...

"Roselyn!" Fergus said with a scowl. He didn't approve of Ivone's ways either, but he wouldn't tolerate disrespect.

"I beg your pardon. My da always says my mouth runs away from me."

"There is no need to apologize. Thank you for coming to my aid."

It took several minutes before she could usher her rescuers out of the room. Roselyn fluttered about like a mother hen, checking

Verena's temperature several times and readjusting the blankets. When they finally left, Jon slowly climbed from his hiding place, wincing and stretching cramped muscles. He eyed her untouched breakfast with longing and she gestured for him to take his fill.

"Lord!" said Jon with his mouth full of sausage. "Your room is busy!"

"I assure you this was not planned, but it is interesting. I thought the clan hated Lady Ivone, and though that might still be true, she must have some very skilled followers, perhaps her own band of spies. I need to know how she learned of last night's events and why she hasn't brought her suspicions to Cairn."

"I bet she wants the treasure for herself and will leave the clan to starve. It is no secret that she plans to return to France."

"If Cairn knew the treasure existed, he wouldn't let her near it."

"I know I wouldn't."

"Even if she plans to steal the treasure, letting the agent of your sworn enemy work unmolested in your home is a foolish risk."

"Gundy is the McPherson's enemy," Jon pointed out, picking his teeth with his knife. "Lady Ivone never considered herself a McPherson."

"Follow Ivone. I want to know everything about her and everyone that comes in contact with her. Use extreme caution. We should assume she has help."

Chapter 36

Three days passed before Cairn visited Verena. She spent the time imagining intrigues between Gundy, Thomas and Lady Ivone. What was the relationship between them? On the surface they appeared to be enemies, yet they were each connected to the treasure. Each of them sought to keep the silver from the McPherson clan.

Jon proved to be a valuable ally and had one of the kitchen boys follow Thomas while he shadowed Ivone. He gave Verena daily reports on their activities and they spent the evenings debating their next move.

Aside from his earlier trip to the Old Lord's burial mound, Thomas' actions were completely normal. He was as cantankerous as ever, but his behavior was not suspicious. If Thomas was hiding the treasure, his actions wouldn't lead them to it. Eventually they would have to search Thomas' cottage, but so far Jon hadn't had the opportunity.

A new maid appeared in Ivone's solar one day to bring the ladies a pitcher of wine, and then disappeared. The kitchen boys were quick to tell Jon of any changes in the castle, thinking it all a fun game. None of the servants Jon questioned knew the identity of the mysterious woman, but he was able to get a description.

In spite of the danger, Jon was ecstatic by these developments. He had never pitted his skills against a rival spy and was eager to prove Hadran's team was superior. Verena repeatedly warned him to be cautious, but she feared Jon was taking too many risks. Several times he narrowly avoided Lady Ivone's attention and would later boast of his ingenuity to Verena.

"You should be careful," she admonished.

Jon shrugged. He had been trained by Hadran and knew what

he was doing. He had worked hard to create an image of himself as a reformed rascal. The kitchen brats worshiped Jon for the incredulous history he had created, and even the gruff Fergus had softened toward him. Jon insisted Ivone was too pretentious to notice a servant boy and wouldn't suspect him.

There wasn't much she could do while trapped in her chamber. She relied on Jon for all of her information and couldn't help him with anything but strategy. Thankfully it didn't take long for Jon's story of her illness to spread through the clan. Almost immediately gifts started to arrive for her. Honey, small embroidered trinkets, sachets of sweet-smelling herbs and woven trim soon lined every surface in her chamber. As Jon predicted, the clan appreciated Verena saving their laird in Langthorne and her efforts to gain their trust.

By the evening of the third day, Cairn burst into her chamber, glaring at her gifts with disdain. It was disconcerting that the sight of him, unshaven and furious, could cause her heart to beat in excitement. There were new lines beneath his eyes, as if he had not slept since that night in the woods.

She knew he would come for her eventually and had diligently prepared for his arrival. A cheery fire burned in the fireplace, bathing the chamber in soft tones. A platter of Cairn's favorite dishes and wine was laid on a small table. Resplendent in an ivory gown that did wonders for her figure, she sat crosslegged in the middle of the bed, plucking the melody of a tragic love song on a lute.

"You have the whole castle fooled." With a swipe of his hand Cairn knocked several trinkets to the floor. "I can't walk ten feet without someone asking after your welfare or reminding me to thank you for something on their behalf. I don't know half of my clan, but you are here five minutes and everyone loves you. Everyone thinks you are so kind."

"I didn't wish to deceive you."

Verena stretched across the bed to put the lute away, giving Cairn a good view of her cleavage and bare calves. This was no time for underwear.

Cairn exhaled, running his fingers through his hair in frustration.

"Do you love him?"

A few weeks ago she might have said yes. For years Owen had been like her older brother, guiding and protecting Verena through her perilous life. He was her friend, but she could never allow him to touch her as intimately as Cairn. She shook her head.

"You don't understand. Owen and I have always been close. Once I thought we would marry, but that was a long time ago ..."

Cairn growled low in his throat and slammed his palm into the wall.

"Is that why you ran from me?"

"I didn't!" she exclaimed. She reached for Cairn, but he flinched away. She forced her fingers to curl into fists. For days she had planned this moment, but her preparations would be for naught if he didn't believe her story. "You have been kinder to me than any man I have ever known. The things we have shared mean so much to me."

"What did we share, lust and a few laughs?" Cairn stalked her, forcing Verena backward until she felt the cold stone wall at her back. He pressed against her, rubbing his swollen erection between her legs. "Was that all it meant to you?"

Her mouth went dry. Cairn vibrated with energy. She wanted to melt into his embrace and kiss the scowl from his lips. He was like a whirlwind, switching from rage to lust in an instant.

Before she could take a breath, Cairn's head swooped down, capturing her lips. He was passion and fire in her arms, kissing Verena like he was starved for the taste of her. No other man could make her feel like this. She drowned in the sensation, uncaring if the kiss lasted until the end of the world.

Abruptly Cairn wrenched his head away. Verena was trembling from the force of his passion; her weak knees were unable to support her weight. She knew she should say something, perhaps beg Cairn to forgive her or weep tears of sorrow, but she felt too numb to act coy or cunning.

"You cannot remain here. Already my clan has begun to wonder, and I will not have disharmony in my household. You will stay in Scotland until the child is born. Once I have dealt with Gundy, I will deal with you."

Before she could stop him, Cairn stormed from the room, leaving her to crumple silently to the floor.

Chapter 37

Suppers among the McPherson clan turned into strained affairs. Verena was forced to sit between Cairn and Ivone and bear the wrath of their thinly veiled contempt. Several days had passed since that disastrous night and though she was no longer confined to her chambers, Cairn insisted a guard follow her at all times. This meant she was unable to resume her duties for Lord Gundy and couldn't speak to Owen again. Knowing that Jon was also unable to contact Owen since that night made her stomach twist with worry. Were his words frustrated ramblings, or was Owen truly planning to overthrow Gundy's authority?

Cairn spent his days making plans for England and the winter. For the sake of the clan he strove to maintain the illusion of stability. She had grown close to the McPhersons so Cairn granted her a measure of freedom, though he no doubt longed to lock her away. They never spoke about the child, but sometimes she would absently rub her flat stomach, imagining a boy or girl with bright curls and Cairn's eyes. She would glance up and find Cairn watching her with an inscrutable expression. Verena knew he wanted the child, otherwise he would have banished her from the castle, but he was not ready to trust Verena again. She set to work trying to repair their relationship.

If the clan liked Verena before, she was determined to make them love her now. She assisted the midwife and the apothecary. Verena distributed medicines to the sick and found old bolts of wool to make warm clothes for the village children. Recipes were exchanged with the cook and she never missed a church event. Verena was beyond reproach, but Cairn still maintained his distance. He didn't visit her chamber or attempt to kiss her again.

Verena was cut out of his heart, but she was determined not to lose hope.

With Gundy's forces expected in less than a fortnight, she knew she was running out of time. Unfortunately, she was no closer to finding the treasure. There were too many unknowns and she hated her precarious position. Owen was an opportunist and might try something without her knowledge. He wouldn't dare approach the castle for fear of being recognized. Instead Owen would work his mischief from a distance, perhaps employing another to take his place.

Lady Ivone also had at least one operative working within the castle for a purpose she didn't yet understand. There were too many actors on the stage and she was no longer sure of her part. All she knew was that she must be careful lest she be caught in another scheme.

Verena scanned the faces of each person entering and exiting the hall, looking for anyone who seemed out of place. She needed to identify all unknown agents immediately, in case Ivone employed more than one.

A young servant quietly entered the hall, carrying a pitcher of wine. He seemed removed from the chaos in a way only someone outside the household would be. He stayed close to the walls with downcast eyes, trying not to draw attention to himself.

"My lord?" she bravely asked Cairn, despite his less than social mood. "Is that a new server?"

"How should I know?" he snapped, draining the contents of his goblet for the third time. "You know the servants better than I."

Undaunted she repeated the question to Lady Ivone and received a similar response. She surreptitiously signaled to Jon. He would know if a new servant was working. Ever watchful, Jon immediately caught her eye and subtly shrugged his shoulders. He didn't recognize the lad, but would certainly know his story by the end of the evening.

There was something about the servant that bothered Verena. There was a slight hesitation in his step as if he was unfamiliar with his role. His eyes darted about, watching the other servants and imitating their movements. When he approached the head table Verena knew something was wrong.

Unless the boy was extremely ambitious or foolhardy, a new

servant wouldn't dream of approaching the head table without a summons. He only refilled Cairn's goblet, ignoring Verena and Lady Ivone's half-empty ones.

"What is your name, boy?" she asked, nearly causing the lad to drop his pitcher in surprise.

"My ... er ... my name?" he stammered. "It's uh ...umm ..."

"Leave the poor boy alone," interjected Ivone. Verena was astonished to hear her come to the rescue of someone so far beneath her. "You may go now."

The boy bowed nervously and started to run from the hall, but her voice stopped him.

"Won't you refill my goblet?" she prodded. He clutched the pitcher to his chest as if it were made of gold. "Why don't you leave that here?"

"I ... Um ..."

She could see the perspiration gathering on his forehead and silently rebuked Owen. This lad should not have been dragged into their shady business. He looked barely sixteen years of age. Verena noted his gaunt features and the way his ragged clothes hung loosely about his skeletal frame. He was probably a runaway.

"It's empty," he lied. "I'll bring another."

Cairn reached for his re-filled goblet and she snatched it. Her move was instinctive and she grimaced in horror at her stupidity. Verena knew she was beginning to care for him, but until that moment she didn't think her affection would hinder her ability to act.

Why did she take the wine from Cairn? According to Gundy's plan, Cairn had to die. She knew this would come and should be relieved someone else found a way to do it. Verena should have calmly watched the boy do his business, but now it was too late.

She couldn't give the wine to Cairn after she had drawn attention to it. She would no doubt be suspected of participating in the murder. There were many opportunities for an assassin to strike and she was certain they would try again. Next time she must not allow her emotions to dictate her actions.

"That is my cup," said Cairn as he reached for the goblet again. Verena handed him the drink, but before he could grasp it, she allowed the cup to slide through her fingers, spilling the wine into the floor rushes below.

"Oh!" she exclaimed. She made a show of leaping back so the wine didn't soil her gown. Cairn was not so lucky and some of the liquid splashed his hose. "I am terribly sorry. The lad said he would return with another pitcher, but I was impatient."

"It is fine," said Cairn, irritably dabbing his tunic with a cloth.

"I think I shall retire for the night."

She excused herself from the hall, retreating quickly before Cairn or Ivone could question her unusually clumsy behavior. Verena scanned the faces of the assembly, but the servant was nowhere to be found. Jon had also slipped away, probably in search of this new agent. If Owen had orchestrated the attempted assassination, he wisely kept out of sight.

Chapter 38

A surprisingly warm sun bathed Verena's cheeks. It reminded her of the glorious summer she spent in Southern France with the Duc de Ravenna. Every morning she had risen early to bathe in the ocean and feast on imperfect breakfast rolls, deliciously dripping with butter, yet deemed unworthy to grace the lord's table.

Suddenly her door flew open, slamming against the stone wall with a loud bang. She sat up in bed, grabbing the knife under her pillow, and ready to fling it at her attacker.

"Come with me now!" Cairn growled.

"Milord? Is something wrong?"

Verena scrambled from the bed. She threw on a dressing gown and slippers, never loosening her hold on the knife.

"Aye."

Cairn grabbed her arm and propelled her through the door. She had to run to keep up with his long strides as they hurried toward the feast hall. Several knights were gathered around the head table, grimly examining the floor and shaking their heads.

"What is it?" she asked, but she feared she already knew. The floor rushes had not been cleared since the night before and two enterprising mice had snuck into the castle while everyone slept. Their corpses littered the floor where she spilled the wine. It was obvious they had been snacking on the liquid.

"Why did you keep me from drinking the wine last night?"

"I spilled it."

"Did you know it was poisoned?"

What should she say? If she told him the truth, Cairn would be furious, but what if she lied and the assassin struck again? Verena hoped as long as she carried his child, Cairn wouldn't harm her, but she couldn't be certain. If he knew the truth, would Cairn still want the bastard child of a spy?

"I didn't know, but I suspected."

"What did you suspect?" Fergus demanded. "Why did you not say anything?"

The clan had come to respect Cairn during his months as their laird. None of them would see him harmed, especially not after the sudden death of his father and the coming war with Langthorne.

"I wasn't sure. All I knew was that the lad was unfamiliar and he only refilled your glass. Did you question him?"

The knights exchanged looks. They were expecting Gundy to send his army, not an assassin, and had not been vigilant against such a threat.

"We found the boy outside the village. His throat was cut."

"Oh my!"

"It was Gundy, milord," Fergus said. "I knew that whoreson was still plotting against you. There will be another attempt. I am sure of it. If he could turn Jon ..."

"Jon, the new stable boy?" She tried to keep her voice as even as possible. What happened after he left the hall? He probably confronted the lad, but that was no reason for Fergus' accusation. Verena was closer to Jon than anyone else on Hadran's team. She had to find a way to help him.

"Aye. We found him sneaking away from the lad's body. He said he was innocent, but he was holding the bloody knife!"

"I don't believe it. Why would he do such a thing?"

"I bet they were conspirators. They fought once they saw laird Cairn didn't drink the poison and Jon stabbed him ..."

"We do not know who was behind this attack," Cairn lifted one hand to stop the argument before it could turn into a shouting match. Everyone was upset by the poisoning and Jon's possible involvement. Cairn worked hard to give the clan the illusion of stability, but now everything was crumbling apart. "Jon will remain in the dungeon until I am assured of his innocence."

"Fergus is right. There may be another assassination attempt. We must be vigilant."

The knife was still clutched in her hand. She surreptitiously slipped it into the sleeve of her dressing gown. She and Jon were the only outsiders in the household and Jon was now being held for suspicion of murder. He was so sure no one would suspect him of working for Gundy, yet now he was locked in the dungeon.

She didn't believe Jon was behind the murder. He had no reason to kill the lad and unlike Owen, wouldn't act so rashly on his own. Unfortunately she couldn't tell Cairn that. If they suspected him, despite her pleasant demeanor, the clan could very easily begin to suspect her.

"Milord," she asked. "Do you truly believe Lord Gundy is behind this?"

"He is certainly capable of such a deed and has the most to gain from my demise. I don't know how he gained access to my castle, but I will ensure other assassins are not so lucky."

"How? There are so many people working here. You cannot watch everyone."

"We will do our best. Don't worry. Last night I was not expecting an attack. Now I know better."

With Cairn's soldiers on guard, an assassin would have a harder time reaching him, but it was also one more obstacle in her path to finding the treasure. Discovering the silver seemed less likely as time passed.

Would Owen make an attempt on Cairn's life without contacting her first? If he was behind the attack, he should have notified her first. But what if Owen didn't orchestrate last night's attack? Who else would benefit from Cairn's demise?

"Milord," she asked suddenly. "How did your father die?"

Cairn shrugged. His mind was clearly on other matters.

"He was sick for a long time. Six months ago he passed away."

"What were his symptoms?"

"What difference does it make?" asked Cairn. "Ivone nursed him."

Chapter 39

The McPherson dungeons were not the most elaborate she had seen. They consisted of a large room for prisoners and a smaller one for the guards. Rather than separating the inmates, Cairn's ancestors derived great pleasure in having them watch their companions being tortured, knowing their turn was coming soon.

Elaborately sinister machines were stacked in one corner of the large cell, making her grateful she couldn't fathom their uses. They were all covered in a thin layer of dust and rust. Though not old, it had been several months since most of the equipment was used.

Jon was fast asleep on a dirty straw mattress, but he came instantly awake when he heard her pick the lock.

"Who is there?" he asked warily. "Tell me quick or I'll bash your head in!"

"Tis I, Verena," she answered, puzzled. The lad sounded terrified, but as she lifted her candle, she couldn't see any bruises on him. What was he afraid of if not Cairn's questioning?

"'Tis good to see you! I thought they were coming for me."

"They? What happened last night?"

"I followed the boy, as you asked. He went directly to see his contact, not caring if half the world saw him –he was obviously not a real spy. At first I thought Owen sent him, but he didn't meet Owen. I couldn't get a good look at the other man, but I would have recognized Owen's bulk anywhere.

"He asked if the boy delivered the poison and the lad said yes. He thought he was so clever for escaping your questions and was foolish enough to boast about it. Quick as lightning, the other man took out a knife and slashed his throat.

"I must have made a sound because the killer ran away as fast as he could. The lad was still alive so I tried to stop the bleeding. I hoped he could tell me who sliced him. That's when Fergus came along and I didn't get a name. Isn't this a fine mess?"

"You think they will come after you here?"

"Certainly," Jon replied, calmly cleaning his fingernails as he imagined an unknown assassin making an attempt on his life. "They know they were seen and the whole castle must know why I am in the dungeon. They'll think I saw their face and try to silence me."

"I wish we could contact Owen. He would see you to safety."

"Don't worry about me. I'll find Hadran and bring him here. If anyone can straighten Owen out, it is him."

"I hope you are right."

The spies slowly tiptoed up the winding stairs. It was late enough that most of the castle was asleep, but she laced her guard's wine with a sleeping powder just in case. The same powder was liberally added to the prison guard's soup during the evening meal.

They decided not to attempt the front gate and instead made their way to the Old Lord's rooms. They could easily sneak out of the castle through the secret passage. Unfortunately someone had other plans for them.

A large shadow detached itself from the wall as they neared the entrance to the dungeon. The two spies separated, giving each other enough space to fight. Knives were clutched in their hands and before she could think, she instinctively blocked the upward thrust of a shiny metal object.

If she were less trained, the knife would have plunged into her belly, killing her and her unborn child. That knowledge enraged her. She struck back furiously, slashing at her attacker with ruthless precision.

They stepped backward through the open doorway, falling under the light of a hall torch and she gaped in surprise. This was no man striking her with the skill to match Hadran's best agents. A woman stood before her, dressed in tight hose and a nondescript black tunic. She was older than Verena, with a face ravaged by a hard life. Her affinity for drink was evident in bloodshot eyes. It took she but a moment to assess her attacker, committing her face to memory. Though older, this woman more than matched Verena in skill.

"That's her!" Jon exclaimed as he recognized the woman. "She's the servant that visited Ivone."

What did Ivone need with such a ruthless agent? This was much more serious than watching Gundy's spy. This woman was a killer, perhaps the same killer that murdered Cairn's would-be poisoner.

Her head was reeling and the assassin quickly took advantage of her distraction. Seeing an opening, she cut Verena below her rib. If not for the thick woolen gown, she would have been seriously injured. The wound was not deep, but it was painful.

Jon tried to sneak behind the woman, but she was wise to that trick and danced around them, positioning them so they couldn't attack at the same time.

"Who are you?" she demanded. This woman was not part of Hadran's team so couldn't work for Gundy. But why else would she try to assassinate Cairn? Their knives scraped loudly against the stone as they parried and struck at each other. The woman kicked a brazier of coals into Verena's path to distract her. It wasn't long before the noise drew the attention of the awakening castle and she heard running feet.

"Jon, run!" she demanded, parrying another deadly attack. "Take the passage and find Hadran. He'll know what to do."

The assassin struck at Jon as he ran past, but she punched her hard across the face, making her miss her target. She was only dazed for a moment and then redoubled her efforts, seeing part of her quarry escape.

"You'll pay for that."

Verena shivered at the words. She thought she was used to ever-present danger, but the certainty in this woman's voice sent chills up her spine. She meant what she said. A flurry of strikes was sent toward her face. It took all of her concentration to block them. She was dimly aware of the knife slicing into her forearms, but was too focused on the fight to feel pain.

Cairn appeared then, followed closely by several knights. He gaped in astonishment at the skilled knife fight. She could sense his confusion and swore profusely. How would she convince him of her innocence now?

"You chose your allegiance last night," continued the assassin. "But you chose the wrong side. I look forward to seeing how Gundy reacts to your betrayal."

Abruptly the woman switched tactics and swung low toward Verena's legs. The knife sunk deeply into her skirts and the soft flesh of her thigh. She then spun on her toes, wrenching the knife from her leg, and flinging it at Cairn as she charged past. She was much faster than she anticipated and she barely managed to clumsily push the assassin, making the knife clatter harmlessly against the stone wall.

"After her!" Cairn yelled, but she knew it was too late. This woman doubtless had several places to hide and more than one way to get out of the castle. Once she was out of sight, they would never find her.

The hall was quiet following the knights' departure. The adrenaline slowly ebbed from her body and she felt the lateness of the hour and her exhaustion. She had to grab the wall to keep from falling as the pain in her thigh and forearms flooded her.

Cairn stood before her, watching her with a mixture of horror and disbelief. No matter what she said, he would never believe she was the innocent she claimed to be. Verena said her brother taught her how to use a knife, but no mere guard would have skills like hers. Nor could she explain her presence in the dungeon. Once he discovered Jon was missing, she would be in serious trouble.

"Milord," she began slowly, not knowing what to say, but knowing she must say something. "I can explain ..."

"You work for Gundy."

That was a fact she could no longer deny. There was no way to salvage her persona, no pretty lie to make Cairn love her again.

"I saved you last night," she pointed out, but Cairn cut her off. That one act had come after weeks of deception.

"Why? Isn't that why you are here? Did you kill the boy?"

"Nay! The woman did. She came to kill Jon because he recognized her."

"Who was she? Why would she try to murder me?"

"I don't know."

That was the flaw in Hadran's reasoning. He thought it was safer to tell his agents only what they needed to know—safer for Gundy. If they were captured, there would be little danger to Gundy's plans. But now she had no way to save herself, no useful information to barter for her freedom. The treasure was still lost and she knew few details about Gundy's plans. She didn't even know the identity of the assassin, and had little more than conjecture to tie her to Lady Ivone.

If she told Cairn the truth about his stepmother, would Cairn believe her, or think she was lying to save herself? Knowledge of Ivone's deceit was all she had gained during her stay in Scotland, but how would that help her?

The cut on Verena's thigh was deep. Even without looking, she knew it would require stitches. She no longer had the strength to stand and slowly lowered herself to the floor. Would he let her die? Would he let their child die in anger?

"Everything you said was a lie."

"I'm not lying now. Please ..."

"Don't say another word! No matter what I do, Gundy's treachery follows me. No longer!"

Without warning, he scooped her into his arms and carried her down the twisting stone staircase. He unceremoniously dumped her on the same straw pallet Jon had used only a few minutes before.

"Do not speak," he cautioned, digging his fingers painfully into Verena's arms. "Do not move. You betrayed me before and I forgave you. I never thought the mother of my child was capable of such deceit."

"You still want our child?"

She couldn't help the hopeful catch in her throat. He knew she betrayed him, knew she was his assassin, but he still wanted their child. She didn't know what to make of that.

"It is my child!" he growled. "And I'll ensure a devil like you never comes near him."

Chapter 40

The hours passed slowly in the dark, cold dungeon. Verena didn't know how long she lay on the straw pallet, creating plans and then discarding each of them as silly. Cairn had stripped her of almost everything but her gown. She had one long hair pin, tucked into her elaborate coiffure, but that wouldn't pick the dungeon lock.

Long ago a nervous Roselyn had seen to her wounds. She was clearly puzzled by Verena's change in circumstances, but knew better than to ask with Cairn standing over her, glaring daggers at them both. She thought briefly of having Roselyn sneak out a message, but was unsure of the maid's loyalty. Even if she agreed, she had no one to send a message to. Jon was headed to England and she hadn't seen Owen in days. There was no one left to help her.

At least Cairn left her a candle. That was a courtesy she didn't expect, but it was also torture. Hadran repeatedly told his agents to never accept defeat. There were ways out of every situation. Verena spent her time carefully examining the cell, looking for any tool that might help her escape. Unfortunately the cell was impenetrable and instead of spending the night resting, she exhausted herself with a futile search. She finally admitted defeat when her candle grew low, but was afraid to extinguish it, lest the dungeon's rodents decide to pay her a social visit.

The next morning Cairn discovered her curled in a ball on the uncomfortably thin pallet, caught in an exhausted slumber. He shook her awake, ignoring the dark circles beneath her eyes which mirrored his own. He probably spent the night searching for Ivone's assassin.

"I need answers."

Verena blinked to clear her mind. She had not slept well since arriving in Scotland. Her days were spent with the clan while the nights were filled with Cairn's energetic lovemaking and searching for the treasure. Even the days locked in her chamber were spent working on projects to win the clan's support and scheming with Jon. She had maintained this brutal schedule because of training and the knowledge that it wouldn't last forever. Perhaps because of the baby or her injuries in the knife fight, her body chose this moment to rebel. Opening her eyes was a Herculean chore and though she sat up, she couldn't seem to focus.

"Verena! Who was the assassin? How did she get into the castle?

Slowly her mind began to clear. Jon had left for England, Hadran was miles away, and Owen was plotting against their employer. Ivone's assassin would return; she was certain of that. Only Cairn, the man she sought to destroy, could protect her until Hadran returned. Maybe if she told him the truth, Cairn would think she was worth saving.

There was little hope of salvaging her mission at this point. Now she needed to focus on survival. There was a measure of safety as long as she carried Cairn's child, but she would never allow him to take the baby from her. She would live until Hadran came, and pray the old man could make things right.

"She works for your stepmother."

"Lies!"

"It's true. Jon saw her in Ivone's solar. That's how she knew I worked for Gundy."

"Ivone knew you were a spy and didn't tell me?"

"Aye." She rubbed her forehead to clear the raging headache that was forming. Not since she was a little girl had she felt so alone. No matter how dangerous the assignment, she could always rely on Hadran, Owen and Jon for help. Now she had nothing but her wits and a hairpin. "Gundy isn't the only one to profit from your death."

"Ivone has her faults, but she isn't a murderer."

"She murdered your father, though that wasn't very wise."

"Explain yourself."

It felt good to tell Cairn the truth. She had been carrying her deception like an unwieldy burden for weeks. Though Cairn was incredulous, he was at least willing to listen to her story. Once she started, she wanted to tell him everything. Perhaps a part of her still trusted this man. Despite everything, she wanted to be close to him

"Your father was ill for years while you were in France. That was perfect for Ivone as she could rule the clan with impunity. It was the arsenic she fed him in small doses over the years. The same arsenic Ivone keeps in a vial around her neck to protect her from the plague. His death was probably accidental, but he was sick for so long, no one suspected foul play.

"She didn't intend for your father to die. When you returned, Ivone had to relinquish her power to you. Now she wants it back."

"This is too much. Why should I believe you now? You can't prove anything and I have known Lady Ivone much longer than I have known you."

"Ivone's agent said she would come after me, and I believe her."

"Why?"

"Because she thinks I have information about your grandfather's treasure. I believe your stepmother has a plan for the silver that does not include you or your clan."

Cairn had to sit down. He lowered himself to the filthy dungeon floor on shaky legs. The stone wall at his back felt reassuringly solid. These age-blackened walls had survived centuries of war and plague, but he knew only too well that a castle was only as strong as its defenders. Faced with Jon's, Ivone's, and Verena's betrayals, Cairn felt shaken and terribly alone. How could he protect his clan when he was so easily fooled by the people closest to his heart?

He didn't want to believe his stepmother was capable of such treachery, but Cairn had heard too many stories about how she led the clan before his arrival. While Angus was ill, she had squandered their funds and increased taxes to pay for vain projects. Not long ago this dungeon had been filled with people incarcerated on petty charges. The McPhersons were severely chastised for not showing the proper respect, or offending Ivone in a million different ways. He knew she was cold and selfish, but that didn't make Ivone's betrayal easier to bear.

"Ivone left for France this morning."

"Of course. With Gundy's army coming, she probably thought it was no longer safe to stay in Scotland."

"Tell me everything."

Verena took a deep breath and began her story. The information wouldn't save the McPhersons, but it would teach Cairn the depths of Gundy's deviousness. Maybe if he knew a little about her history, Cairn would take more precautions to keep her safe.

"For the past twelve years I have worked for Lord Gundy, with a small group of assassins and spies. We were hired by Gundy to find your grandfather's treasure, but a few days ago the rules of the assignment changed—or perhaps I was finally told the entire plan. The treasure was not enough for him. You had to die in order to pave the way for Gundy's invasion. Owen, the man you saw in the woods, was not my lover; he was my assistant."

Cairn felt numb as her damning words washed over him. She was working with Gundy all this time, plotting against him and his people. She planned to murder Cairn and open his clan to an English massacre. Despite her guilt, she looked at him now with something akin to trust.

"When will his men arrive?"

"I do not know. Owen was keeping me informed, but he left a few days ago."

The man in the woods was not her lover. Cairn felt his heart thaw a bit at that news. Could he believe her now that she was finally exposed? He was surprised by his desire to trust her. Even now Cairn cringed to see her locked in the dark, filthy dungeon. This woman had taken control of his heart with terrifying ease. Were her kisses lies; and the way she moaned in his embrace? Cairn wished he had never laid eyes on this viper.

"That night I told him of the child and asked to be removed from this assignment. It was too dangerous for the babe. At first he was enraged. Then he ordered me to go back to the castle and find the treasure—not for Lord Gundy, but for us. I believe he plans to overthrow Gundy and take his place."

"If he murders that English bastard, it will be a blessing."

"Believe me, this is not good news. Owen is volatile and ruthless, but was always willing to follow Gundy's orders. Not anymore. He hasn't tried to contact me since that night and I am afraid of what he might do.

"I know what kind of man Lord Gundy is, but I owe him my life. Without Gundy's patronage, I would have starved long ago."

"Patronage?" shouted Cairn. He looked like he wanted to throttle her "What type of man would force you into such labor? You gave your body for him, you would have murdered for him."

Verena thought she had come to terms with her profession. As long as she had the support of Hadran and her family of spies, she could ignore her conscience. Now Cairn glared at her as if she was the vilest of creatures.

"You were born into wealth and privilege. I had nothing. You can't possibly understand what it means to have someone look at you, filthy and starving, and see potential. He turned me into a spy, and I thank God every day for that. He gave me my life."

Forcing herself to look him in the eye, she squared her shoulders. Cairn didn't love her like Hadran and the others; he had not been with her for years, fighting beside her. He couldn't understand how perilous life could be for a peasant girl without a family.

"And you would have taken mine. Why didn't you let me drink the poison?"

"I don't know."

Cairn's features were still, but she could see the storm brewing in his eyes. Cairn wanted her before; he wanted their child. How much did her answer mean to him?

"This is the knife your brother gave you," he said, pulling out the blade he confiscated the night before. "The one he taught you to use."

"I don't have a brother. Owen made it for me. Hadran, the leader of our group under Gundy, taught me how to use it."

"How many of you are there?"

Cairn's voice was a low, deadly growl. Months ago he had sworn to never fall for Gundy's tricks again, but suddenly found himself back in Gundy's trap. The lovely woman before him, the woman that so neatly captured his heart, was accomplice to it all.

"Four," she replied, watching him cautiously. She could see the rage within, but Cairn kept his emotions in check. She forced herself not to think of what Gundy had done to a spy he discovered in Langthorne.

"I am the primary agent, Owen and Jon are my backups, and Hadran acts as our liaison to Gundy. Hadran put our group together at Gundy's behest. He delivers our assignments and keeps Gundy informed of our progress."

"Why didn't he kill me in Langthorne? Why send you?"

"Our mutual suffering made it easy for you to trust me," she replied. "I needed unrestricted access to search for your grandfather's treasure—a servant wouldn't have such freedom. Once I found it, I was to kill you before your brother returned with reinforcements and supplies."

Cairn was so angry it was difficult to see. His fists clenched in fury, desperate to slam into Gundy's face, to shake the woman in front of him and make her take back everything she said.

"My men are dead because of you!" She could feel the emotions pouring off Cairn in waves. "You came here to destroy me. You gave your body to me for Gundy."

"No," she replied softly, no longer able to look him in the eye. She had long tried to deny it, but the passion between them was real. It had nothing to do with Gundy or her mission. Verena genuinely cared for Cairn and was tormented by the thought of what would become of him. "That was not for Gundy."

"Then why?"

"You were kind to me," she explained, trying not to fidget under his uncompromising stare. "And ... I wanted you."

Cairn had been through so much. She could see the distrust in his eyes. He reached out to lightly grasp her arms. His fingers caressed her biceps as if he couldn't believe she was real.

Though his heart raged against it, and his mind didn't want to accept it, Cairn believed her. He recognized the desperation that must have driven her to confess the truth.

"Who are you? What are you?" His fingers pressed harder, but she didn't cry out from the bruising pressure. "Why are you telling me this?"

Verena tried to halt the tears that threatened to spill, but she couldn't stop her traitorous body from swaying toward him. She needed to believe he still wanted her, and not just for the baby. She saw a raw hunger build in Cairn's eyes, slowly replacing his simmering ire. Her body yearned for him. Though it had only been days since they had last come together, to Verena, it felt like an eternity. She wanted to touch him and taste him. She wanted to lick the salty sweat from his skin and stay with him forever.

An instant later Cairn's lips hungrily descended on hers. She could feel the desire in him that was for her alone.

"Damn these clothes!"

A cord snapped in Cairn's impatient hand. She was so fixated on his wonderful kiss that she didn't notice Cairn had nearly undressed her. Verena's fingers were actually shaking with need. She frantically kissed his lips, his cheek, his ear—anywhere she could reach. Finally Cairn swore in frustration, grabbed her knife, and sliced through the stubborn knot in her bodice.

He paused to look at the knife in his hand. Owen had made it for her; Hadran taught her how to use it. Verena's shady past was represented in its crude handle and sharp blade.

How could he have so quickly forgotten the deadly accuracy of Verena's fight? Her very presence was intoxicating, making Cairn long to forget her past. He hated what Gundy made her become, but she was not innocent. She willingly chose the life she led. He could never trust her, but Cairn's throbbing body didn't care.

"You are poison. You confessed your sins and yet I still hunger for you. I am throbbing with the need to take you again. Why it is so difficult to see you for the temptress you are?"

Still caught in a haze of passion, it took her a few moments to understand his words. Cairn was leaving her. Slowly his arms released her naked, trembling flesh. She tried to collect her thoughts to call out to him.

"Cairn please, the woman will kill our baby!"

Those words made him pause as he reached the door. What was Cairn to do with this minx? He knew he should punish her, or at least banish her from his clan, but how could he reconcile his heart with reason? Could he give up his child because of its mother?

"No one will touch my child," he called over his shoulder before the door slammed shut. "I promise."

Chapter 41

Roselyn came several times to bring food and change Verena's bandages. She was always escorted by a guard and instructed not to speak. There was so much she wanted to ask the maid. Had Jon been captured? Did they find the female assassin? All she could infer from the sympathetic looks and sweets Roselyn snuck into the dungeon, was that she still had a friend.

Roselyn's visits gave her a schedule to orient her time. The days were spent exercising and practicing her knife skills for her next encounter with the assassin. The long, awkward hairpin was her only weapon and she was determined to be as comfortable with it as the knife Cairn confiscated.

Despite Cairn's precautions, she knew someone would come for her eventually. She was in the middle of this entire mess. She probably knew more about the Old Lord than anyone, thanks to her research. If she only had a few more days, she was confident she could find the treasure, but she couldn't do anything inside the dungeon.

Being confined gave her ample time to think and her mind invariably went back to the missing silver. She had searched every likely and unlikely hiding place in the castle and countryside. She had identified Thomas, Father Simon and Lady Ivone as the most likely caretakers of the treasure, but had long ago discarded Father Simon as a candidate. He was too kind to keep the treasure from the clan during these difficult times. Lady Ivone couldn't know the location either; otherwise she wouldn't have attempted to question Verena. That left one suspect.

Thomas knew something. His obsessive care of the Old Lord's tomb indicated he was closer to the old man than anyone. He had to be hiding the treasure.

Should she tell Cairn her suspicions? If he was to repel Gundy's attack, he would need the treasure to pay for supplies. If he was to protect her and their child, he needed the silver. But what if she was wrong? Would Cairn think it was another lie to shift the blame from herself? He certainly had not thanked her for airing her suspicions about Lady Ivone. When she found a way out of the dungeon, she would search Thomas' cottage, but would say nothing until then.

It was nearly a fortnight before someone came for her. She heard the soft scrape of someone trying to pick the dungeon lock, and prepared her defense. One of the heavy torture devices was laboriously moved beside the door to provide a space for her to hide behind. She intended to push it onto her would-be attacker as soon as they stepped through.

"Verena?" called a low, familiar voice. A candle was briefly unshielded so that a single ray of light shone on her empty pallet. "Where are you?"

"Hadran?" Verena stepped from behind her hiding place to greet the old man—who wisely refrained from entering the dungeon. He had taught her to be prepared, so he was doubtless expecting an ambush.

"I taught you well," he said, studying her use of the torture device and hair pin. "Although in the future make sure you use two hair pins. You were always the best with double blades."

"I'll remember that," she replied, smiling her first genuine smile in weeks. To the old man, everything was an opportunity for instruction. She threw her arms around him, forgetting herself in the joy of reunion.

For a moment Hadran allowed the embrace, holding her tightly as if he were the surrogate father she envisioned him to be. All too soon she felt him stiffen in her arms. He pulled back self-consciously, remembering his rule that no matter how close they became, a spy must never be coddled.

"Are you alright?" he asked, peering closely at his ward. "I have heard the strangest tales."

"What did Jon tell you? Why isn't he here?"

"Jon is guarding the entrance." Hadran shook his head at the foolishness of his other protégé. "At first I didn't believe his story, but Owen confirmed it. Owen is determined to leave Gundy's service and take us with him.

"I knew he was not happy in Gundy's employ, but I never thought Owen would turn against us like this. You were both so gifted. I think I was more indulgent that I should have been."

"There was nothing wrong with your instruction. You taught us to be strong and loyal to each other. No matter the assignment, we would do it because of what it meant to the group, our family."

"And now Owen wants to tear our family apart."

"I don't understand him."

"Owen wants you," replied Hadran with a slow shake of his head. "I taught both of you to be tenacious in pursuing your goals. We never failed in an assignment, nor let circumstances keep us from success. For him, this is no different. There is only one thing he needs that will make his plan a success —the very thing you were sent here to obtain."

"The silver," she finished. Everything hinged on the cursed treasure. She thought she knew where it was hidden, but what if she was wrong? Gundy needed the money to finance his invasion, Cairn needed the money to defend his home, and Owen needed the silver to create his vision of their future. Everyone's dreams depended on a treasure that might not exist.

She had run out of time to search and was terrified of what would happen if she returned to Gundy without it. He certainly wasn't the most forgiving master. Child or no child, she would be severely punished.

Staying in Scotland was no longer possible. Hadran had proved how easily an assassin could reach her. She had always felt safest when Jon, Hadran and Owen were together. She had to trust they would protect her from Gundy's displeasure.

"I don't agree with Owen's plans," said Hadran thoughtfully. "But over the years I have learned to pick my battles. Give Owen the treasure, play along. We'll think of a way out of this when the time is right. There is always a way to rectify a situation if you are patient."

"There is something you need to know." She didn't know how to explain her relationship with Cairn, but needed Hadran to understand her feelings before he started making plans. "I cannot kill Cairn McPherson. If it needs to be done … I cannot be responsible."

"I don't understand."

"Throughout this assignment, we have become close. I believe he cares for me despite everything that happened. He knows the truth. He knows I work for Gundy, yet he didn't harm me. He promised to protect me and our unborn child, and I believe him."

Hadran was silent for a long moment. He stared at her as if she were a stranger. Hadran taught her to never fall victim to her emotions. He schooled her repeatedly on the dangers of getting attached to an assignment, yet that was exactly what she had done. She couldn't murder Cairn because she had fallen in love with him.

"This Scot has turned your head."

"Aye."

"This is madness! I taught you better than this."

"I love him."

"Love him?" Hadran spat the hated words. "How could you love a rich, spoiled noble? He is not like us. He is another Gundy!"

"You are wrong. Cairn is not shackled to this land. He could have left any time and returned to France with his brother. He chose to stay here and take on the responsibility of his clan, for no other reason than they need him. There is no glory in what he does, no wealth or prestige. He has emptied his coffers to stretch the clan's finances. He is the bravest, most compassionate man I have ever known and I would never do anything to hurt him."

"I cannot believe my ward. You are like Owen, turning against family."

"Any punishment shall be mine to bear," Verena said. "The failure is mine."

"If you think I will let you face Gundy's wrath alone, you are mistaken." Hadran tugged on his thinning hair as he paced the confines of the dungeon. He was shocked and disappointed, but She hoped some part of him would understand her feelings. They had been through so much. Surely Hadran would be sympathetic. "Foolish girl, he locked you in a dungeon."

"Gundy would have done much worse. Cairn knows the truth. He knows I betrayed him. He knows I work for Gundy, yet he didn't hurt me. I don't think he could ever harm me."

"Does he love you?"

She paused, glancing guiltily to the side. She wanted to say yes. Verena knew he cared for her, but was it love? So much had changed since he discovered the truth.

"I believe so."

"We don't have time for this. Owen is not far away. We'll meet him and then devise a new plan."

"Thank you, Hadran."

"Don't thank me yet. We'll speak again when this is over."

The sound of footsteps on the stone stairs made the two spies spin around. Their conversation had been so animated, they lost track of time. There was so much to discuss, she forgot Roselyn would be returning soon with her meal.

The terrified maid stepped through the open doorway, followed by a grim-faced guard and Jon. The young lad was holding a crossbow in his arms, trained on the back of the guard's head.

"Roselyn?" she asked with a sinking heart. She had not wanted to involve her in this nasty business, but it seemed she had no choice. "Are you alright?"

"Who are these people?" asked Roselyn in wide-eyed terror. "Are you going to kill me?"

"No one will touch you."

"If you do what we say," broke in Hadran. He pulled out another crossbow and aimed it at Roselyn. "Turn around and march back up those stairs. Good work, Jon."

As he led their small group out of the dungeon and to the Old Lord's secret passage, Jon spared Verena a curious look. What did he think of these developments? Roselyn had taken a special interest in Jon before he was forced to flee Scotland. It must be terrifying to find out the sweet lad was in the employ of her hated enemy.

Chapter 42

Verena and her prisoners walked quickly toward the village. Winter had come to Scotland while she was in the dungeon. Thick snow flew sideways across the land, carried by a freezing wind. This was the first real storm of the season and promised to be an ugly one. Only a fool would fight a war in such weather, but Gundy didn't care for the comfort of his men. If he thought the unseasonal invasion would give him the element of surprise, he would use it.

Although their presence exiting the Old Lord's woods might look strange since aside from Jon and Hadran, they wore no cloaks, their group drew little attention. The few villagers outside in such abysmal weather were hurrying home.

 Once they had to duck behind a cottage as a small group of soldiers came toward them. Their guard looked like he would call out, but the sharp prod of her hair pin silenced him. The small weapon worked, but she sorely missed her knives. As soon as they were out of sight, the weary group continued their trek.

She was surprised at first when Jon led them to Thomas' cottage, but the same factors that made him the most likely candidate to hide the treasure, also made Thomas the perfect man to hide them. He insisted upon his privacy and independence so the villagers were unlikely to disturb him. It also gave her the opportunity to test her theories about his involvement.

Inside the cottage was virtually unchanged since the last time she was there with Roselyn, to dispense bread and soup from the castle. A large table was placed directly on top of Thomas' incongruous rug, forcing people to walk around it. Owen sat upon a three-legged stool, calmly helping himself to Thomas' supper while the old man lay in a corner, tied and gagged.

"Owen?" she asked, checking to make sure Thomas was unharmed. Aside from a nasty bruise on his cheek, he seemed fine. The old man was conscious and glaring at her as if she were the wife of Satan. "What have you done?"

"You know I had to keep him from making trouble," Owen replied. "You are looking well. I heard that whoreson locked you in a dungeon."

"I am fine."

"What shall we do with them?" asked Jon, pointing to Roselyn and the guard. She finally remembered his name was Stephen. He also glared at her as if all of this was her fault.

"Too many hostages are difficult to handle," replied Owen. He wiped his knife on his thigh and menacingly approached Roselyn. "We don't need them all."

"We made it here without killing anyone," she pointed out, horrified that her former friend would casually murder for no other reason than convenience. "And we won't be here long enough for them to create trouble for us."

"Did you find the treasure?"

Verena froze. What should she tell him? If Owen knew Thomas had the silver, he would do anything to get the truth from him. The nasty old man had caused many people, including his clan, a lot of trouble, but did that justify torture? She hesitated to point fingers at a frail old man no matter how unpleasant he was.

"Why should I give it to you? All you care about is yourself. Have you considered what this betrayal will mean for the rest of us?"

"This is for us. We don't need a spoiled noble controlling our lives. With our skills we can control the world. We can create a web of intrigue that will engulf England and the continent. What do you think these nobles will pay for the secrets we can uncover?"

"That is blackmail."

"It is too late for an attack of conscience. We have been doing this for Gundy for years. This time it is for us. I want us to obtain the riches we deserve."

"You will get us killed," interrupted Hadran. "There is a reason Gundy limited our activities. If anyone uncovered the truth, they wouldn't rest until we were dead. Your plan will destroy us."

"No! I will save us. We will live like kings. You'll see.

Owen crossed the room and grabbed Roselyn roughly by the arm. He twisted her until she cried out in pain. Verena made a move to stop him and he struck out, knocking her to the ground.

"Stop, Owen!" yelled Hadran. "We don't treat each other this way."

"Don't tell me how we treat each other. From now on you'll do as I say."

"Verena, please," whispered Roselyn, as Owen twisted her arm until her eyes rolled backward in pain. "Make him stop. I'll do anything."

"Is this a friend of yours?" asked Owen with deceptive sweetness. She bit her lip. If she displayed concern, Owen would try to use her emotions against her, but it was too late. He knew she cared for Roselyn. "I have watched you interact with these Scots. I see they way they treat you, the way the McPherson treats you. This assignment is different, he is different to you. Do you think I cannot see how you feel about them?"

"I don't know what you are talking about."

He was toying with Verena the way he toyed with all their targets. It was the same maddening impulse that led Owen to leave the bloody dagger in Queen Anne's chambers and let himself be seen by Cairn in the Langthorne woods. The wild recklessness would never allow Owen to calmly accept his role. With or without the treasure, in Gundy's employ or independent, Owen would always feel the need to push and tempt fate.

"Owen," broke in Hadran, stepping forward to try to diffuse the tense situation. "This is not necessary. Verena will tell you where the treasure is."

"I'm waiting."

Verena knew Thomas had the treasure, but she didn't know where. Everyone was watching her for an answer, but her mind was blank. If she told Owen her suspicions, he would likely torture the old man. If she was mistaken, it would cost Thomas his life.

Why did he stubbornly insist on living alone? Surely someone would shelter Thomas despite his grumpy nature. For years he had refused to leave this cottage, steadfastly maintaining his independence. She peered into the shadowy corners, trying to fathom what in this cottage had kept him for so many years.

As she climbed to her feet, she felt the ground change beneath her. Under the rug, she heard the soft, but distinctive creak of wooden beams.

Some peasants built extra storage space beneath their cottages. These recesses were often used to hide valuables during times of conflict. What would Thomas chose to hide under his floor?

"You are taking too long. Perhaps you don't know where the treasure is and are seeking to delay me. Or perhaps you do know and are seeking to test my resolve."

The knife rose to Roselyn's throat and gently pricked her skin. Roselyn squeaked in alarm as Owen's intentions became clear. He would kill her to prove he was serious. He would probably kill all of the hostages regardless of what she did because they were taught to leave no witnesses.

It was hard to believe Verena had once passively accepted such knowledge, allowing Owen to clean up after her clandestine work. Now the thought of what was to come made her sick. She had to do something fast.

"I will give you what you want, if you give me what I want."

"What do you want?" he asked intently.

"Their lives."

"And what do I want?"

"The treasure … and me."

"What of your lover?"

Verena looked Roselyn directly in the eye, hardening her voice so there would be no mistaking her next words. "He will not follow."

Owen took his time responding, staring at her, and judging her motives for any sign of treachery. She saw Owen's distrust, but also his excitement. He was so close to getting everything he desired, but he had learned over the years to be wary.

"Do we have a deal?"

Ever so slightly, Owen nodded in agreement. Before he could change his mind, she reached down and tossed the table and rug aside, exposing the trapdoor beneath. She pulled it open, ignoring the splinters that dug painfully into her palms. She made a show of her struggle, trying to get Owen to release Roselyn and come to her assistance, but he was too smart to fall for that.

"It was here the whole time!" said Jon in surprise. "I knew the old bugger was hiding something."

Tucking her skirts into her girdle, she descended the rickety ladder. At first glance the room looked like an ordinary storage room. Old blankets and sacks of moldy grain were piled up and most likely forgotten as the years wore on. She was not convinced. The McPhersons had been through too many hard times to leave piles of food to rot.

She approached one sack and lifted out a few handfuls of dusty grain. There was nothing there.

"S'wounds!" she hissed in frustration. This was her last hope. If the treasure was not hidden here, she had nothing left to bargain with. She threw the heavy sack to the ground in frustration and watched as the dusty grains spilled across the floor. She was about to turn away when something caught her eye.

Lying among the spilled granules was a scrap of dirty fabric. She leaned down to tug on it and realized the cloth was actually a smaller, separate bag concealed within the larger one. Her heart was pounding as she pulled it out and spilled its contents into her hand. Dozens of Roman coins glinted dully in the light of her candle.

Thomas was living on top of a fortune! Why didn't he take the silver for himself or turn it over to the new laird? Whatever his motivations the treasure was in her hands now, but instead of feeling triumphant, she felt only a dull ache of regret. This treasure had cost Cairn so much pain, yet he would never see it. The McPhersons would have to survive this winter without it.

"This is what you want," she said when she climbed up the ladder. She held up a silver coin to Owen's hungry gaze.

"Aye."

How could she have considered marrying a man like him? Owen was so selfish, so transparently greedy. She looked down at the silver piece resting innocently in her hand. Gundy would destroy the McPhersons for this treasure. Countless lives would be lost because of one man's selfishness and she was complicit to it all.

"Let her go."

"Your time in Scotland has made you soft," Owen chided as he released Roselyn. She could see the indecision on her friend's face. She was torn between staying to help and running for her life.

Owen quickly took the decision out of her hands. Before

Roselyn could move, Owen cuffed her hard across the face. She crumpled unconscious to the ground.

"You could have tied her up," she pointed out. Owen shrugged. Both methods were equally effective in keeping the maid quiet. "We'll need several horses to carry it all."

They decided Jon would go in search of the horses while she, Hadran and Owen brought the sacks of silver up the ladder. Even with horses they would have a difficult time transporting all the silver. The amount of treasure was enormous. As soon as Jon returned with the first of his purloined mounts, they sent him for more.

"Verena," whispered the lad while Owen was occupied checking the distribution of their baggage. "Did you mean what you said in the dungeon about laird Cairn? Do you trust him?"

"With my life. He was furious, but he didn't hurt me, nor do I think he would."

"Would you stay with him?"

"If I could, aye."

"I believe you. If Gundy found out we were conspiring against him, he would do more than lock us in a dungeon. Laird Cairn is a fair man."

"He is an angry man and likely to explode when he finds out I escaped."

"What are you two whispering about?" Owen demanded, seeing the two huddled in deep conversation.

"I asked how many more horses we would need," lied Jon. "There should be some old nags in the southern pasture that no one will miss."

"Bring as many as you can. Quickly."

Hadran helped Verena carry Roselyn to Thomas' bed and cover her with a blanket. She had expected her to awaken long ago and was beginning to grow worried.

As the minutes ticked slowly by, no sound of horses were heard from the castle. She paced the floor in frustration imagining the millions of things that could go wrong. Suppose Owen didn't keep his end of the bargain and decided their hostages were too much of a liability? What if Roselyn never woke up? What if Cairn saw her leaving with Owen and assumed the worst?

"Tie her up," Owen commanded, gesturing to Roselyn's still

form. "She is not dead yet and we can't wait any longer for Jon."

She looked at him sharply, stunned by his callous attitude. Owen was going to leave Jon behind knowing the whole castle must be alerted to his treachery. Hadran taught them to protect each other, but for Owen things had changed. The treasure was more important than his companions.

"We cannot leave Jon."

"If the Scot catches him, they will soon have us all. We must leave before it is too late." Owen hefted Roselyn onto his shoulder. He adjusted her small weight and she imagined she heard the girl groan in protest as his shoulder dug painfully into her abdomen. "You may hate me now, but in time you will realize everything I have done was for you."

She wanted to scoff. She would never believe Owen acted selflessly. She saw the way his eyes lit up when she showed him the silver coin. Owen wanted the treasure as badly as Gundy and was just as ruthless in obtaining it.

"I will not leave her in that cold, dark pit."

"Would you rather I kill her now?"

She snapped her mouth shut, hating her powerlessness. She had bargained for Roselyn's life, but could push Owen no further. Verena had to think of what she could do for her friend.

She gathered several blankets to place around Roselyn's body and left a long candle burning near her. At least Roselyn would have a few hours of warmth and light. With Thomas and the guard, she wouldn't be alone. Hopefully someone would discover them soon.

Roselyn finally awoke when Owen stuffed a cloth into her mouth. It seemed he was taking no chances. Though she tried to scream through the gag, Roselyn could only make a tiny, muffled sound. Owen brought his hand back to cuff her again and Roselyn wisely quieted.

The weather outside had grown steadily worse while they loaded the horses. There was a chill to the air that cut through her woolen gown as if she wore nothing at all. Hail plastered her garments to her skin. Her cloak was still in the castle, but she had purloined a few blankets from Thomas to wrap around her shivering frame. Owen tried to place his cloak around her shoulders, but she stubbornly refused the gift.

Before they reached the forest, she turned to look on the castle one last time. Within its foreboding walls she had experienced such joy and pain. Verena would never forget her experiences there, the friends she made and the man she had come to love. She would worry about Jon until they reunited. The little imp was constantly getting into trouble, but she knew even if he was captured, Cairn would treat him fairly.

Chapter 43

"Milord!" came a familiar shout from behind. Cairn was far from the castle, overseeing the slaughter of the McPherson sheep. Animals that wouldn't survive the winter had to be killed and their meat preserved. It was a yearly ritual, but this time there was an air of desperation to the act. The Scots were furious warriors at close quarters, but if Gundy was planning a long siege they would need more than their current reserves to survive.

Jon, who had recently escaped Cairn's dungeon, ran toward him as if he had not been implicated in an assassination plot. He nimbly approached, leaping over dead animals and dodging the soldiers that tried to detain him.

"Milord! You must come quickly!"

"Are you daft, boy?" Fergus asked, trying to grab Jon as he ran past. He missed and fell into a pile of steaming entrails.

A prickle of unease lodged in Cairn's throat. He knew Jon was one of Verena's associates. Why then would he openly seek out his enemy? Whatever Jon was running from must be more frightening than Cairn's wrath.

"It is Verena," Jon exclaimed as he skidded to a stop, panting and holding his sides in pain. "She has been kidnapped by Gundy's men."

"You are Gundy's men! All of you have deceived me and now you wish to lead me into another trap? Guards, seize him!"

"No! Not this time. Verena loves you. Owen would have killed Roselyn if she didn't come. You know I am fond of Roselyn. I wouldn't hurt her for the world."

Something inside Cairn stirred at Jon's impassioned speech. For days he had tried to push her from his life. As soon as the child was born, he planned to banish her to France. Let Andreu care for her in one of his castles. But no matter how he tried, each moment away from her was torture. Everywhere he looked there were reminders of her presence, from the cook's improved menu to thoughtful gifts she had distributed to the clan.

If she was the calculating spy Gundy wanted her to be, she would have let him drink the poison. There was softness to Verena she couldn't pretend; the way she melted in his arms and hungered for his touch. He couldn't convince himself that was all pretense.

"Explain yourself."

"They are headed to Gundy's camp across the border. If you leave now, you might catch them."

"How did she escape?"

Jon's fists clenched at his sides. Verena was captured while rescuing him. He brought the unstable Owen to her. If Jon truly believed she was in love with Cairn, perhaps this was his way of making amends.

During her confinement she told Cairn about her family of spies, how Hadran picked them off the street and taught them how to work together. She insisted they were selected because Hadran glimpsed something special in each of them, but Cairn suspected that special quality had more to do with desperation. They were united in their need to belong. Hadran's genius was his ability to recognize this need and exploit it for his employer.

Cairn would never pity Verena's family because he knew what lengths they would go to in order to protect each other. He had little reason to trust the young spy, but knew he had no choice. She was in trouble.

"If any of my clan suffers because of you ..."

"I promise, sir. We didn't hurt anyone."

"Milord?"

The soldiers were watching him anxiously. Most of them didn't know the whole truth, but rumors of her deception had been circulating since her imprisonment. Although they didn't dare question him, Cairn had seen the heaping plates of food Roselyn brought to her, the sweets, comfortable bedding, warm clothes, candles and cushions. He didn't understand how they could still care for her. Perhaps they, like Cairn, longed to believe she was Gundy's victim rather than his accomplice.

"If this is a trap you will not live to regret it."

"I know." It was difficult not to marvel at this young lad. He didn't even blink at the threat. Cairn didn't know if he was brave or merely resigned to a world of violence. "I will explain everything on the way."

"You aren't going anywhere without me," insisted Fergus, climbing to his feet. "Someone needs to keep this little rascal in line."

"Who else will ride with me?"

"I will!"

A chorus of enthusiastic affirmations greeted Cairn's question. These men were strangers a few months ago, but were now willing to fight and die beside their laird. They accepted Cairn not because he was Angus' son, but because of the close bonds that had forged as they worked together.

"We don't have much time."

They raced toward Thomas' cottage, but the spies were long gone by the time they arrived. They found Roselyn, Thomas and the guard, Stephen hidden under a trapdoor in Thomas' cottage. The rhythmic thumping of Stephen's foot against the wall alerted Cairn to their presence.

"Let her go," spat Thomas as soon as his gag was removed. "She is not one of us."

"Quiet, old fool!" Roselyn said. "This is your fault! They took the silver and Lady Verena."

"The treasure was here?"

"Aye, hidden in those sacks of grain."

Cairn swung his shrewd gaze toward Thomas and the old man backed up in fear. All of Gundy's scheming was for the treasure. Even if Thomas didn't know of Gundy's plans, he knew the clan's state of affairs and how desperately they needed that money. Months of struggle could have been avoided if he had spoken up. Yet Thomas was unrepentant.

"You were my grandfather's personal retainer."

"Aye, and I have done my part to keep this clan safe."

"More than was wise. I never thought I would see the day when a McPherson put himself before the needs of our clan."

"I am not a traitor," replied Thomas stubbornly. "I have always put the McPhersons before myself."

"And now?"

"Now more than ever. You call me a traitor, but you are a stranger to this clan. You haven't set foot in Scotland since childhood and now you think you are one of us?"

Fergus drew his sword, but Cairn waved him down. He listened to Thomas' rant, curious about his motives.

"That English woman is like your stepmother, dazzling us all with her beauty. Soon enough you will see what a viper she is. That is why the Old Lord trusted me. He knew I would never let a woman turn my head, particularly a foreign witch."

Cairn grabbed Thomas' scrawny neck and pressed him against the wall of his cottage.

"I didn't ask to be laird, but I accept the responsibility placed upon me. I have worked from dawn to dusk for my clan. Every day I repaired walls and trained men. Verena has assisted the sick, given aid to the poor and cared for my people as if they were her own. What have you done?"

Thomas didn't dare answer. He couldn't breathe with the pressure of Cairn's fingers on his throat. No one made a move to stop him, or said anything in Thomas' defense. The old man would have let his clan starve rather than risk Ivone touching their silver.

After a tense moment Cairn stepped back, dropping him to the floor.

"Take him to the dungeon."

"The Old Lord asked me to keep the treasure safe," shouted Thomas as Stephen pulled him toward the ladder. "I made sure Ivone never found it and she didn't take it all. There is plenty left for us. We don't need the paltry sum she stole."

Cairn turned back to Jon, who had watched the exchange with interest. Jon had taken a considerable risk in trusting Cairn, but it wasn't until he saw Cairn release Thomas that Jon knew he make the right decision. The old man would be punished, but fairly and not in a fit of rage. Cairn was not like Gundy.

"We have wasted enough time here. Let's find Verena."

Chapter 44

Verena's group made swift progress despite the abysmal weather. The land was much different from her last journey, when there was still a bit of green to the countryside. Now the trees were completely barren, the leaves lay strewn on the ground in muddy piles. Where the trail was not slippery with frozen ice, it was churned to thick mud by the hooves of many horses.

Taking her words to heart, Cairn had instructed his men to vigilantly watch the roads to give his clan as much warning as possible for Gundy's attack. Several times they had to duck behind a scraggly copse of trees to escape the patrols. Owen and Hadran had nothing to fear, but she was too recognizable after her time in Scotland. If anyone saw her, their group would be detained.

The blow came before she could flinch, knocking her off her horse and onto the frozen ground. She just managed to break her fall with her arms so not to jar the baby.

"Owen stop!" said Hadran, but Owen paid him no mind.

"Stay out of this, old man."

Owen dismounted and stalked over to where she lay in the mud holding her injured cheek.

As they neared the border, Owen had led them off the main road and along an old deer trail. From the dead branches nearly covering the path, she assumed few knew its existence.

"You are marking a trail for him!" He stood over Verena's huddled form with clenched fists. She shook her head, but Owen continued angrily. "Don't lie to me."

Owen lifted her off the ground, dangling her before him like a rag doll. He had always used his size and strength to intimidate others, but for the first time she was truly frightened for herself.

She was marking a trail, but not for Cairn. He wouldn't trouble himself over her disappearance. She carried his child, but what would he want with a traitor's bastard? Though it hurt more than she thought possible, she had to resign herself to a life without him. There was no place in her world for love. She needed to be practical.

So she lowered her traitorous eyes, taking comfort in the old habits of the past. Adapt and survive, that was what Hadran taught her. "Do not lose yourself in futile emotion. Rise above it." Verena needed that advice now. She took comfort in the cold words. She would adapt and survive because much more than her life was at stake. She must think of her child.

"Are you that desperate to return to your lover? You are pathetic."

Owen raised his arm to hit her again, but was stopped by Hadran's restraining hand.

"That's enough!" he said with some of his old authority. Owen flicked a contemptuous glance at his former mentor before pushing him away.

"I told you to stay out of this, old man."

"No! I raised you, clothed you, fed you, taught you everything you know and now you will listen to me.

"What you are doing now is beyond reckless, it is stupid. Stealing the treasure, betraying Gundy, and now your behavior … You are out of control and I should have said something long ago."

"I thought you were with me."

"I love you like a son, but think about what you are doing. If we follow this path we will be running for the rest of our lives."

"I will no longer live as a slave."

"Go back to Scotland," she suggested. "Cairn will listen to me. This silver means the survival of his clan. No matter what we have done, he will be lenient."

"I can't do that. I was meant for more than to spend my life as some nobleman's lackey. With this silver I won't have to be. Don't you see I am doing this so that we can live the lives we deserve? The finest houses in England will bow before us; they will tremble at our knowledge and power."

"I will ask you for the last time," Owen's eyes burned into Verena's. She was frightened of what he might do in anger, terrified that his unrestrained violence might cause her to lose her baby. "Are you with me?"

She choked back her natural response as she remembered Hadran's words in the dungeon: "Give him what he wants." Owen was dangerous, ready to murder anyone who dared to stand in his way. She couldn't risk his wrath. For the sake of her unborn child she had to find a way to pacify him.

"You are right," she announced demurely. Both men stilled at her words. "The McPherson was so kind, I wanted to believe it was love."

She sighed, allowing a tear to carefully fall from one eye.

"I was willing to give up my life for a lie. Hadran taught me better than that. He is not my family, you are. I'm sorry."

She slowly climbed to her feet, awkwardly brushing off her muddy skirt. She forced herself not to wince as Owen roughly grabbed her chin and forced her to look him in the eye.

"If this is a trick ..." he warned.

"You would know. I never could lie to you."

Owen stared at her for a long time, trying to gauge the truth of Verena's words. He wanted to believe her, but was afraid. If he felt so strongly perhaps she could still influence him.

"Are you with me?" he repeated softly. This time there was no threat in his voice, no anger, just the earnest pleading from his heart. Verena swallowed the guilt that threatened to choke her. This was Owen, the man who had been like a brother to her. She wished they could return to the way things were when she had idolized his gruff competence and he had diligently taught and protected her.

"You know I am."

Owen lowered his lips to hers and though she initially froze, she forced herself to respond. She opened her mouth to Owen when all she wanted to do was run away. Her body was acutely aware that it was not Cairn that held her in his arms. His taste, his smell, the very feel of Owen was wrong. Yet somehow she endured his alien touch.

After what seemed like an eternity Hadran cleared his throat, reminding them of the danger they still faced.

She gazed sheepishly at Owen. In his eyes was a promise she had no intention of fulfilling. She wanted to wipe her hands across her lips and erase the taste of him. Owen believed her, but that didn't ease the sick feeling in her stomach. Why was it so difficult to pretend now? Her entire life was built upon lies.

"We can rest once we've crossed the border," said Hadran. His censorious gaze raked Owen as if he were still an oversexed teenager.

She nodded and allowed Owen to help her remount. If Jon was following the trail she marked, he would be careful crossing the English border. She knew he could take care of himself, but that didn't stop her from worrying.

She had found a way to make Owen lower his guard, but in doing so she had created a new danger for herself. Once they reached safety, she didn't know how long she could keep Owen away.

Chapter 45

Owen called a halt not long after they crossed the border. They had ridden through the night and Verena's muscles were aching with fatigue. She gingerly swung her leg over the saddle and Owen was immediately by her side to help her dismount. She silently cursed the weak muscles that forced her to cling to him to keep from falling into the mud.

"Gundy's army is through those trees," Owen explained. "He put us uncomfortably close to the center."

The nobles liked to stay in the middle of their army camps where it was safer and everyone could see their importance. Hadran would never have chosen such a spot for the spies. They would be constantly on display, giving them little chance to sneak around.

"He wants his precious treasure as close as possible."

Though this conflict was close to home, there were many families in Gundy's camp. One of her first assignments had been to sneak into an enemy's encampment disguised as a camp follower and assess their strength and numbers. Did Cairn have men hidden in the English army? She didn't recognize anyone.

Perhaps because of their proximity to the noble's area or pleasure at their success, Gundy decided to furnish the spies with a much grander tent than expected. Fabric flaps divided the space into three rooms. Beautifully carved furniture graced rooms hung with colorful tapestries. Mountains of thick furs and blankets were gracefully draped across comfortable beds and chairs.

Weary from traveling through the frigid night, she wanted nothing more than to collapse onto the giant bed. Unfortunately before she had time to remove her cloak, a lad of about fifteen summoned them to Gundy.

"I'll go," offered Hadran, smothering a yawn. He had always been the one to deal with Gundy and had years of practice soothing his easily offended pride.

"He wants the woman," said the lad, gesturing to Verena with his chin. He no doubt thought she was a new leman being summoned for his lord's pleasure. He opened one of the chests to reveal a wine-colored dress of flimsy silk. She shivered just looking at the fabric. The fine cloth would be as warm as gauze in this weather.

"He can't be serious."

"My lord has also generously provided a fur cloak for your comfort," continued the messenger in the same bored tone. The tent flap opened behind him to reveal a group of servants carrying a large wooden tub, buckets of steaming hot water and platters of assorted meats, breads, cheeses, and wines. He directed them to set up in one of the smaller rooms. "I suggest using plenty of soap."

"Lady Verena thanks his lordship for this generosity," spoke up Hadran before Verena could box the impertinent boy's ears. After a fortnight in a dungeon making do with occasional sponge baths, She knew her smell was offensive, but he didn't have to point that out.

Deft hands washed, combed and braided her hair into an elaborate circlet while fragrant herbs from the bath perfumed the air. She would have liked to linger in this small respite, but Gundy was probably anxious to hear her report. She didn't know why Hadran couldn't deliver it like usual, but long ago gave up trying to understand Gundy's whims.

She forced herself to climb out of the cozy tub and munched on a crust of bread while the ladies dressed her. When they were finished, she grimaced at her reflection in the small mirror.

The ladies were experts at showing the female figure to the best advantage and transformed her into an expensive courtesan. Her bosom was proudly displayed in an indecently low bodice, tightly laced underneath to accentuate her still tiny waist. The voluminous skirt was parted in the center to reveal a saucy red underdress. Five small puffs decorated the sleeves which were fashionably slashed to show the red fabric beneath.

The effect was just short of decadent. The soft fabrics begged to be touched, the fashionable slashes clearly showed her undergarments. When she left the bathing room, the look Owen gave her made Verena want to cover herself with a blanket.

"You are radiant," he said, scrambling to his feet. The silver had been unloaded and stacked beside the table where Owen and Hadran were busy devouring the rest of her meal.

"You will be fine," said Hadran, stepping forward to wrap the luxurious sable cloak around her shoulders. He gave a wry smile at the two long hair pins stuck into her elaborate coiffure. "Remember what I taught you."

She took a deep breath and forced the worry lines on her brow to smooth.

She gave Hadran a brilliant smile despite the knots in her stomach. Gundy had never touched her in the past, but that was thanks to Hadran's efforts to keep them apart. Wearing this dress, she felt as safe as a chicken in a wolf's den.

"Gundy is still cloistered with his neighbors," said Owen once the last of the servants departed. "That is why he chose you instead of Hadran to attend him. There is nothing suspicious about a new whore following her lord to war. Make note of the tent's layout and any other useful data. When the time is right, we shall need it."

Soon Owen would assassinate Gundy. Strangely, that knowledge no longer terrified her. Did it really matter who became her new master? She would still be a slave. It was Gundy's nature to use his servants as he saw fit. Owen wanted to become just like him.

She desperately wished she hadn't followed Hadran out of the dungeon. Perhaps with a little more time, Cairn would have forgiven her. When she was with him she began to think dangerous thoughts of what life would be like if she wasn't a spy. She wanted to be that innocent and brave lass Cairn met during his flight from Langthorne.

Years of working for Lord Gundy had taught her to be practical. Wishing for Cairn wouldn't change anything. Lifting her skirts free of the muddy road, she allowed Owen to escort her to Gundy's tent.

Chapter 46

They stopped outside the largest tent in camp. Owen bent down to remove the tall wooden chopines that protected her delicately embroidered slippers from the road's mud and filth. The gesture was for the benefit of the curious onlookers staring with unabashed awe at the mysterious lady. Owen's reverence silently told them better than the fabulous cloak, that she was an honored guest and worthy of respect. She wondered what curious role she was supposed to play this time.

Before she was ready, Owen whisked the cloak from her shoulders and pressed a fragile decanter of wine into her hands. Like her flimsy dress, it was entirely unsuitable for a war camp.

"Relax," he whispered into her ear.

Verena gave a curt nod and stepped into the tent. If her arrangements were grand, Lord Gundy's were nothing short of opulent. The colorfully draped hangings gave the space an oriental look. It was probably Gundy's intent to remind his associates of the foreign crusades, though the lords would be foolish to mistake themselves for crusaders.

Fabric in every shade hung from the canvas walls. Everywhere she looked there were gilded ornaments and furniture more suited for a palace than a war tent. Thick imported rugs hid the mud beneath her feet.

Six lords sat in a circle debating battle scenarios and venting their unease. Gundy looked like he would like nothing better than to banish them all from his sight, but he knew he needed their support to win.

"S'wounds!" came an appreciative exclamation when she stepped into the room. She dipped low into a respectful curtsey, giving them all a generous view of her bosom.

"Ah, Verena!" exclaimed Gundy happily. "It is so good of you to join us. And you brought wine. You were always such a dutiful child.

"Milords, allow me to introduce Lady Verena, my ward from France. She is a distant relation of my late wife. Do be kind. This is her first trip away from the continent."

His ward? What game was Gundy playing today? Putting Verena on display like this guaranteed she could never again work in any of these lords' households. Like Cairn, he was giving them the impression of nobility, but Gundy always had an ulterior motive. Did he seek to use Verena's beauty against these lords in some way?

"It is a pleasure," gushed a florid man who introduced himself as Lord Oswald.

Verena remembered his lands bordered Gundy's and he had been anxious to form a more permanent alliance for years. He kissed her fingers as if she were the grandest lady.

"I'm sure your ... er ... ward shall find England most diverting."

That was said by Lord Reginald, a man surprisingly cunning to be in Gundy's camp. Verena had once played a servant in his household when the king had come to visit. Gundy must not trust him if he felt the lord needed to be watched. She wouldn't be surprised if he had his own ideas for the outcome of this expedition.

They reminded her of Owen's gambling partners. The lords were the most casual allies, united only in purpose. They came together for supposed friendship, but each greedily sought to benefit from the other's downfall.

"Come and sit by me," crooned Gundy in the gentlest voice. He placed an elaborately embroidered pillow on the carpet next to his chair. Verena gracefully sank into it and just barely kept herself from flinching as Gundy began idly playing in her hair.

"We should push on," demanded Lord Oswald. He was the most impatient of the bunch and ignored his chair to pace the room in agitation. "The McPherson must have seen our army by now. He is probably preparing for a siege as we speak."

"There will be no siege," insisted Gundy. "Our battle shall be quick and decisive."

"How do we know that? You are so bloody secretive. I have a mind to withdraw my men until I get some answers."

The finger that was gently playing in her curls suddenly jerked. Gundy wasn't always so powerful. He had built his small empire through conquest in war and intrigue. Though he had vastly expanded his lands and purse, Gundy continued to push Hadran's agents. He still felt the need to prove his dominance over England and Scotland. Gundy would never allow one of his allies to withdraw and leave him vulnerable.

The hand in her hair lowered to caress her cheek and then gently squeeze her shoulder. Taking the hint, she rose to her feet and approached Oswald.

"Your wine glass is empty," she observed sympathetically, allowing her voice to thicken with a sultry French accent. "Allow me."

One drop of wine spilled down the side of his glass. Verena caught the drop on her finger and seductively sucked the digit into her mouth.

"An excellent selection. My lord is most generous."

The room lay in shocked silence after that brazen display, only disturbed by Oswald's audible gulp. When she was reseated next to Gundy, he once again placed a proprietary hand on her shoulder, giving it a quick squeeze to show he approved. She wanted to vomit.

"It would be a shame if you decided to leave us," said Gundy with affected nonchalance. Oswald was quick to recant his threat.

The meeting continued and no more was said about withdrawing. When the lords began to grumble about Gundy's demands, he would skillfully use her to distract them. He presented a platter of succulent delicacies for her to nibble on. When Lord Reginald complained that his troops would be on the front lines, Gundy allowed one sleeve to innocently fall from Verena's shoulder. The men were enthralled.

When they finally left, Gundy was ecstatic from his success.

"That was the most fun I have had in ages! If I knew you were so effective, I would have brought you in from the field long ago."

"Milord is too kind."

The inner flap dividing the large tent into smaller rooms was pushed aside to reveal Ivone's grim-faced assassin. She glared at

Verena as if she longed to carve her in two. Ivone lay beyond, posed provocatively on a massive rope bed, wearing only a blanket and a smile.

"That sounded productive," she purred as Gundy came forward to stroke the inside curve of her thigh. Ivone stretched contentedly on the bed, drawing Gundy's hand up under the blanket. She giggled like a young girl, and then moaned. She quickly looked away.

"It has been too long."

"Indeed, my love," replied Gundy, leaning down to kiss her puckered lips. After a moment, he forced himself to straighten. "Unfortunately now is not the time to dally. There is much to be done. Verena, tell us about Scotland."

"I have found the treasure." Her attention was focused on the bump on Gundy's nose, pointedly ignoring the naked woman and assassin. Gundy whistled low as she produced a small pouch of silver coins. "Owen, Hadran and I brought most of it with us. We were able to fill eight sacks, each weighing about fifty pounds. The McPherson is still alive."

"What?" Gundy slapped her hard, but his heart was not in the punishment. He was too distracted watching the candlelight skim over the surface of the coins. "That was not the plan."

"I know, milord. The fault was mine."

"Why couldn't you murder him?" interrupted Ivone.

"I became pregnant and needed to be removed from the assignment."

"Pregnant?"

Gundy cocked his head to one side, astounded that the woman he thought of solely as a tool could be a mother. From the corner of her eye she saw a slight jerk of the assassin's blank visage. It passed as quickly as a blink of an eye, but she was certain. Something in the assassin had reacted to news of the child. Perhaps it triggered a memory of her past.

They were like two sides of the same coin. She was soft where the other woman was hard. She was trained to infiltrate, preying upon people's emotions and expectations. Verena was like water where the assassin was stone.

There was no softness in the assassin. She skulked through the shadows until coming close enough to strike. The hard life she must have faced was clearly evident in her blank eyes, completely devoid of emotion. She knew that look well and often feared the day she would wear a similar expression. Hers were eyes that had seen too much.

"Your female problem could have cost me the entire war!" Gundy exclaimed, clenching his fists in indignation. "Get rid of it. I still have need of you."

She dutifully bowed but didn't answer. Of course she would do no such thing. She would never let someone take her child away.

"I'm sure you noticed my esteemed neighbors' reaction to your beauty. Those vipers would cheerfully plant a knife between my ribs. I will need you to make sure that doesn't happen."

"I am ready to serve, milord."

"When this is over I may give you to one of them. Wouldn't that be nice? Imagine marrying a penniless spy to a lord! Mind you don't get a brat inside you next time. That is all."

With a short nod she turned and left the tent before the ever-watchful assassin noticed her shaking limbs. He meant to get rid of her child and pass Verena off to another lord. The thought of one of the geriatric English lords touching her made her gag. She never thought to have children but suddenly couldn't imagine living without the tiny person inside her. She had to escape, but how? Ivone's assassin was silent and deadly as a ghost. If she came after her, she wouldn't get far.

Owen was waiting for her outside the tent, holding her muddy chopines like a faithful servant, but his lips were twisted in a grimace of distaste.

"Did you enjoy playing a lady? It took you long enough to leave," he whispered as soon as they were a safe distance from the tent. Did he think she enjoyed being used by Gundy? Owen wasn't concerned for her safety. When did he become so self-centered?

"Ivone was there with her assassin."

"A woman. Jon told me about her. No doubt she is a pitiful creature fallen on hard times. She probably knows nothing about her art besides poisons and whoring."

"I fought her," she pointed out, startled that she felt the need to defend the woman that tried to kill her. "Do not underestimate her skill."

Owen's only response was a dismissive snort.

"I told Gundy about the child. I needed some reason to explain why Cairn is still alive. He told me to get rid of it so he can send me to spy on one of his neighbors."

"That explains the dress. This was merely a test to see how captivating you can be. Too bad Gundy won't live long enough to enjoy your success."

Chapter 47

"Verena! What on earth are you wearing?"

As soon as Owen lifted the tent flap, Jon scrambled off his stool and barreled into her arms. She barely managed to brace herself for the impact. With those familiar scrawny arms tightly circling her waist, she felt some of her anxiety melt away.

"That's enough!" Hadran said, coming forward to pry them apart. "You'll ruin Gundy's dress and I'm not helping you repair it."

"The dress is fine," Verena said with an exasperated sigh. She wished she could burn the infernal thing instead of gently dabbing the mud stains left by Jon's grubby hands.

Hadran demanded to know what transpired in Gundy's tent, so she recited the events almost word for word. They waited patiently until the end and then picked apart her story by asking dozens of pertinent questions. Where did the assassin stand during the interview? Were any of the lords carrying weapons? Were there other servants present? How far away were the guards? Had Gundy actually used the word "love" when addressing Ivone?

She patiently answered each question, familiar with this type of interview. One of the first lessons of being a spy was to know what type of information to look for. Gundy's report was fairly straightforward. He was only interested in the results of her endeavor. Hadran wanted to know every detail so that he could accurately assess Gundy's mood, desires and his next actions.

"It appears I arrived just in time," said Jon, sucking the marrow out of a chicken bone. "Things are starting to get exciting."

"How did you find us?"

"That was easy. Those nags I told you about were being moved just as I approached. I had to wait hours before they were left alone and by then, you had already left.

"At first I thought you would take the treasure back to Langthorne castle. Then I remembered Gundy borrowed a goodly sum to finance this invasion. He needs the silver fast to keep the other lords quiet. So he must have ordered you to bring the treasure to him. The three of you received quite a bit of attention entering the noble's area dressed as you were in rags."

"I always knew you were sharp," praised Hadran, ruffling the lad's unkempt curls. "Anyone else would have wasted hours searching in all the wrong places, but you knew just where to go."

"I learned from the best."

"What of Roselyn? Do you know if Cairn found her?"

"Nay. The cottage was undisturbed when I left."

Was there a brief hesitation in his words? Perhaps Jon wasn't as unaffected by their actions as he tried to appear. The knot in her stomach curled tighter, rising up to form a lump in the back of her throat. More than a full day had passed while Roselyn and the others lay tied and gagged in Thomas' basement. The candle she left burning would be extinguished by now leaving them in a cold, dark pit. Eventually someone would arrive to check on Thomas, but what if they didn't find the hidden prisoners?

Owen poked at his soggy garments drying on a rope strung across the tent. The others had not been provided with a change of clothes and huddled around the brazier in blankets while they waited for their clothes to dry. The smell of sweaty men, wet wool and leather permeated the large tent. Ever the exhibitionist, Owen threw off his blanket, giving them a good view of his broadly muscled back, generously covered with thick hair.

"I need to rest if I am to be of any use tomorrow. Jon, will you help me?" She abruptly stood and walked toward the room she had appropriated as her own. She was a good spy, but it was difficult to pretend around her family.

Jon's deft fingers made short work of her laces. She remembered watching him as he picked the locked door in the Old Lord's tunnel. Any woman would envy such slender hands, shaped for grace and precision. There was a slight tremble in them now as he helped her undress, though his voice was firm when he spoke.

"Did he hurt you?"

Her eyes filled with tears at the young lad's earnest question. Perhaps she wasn't as alone as she thought. Though he would never win a fight against Owen, Jon would do what he could to help her. An image of Roselyn's terrified face suddenly appeared in Verena's mind. She hadn't wanted to hurt the girl, but she had done precisely that. How many others would suffer because of this treasure? Would Jon be the next victim or her unborn child?

"I have endured worse."

Owen knew the value of Verena's face and wouldn't damage her while she could still be of use. Though she tried to make her voice sound flippant, Jon could hear the sarcasm in her tone.

"Not from him," Jon pointed out.

"Nay, I don't know what to do."

Jon led Verena to the large rope bed and lay down beside her. For a moment she forgot she was the elder and allowed herself to be pulled into his embrace. The smell of clean, damp linen and wind clung to his shirt.

"First, you will allow yourself to cry. Then you will sleep. Then we shall figure a way out of this mess."

His voice was so confident, she had to chuckle. No matter how dire things became, Jon could always put a smile on her face, but he wasn't laughing now. The young man's eyes were deadly serious as he stared unfocused at the tent walls.

Though she tried to resist, she felt the tears pour out at this sudden and unexpected tenderness. She clung to Jon, burying her face in his shoulder to muffle the sound of her tears.

"That's it," he murmured, knowing Owen was probably listening on the other side of the fabric wall. "Cry until there is nothing left and you will feel much stronger after."

"How did you become so wise?"

"I know a thing or two about hopeless situations."

His tone was light, but she heard the underlying strength. His easy manner made her assume Jon was much younger, but she realized she didn't know his true age. What had this man-child experienced before finding Hadran? Before she could ask he tucked her face back into his shoulder and she let out a fresh stream of sobs.

She cried until she was completely spent and more exhausted than she could remember, and like magic her mood began to lighten.

For this one moment she didn't have to repress her emotions or pretend to be in control. As her eyes finally drifted shut, her mind began to lift with hope.

She had cried, she would sleep, and then she would find a way out of this mess. She didn't know how the last part would happen, but she was immensely grateful to have such a wise and mature friend by her side.

Chapter 48

"Isn't this a tender sight?"

Owen's rough voice pulled Verena from a deep sleep. She was dreaming of Cairn, running to him through a tangle of dark, twisted trees that scratched at her face and dress. A beautiful infant was cradled in her arms, crying as if his little lungs would burst. She was lost and desperate, but she knew if she could reach Cairn she would be safe.

There were only a few yards to the castle, but it seemed impossibly far away. Cairn stood just in front of the gate, his arms open in welcome, but before she could reach him, he turned away. Verena called out to him, begging Cairn not to leave her, but it was no use. He didn't love her. Cairn didn't want their child.

Strong arms clamped on her skirt. She looked down to find Owen and Gundy pulling at her, drawing her down into the Old Lord's sarcophagus. The beautiful, frightened child with the powerful voice was slipping from her hands and there was nothing she could do to catch him.

She bolted upright in bed. One hand rushed to her belly, desperate to feel the tiny child inside. He was safe and Verena vowed nothing would tear him away.

Jon groaned at the intrusion, pulling a cushion over his head to block out the morning sunlight. They had slept curled in each other's arms. Now Owen stood glowering over the bed with his arms folded across his chest.

"Has Gundy asked for me?"

That was the only reason she could think of for Owen appearing in her room unless he meant to replace Jon with himself. She shuddered at that thought and discreetly reached for the knife she had tucked under her pillow. Her earlier resolve to give Owen what he wanted only referred to the treasure.

"Nay. Get dressed. We have a visitor. You too, Jon."

With one last disgruntled look at the boy lounging in her bed, Owen left the room.

"Poor Owen. He was seething with jealousy."

"That is not funny."

Snatching the pillow, she whacked Jon over the head with it. This was certainly no time for teasing. Where was the mature youth who tenderly wiped her tears the night before? That person vanished with a loud and decisive snore.

She gave a sudden push and shoved Jon off the bed. He lay in a tangled heap of blankets, staring at Verena with murder in his eyes.

"You are lucky you are pregnant," he warned. Those words were like ice water on their play. She was pregnant. Lord Gundy demanded that she get rid of the child. Owen planned to assassinate Gundy and make her his lover. What was she to do?

Jon promised they would think of a plan, but it appeared they would have no time. Owen's mysterious guest awaited them in the front room of the tent. Neither of them could imagine who the stranger could be. It was obviously not one of Lord Gundy's neighbors paying a visit or Hadran would be there instructing her on how best to conduct herself.

Verena could hear the awake and active camp through the tent's fabric walls. Orders were shouted and servants ran about seeing to their lord's comfort. Gundy must have given new orders after she left the night before.

She drew back the flap separating her room from the rest of the tent and paused in shock. A small figure in nondescript dark clothes stood in the center of the room, sizing up Owen and Hadran. Hollow eyes swung to Verena and peered at her as if calmly plotting her disembowelment.

"That is Ivone's assassin."

She desperately longed to draw her knives, but forced her itchy palms to remain at her sides. If she meant to harm them, the woman would have snuck into their tent during the night.

"Assassin doesn't quite describe the full range of my abilities." The self-confident words belied the modest nod of her head. She seemed to be at ease, but her feet were balanced in a fighter's stance. Her hands hovered close to the long knife at her belt. She would bet there were many more weapons concealed in her clothing. "Gundy has sent me to offer my services."

Verena suspected the woman's appearance was due more to Ivone's influence than Gundy's. She was a guest in his camp with only one soul she could trust. The lady no doubt sent her servant to keep an eye on his spies. By placing her own spy with them, Ivone guaranteed she would be the first to know of any changes to the plan.

"We don't need your help." Jon remembered the battle between this assassin and Verena, and wanted nothing to do with this deadly woman.

The assassin lifted one eyebrow, not bothering to respond to the boy's bluster. Regardless of their abilities, Gundy's word was law. If he thought they needed the extra support, they would get it.

"What is your name?" She tried to make the question sound innocuous, but she was burning with curiosity. She wanted to know everything about the woman who vowed to slay her.

"Mary."

"Well met, Mary. Welcome to the team. Are you hungry?"

Verena gestured for her to take a seat next to a tray full of breads, meat and cheese. Without a word, the family of spies circled the assassin. She stood in front, Owen behind, and Hadran and Jon were on either side. They were relaxed, but there was a tension in the air that strained her nerves.

None of them trusted this woman and for good reason. Did she really expect them to welcome her into their fold merely because of Gundy's order? They wouldn't defy him, but neither would they lower their guard around this newcomer.

"You should eat too," said Mary, wrapping a chunk of bread into a napkin for later. How could she eat surrounded by enemies? "Gundy wants us on the road in an hour."

"We are moving camp?"

"Aye. The lords are anxious for this siege to begin. When Gundy gives the signal, you will lead a small contingent of men through the secret passage. I searched and couldn't find it, but I know it must lead to the Old Lord's woods. You were clever to find it."

Praise from this woman? She blinked. Those words, with their semblance of kindness, made her more wary than a direct threat. Mary laughed at her unease.

Jon told Hadran about the secret passage when he escaped from Scotland, and Hadran told Gundy. He was delighted with the news and quickly saw how he could use it to his advantage. With the McPhersons busy repelling the main army, a small group of English solders would infiltrate the castle through the secret passage.

She remembered the anguish she felt in Scotland when Gundy ordered her to murder Cairn. She couldn't hurt him then, and she couldn't harm him now. What would she do when Gundy ordered her to betray Cairn again?

"You are precious! I can see why Gundy has such faith in your team. With those big, innocent eyes you don't look capable of hurting a fly. Muscles over there is probably more than willing to handle the dirty jobs. A young lad is always useful for sneaking into difficult places, and the old man must keep you in line."

"What about you, Mary? Who keeps you in line?" Owen finally spoke up. There was no mistaking the threat in his voice. If Mary gave him any reason to doubt her, he would be ready and willing to end to her career.

Mary laughed again. It was a harsh sound, completely devoid of humor. It made her skin crawl. What happened to this woman? Verena had her family of spies to support her. They uplifted each other when their assignments became too difficult. This woman had nothing but the ruthless job and the coin she received from Ivone.

She couldn't forget that moment when she informed Gundy about the child. A shadow of something crossed the assassin's eyes, a flicker of emotion so brief it might have been imagined. Something was there beneath the impenetrable armor of Mary's heart.

"I need no keeper," boasted Mary with a savage curl of her lip. "I follow milady of my own free will. If anyone tries to get in my way ..."

The words trailed into silence, allowing each spy to imagine the gruesome fate that befell those who dared to control her. At least one person had tried and paid the price.

"There is much to be done if we are to leave within the hour."

Hadran's matter-of-fact words snapped them back to the present. Despite their personal feelings for each other, they still worked for Gundy.

Owen had not mentioned his plot to overthrow their lord, but she knew he was contemplating it with glee. This woman was another obstacle in his path, but Owen would deal with her.

The heady sense of anticipation lay thick in the air. Any moment she expected a calamity to strike. When would Owen make his move?

"We will need water for the journey. Verena, can you help me collect some?"

Sweet, perceptive Jon must have sensed her growing panic and offered her a respite. She was only too eager to grab their water skins and follow Jon to a small stream near the camp. She was dressed in her tattered garb from the dungeon and an old blanket so no one recognized her as the tempting vision that visited Gundy's tent the night before.

"Thank you," Verena said once they were out of sight of the camp. She leaned down and splashed icy water on her face. The shock helped to calm her strained nerves.

"We don't have much time. Give me your water skins and walk through those trees."

"I don't understand."

"Shh! The soldiers will hear you. Go! You'll understand soon enough."

She followed his instructions and headed deeper into the forest. In the distance she could hear their noisy preparations, but felt isolated in the thick trees.

"Verena?"

The knife was in her hand before she spun around, but she dropped it when she saw her visitor.

"Cairn! What are you doing here?"

She flung herself into his open arms, kissing him as though her life depended on each brush of their lips. He was trying to say something, but she was so intent on the glorious feel of him in her arms, it took her a while to understand his words.

"You love me?"

"Aye, and I should have realized that long ago."

"But after all I have done ..."

"You saved my life. That's all I care about. You risked Gundy's wrath for me and I repaid you by locking you in the dungeon. I am an ungrateful cur."

"Nay! You were right to be angry. Oh Cairn, you must return to Scotland immediately. Gundy has ordered his army to advance. They know about the Old Lord's tunnel. Gundy wants me to lead a group of his men through it while your soldiers are occupied repelling the siege."

"His men can't find the tunnel if you come back with me. Once you are in the castle, you will be safe. Andreu should return any day with supplies and men. We can hold out until then."

She wanted nothing more than to go back to Scotland. She wished she could rely on his strong sword arm and the mountain of stone to protect her and their child from danger, but couldn't. She had worked for Gundy far too long to trust her sudden good fortune.

If she returned with Cairn, the spies would come after her, if not Owen, then Ivone's assassin. The family that supported her for most of her life also suffocated her, forcing her into a life of servitude and compromise.

"I cannot return with you." Cairn's fingers tightened on her. It never occurred to him that she might refuse to leave. Cairn was bewildered by her refusal. "We would never be safe."

She told him of Ivone's presence in Gundy's camp and her sinister assassin. Mary wasn't the only threat to their happiness. Owen vowed to keep Verena by his side. If she ran away, Jon would be punished for helping her escape. She couldn't let that happen.

"Let me protect you."

"Who will protect Jon and Hadran? How many people have to die for us to be together?"

"What do you suggest?" Cairn planted his feet, clearly unwilling to abandon her. Verena wanted to weep with frustration. "Am I to leave you to return to being Gundy's servant? What will happen to our child then?"

She forced herself to take deep, calming breaths. She had been pondering those questions since she learned about the child. When the war was over, she intended to run away. She would lose herself in holy lands. It would be hard for a woman alone, but perhaps Jon would come with her. She didn't know what kind of life she would find there, but she and her child would be alive.

"I will run away. There are places so remote no one will find me."

"Unacceptable. I know you are strong, but you need a man's protection. You need me and I need you."

He needed her?   Every fiber of her being vibrated with excitement. She wanted to shout her love for Cairn and beg him to take her back to Scotland. She wanted to wrap herself in his embrace and pretend Gundy and her foolish band of spies didn't matter, but she couldn't. Before she could respond, Jon's overly loud voice rang out from the trees.

"Hey Mary! Have you come to check on us?"

"I'm sorry," the words were whispered as she turned and fled, dodging the hand that reached out to restrain her. She couldn't kiss him goodbye, she couldn't say anything more. If she looked back, all her conviction would melt away.

Verena was a good spy. When plans went horribly awry, Hadran taught her to act with confidence and maintain a level head. Verena grasped at that lesson desperately as she wiped at her tears.

When she emerged from the trees, her face was serene. Her eyes were calm, but puckered with annoyance at Mary's unwanted presence. She irritably adjusted her skirts as she strode to the stream.

"What is taking so long?" Mary asked, glancing about in suspicion.

Verena smiled in mockery of her distrust. "I don't need your permission to relieve myself. The camp has not yet begun to march."

"I don't know how you usually operate, but with me everyone pulls their own weight." Mary grabbed Verena's arm as she walked past, her fingers dug painfully into her biceps, but she didn't flinch. "You aren't a lady anymore."

"I am whoever Gundy wants me to be."

Verena waited, silently counting a full 10 seconds until Mary's hand slipped from her arm. Verena stalked away with her head proudly high. Had she won this round? It was difficult to tell. Mary was too assessing. She hadn't given any ground in their confrontation, only tilted her head to one side, mocking Verena's dignity.

Chapter 49

Despite Mary's words, Hadran quickly saw the advantage in arranging the spies around Verena as Gundy's ward. That status legitimized them in the camp, and ensured they received better supplies for the journey. Mary found a simple though expensive gown and took on the role of her nurse while the others became her guards and assistants.

Their attentions were exemplary. Each spy treated her with such courtesy that she began to feel like an invalid. Gundy insisted she ride in a litter painted in gaudy shades of yellow, gold and green and carried by Hadran and Owen. The sway of the contraption as they carried her over the rough terrain made Verena immediately nauseous.

The massive army traveled at a snail's pace through the forest, clearing much of the ancient trees as they passed. Their passage was agonizingly slow. With every swaying step of her carriers, she was reminded of her first journey through these woods when she was able to comfortably rest in Cairn's arms.

Had he returned to Scotland? He must, for there was no way Cairn could reach her trapped in the middle of Gundy's army. He should be back at the castle, hurriedly preparing for battle. Perhaps she would catch a glimpse of him shouting orders to his men from the parapets.

An alarmed shout cut into Verena's grim musing. It was abruptly cut off and followed by the dull thud of a heavy object falling to the ground. More shouts quickly followed as a thick rain of arrows descended upon them. Contradictory orders were given as each lord instructed his men to see to their own protection. The army's superficial unity disintegrated.

She resisted the urge to lean her head out the window to see what the commotion was about. The wooden walls of the litter gave her a modicum of protection and she would be a fool to abandon it. She heard Hadran order a curt "to the left!" and carried the litter into the shade of some trees. Other servants followed their example, leaving the nobles to the protection of the confused knights. A few soldiers organized themselves into a unit and charged to meet their attackers, but their advance was quickly halted by the deadly accuracy of Scottish arrows.

There was nothing she could do, but cower in her wooden box and pray the archers didn't confuse her for one of the English lords. One small sword was in each hand. Her skirts were raised to her thighs, revealing the knives strapped to them. Should the swords fail, she could fling the knives and buy herself precious minutes to escape. She would be loathe to injure one of the McPhersons, but they may not recognize her in the heat of battle.

She strained her ears to pick out the muffled sounds of battle. The archers seemed to have only attacked the front of the army where the nobles and knights marched—including Verena. If Cairn knew of her role in Gundy's camp, would he have still attacked? She shook her head, forcing the question from her mind. Cairn had a duty to protect his people and she had flatly refused to go with him. She didn't deserve his consideration.

"Run!" Hadran yelled as he pulled the door open. He grasped Verena by the forearm and pulled her from the litter. They ran together through the trees, following Owen and the other servants. Even the most ruthless army would take care of the enemy soldiers first before turning their attention to the fleeing women and servants. Taking advantage of this wisdom, the non-combatants tried to put as much distance as possible between them and the battle.

To her horror, her flight didn't go unnoticed. Taking perverse pride in his new 'relation' Gundy ordered a small group of men to see to her safety. They pursued her in brightly colored livery that was sure to be noticed by the Scots. Predictably a volley of arrows flew in her direction as the Scots suspected a detachment of men was trying to flank them.

"Fools!" Verena shouted as she ducked under an old, gnarled oak. They were protected by armor, but she had naught but the silk dress. "They are following you! Leave me be!"

The soldiers ignored her words. One of them lifted her protesting form onto his horse, but an arrow in his back stopped his brave attempt. Using the soldier's body as a shield, she held him in place with one arm. Her other hand grabbed the reins and kicked the horse into a gallop. She led them in an abrupt left angle, drawing the fire away from the fleeing servants.

"Milady, we must rejoin the others," shouted one of the men. He tried to grab her reins and she irritably slapped his hands away.

"Not yet," she insisted. The arrows finally stopped as the Scots decided against splitting up their forces to follow such a small group, but she didn't feel safe. The sounds of battle had diminished, leaving the forest in eerie silence, but the furious pounding of her heart had yet to slow. They had not recognized her, which meant her group could still be a target.

Should she try to escape? Verena could easily lose herself in the forest. She would be halfway to London before Mary or Owen came after her. It would take only a moment to retrieve the money she stashed near Gundy's hunting cottage. That small savings should sustain her until she found a safe place to settle.

A painful groan cut into her thoughts. Behind her she felt the soldier shift in the saddle. He had not died as she suspected, but merely fainted from the pain. A bitter grimace twisted Verena's lips. If she left now, the solders would have to chase after her. It could be hours before the injured man received medical treatment.

Leaving Gundy's employ meant more than Verena's freedom. It meant she would never have to lie, steal and murder. The small flutter of life resting in her belly urged Verena to be better.

The men helped to lower him to the ground while she hunted for supplies. They were unprepared for the attack and brought little with them. One of the men happened to have a needle and thread while Verena's undergarments were turned into bandages. The men fashioned a travois for the soldier while she cleaned the wound with some melted snow and stitched it shut. Luckily after a few grunts of pain, he passed out again.

"I thank you, milady," said the oldest of the group. Though his tone was respectful, there was coldness in his eyes that made her wary. He was big like Owen, with an apathetic manner as if he found little difference between saddling a horse and snapping a neck. In Verena's line of work, she had learned how to spot a killer. This man was an interesting choice for Verena's guard. "I am Robert, and this is William and Stuart."

"We may not be out of danger yet."

She ignored his outstretched hand. Her attention was not on the men and instead scanned the forest for movement. Although the battle sounded far away, she couldn't be sure they escaped their attackers. They could be silently encircling their group while their attention was occupied with the injured Stuart.

How many men had Cairn brought into England? She expected him to return to Scotland and prepare for Gundy's arrival. She never expected Cairn to bring the fight to the English. This guerrilla attack served to confuse and demoralize Gundy's men and made Cairn's next move unpredictable. He could have men hidden all over the woods picking off the English as fled.

She strained her ears for the army's trumpet signaling it was safe to return. It seemed an eternity before it came, barely audible in the distance. A travois was attached to the back of her horse. Robert insisted she ride in the center of the group as they made their way back. She couldn't tell if it was for her protection or to make it more difficult for her to run.

The lengthening shadows and eerie stillness reminded her of the Old Lord's forest. She felt as if the Old Lord was watching from the canopy, ready to unleash his army of spirits on the woman who dared to betray his grandson. She frequently glanced about to make sure they were alone. She saw nothing, but the sensation of being watched wouldn't abate. The noisy army ahead promised warm food and blankets, but it seemed impossibly far away. Darkness was quickly falling along with the temperature, and the travois forced them to move excruciatingly slow.

Ignoring Robert's command to stay in the center of the group, she urged her mount to the front, careful not to jostle the injured Stuart any more than necessary.

"Should we stop for the night?"

There was no road through the forest and when darkness fell, it would be impossible to find an easy path for the travois.

"Nay. I feel these trees have eyes. Let us push on. Stuart will have to endure."

With one last censorious glance at her, he increased the pace. She glanced back at Stuart and found he had regained consciousness, but was gritting his teeth in pain, determined not to be more of a burden on their small band.

"We should rejoin the others soon."

Stuart nodded, but he knew they were far from safety.

"Verena," called a familiar voice from the trees. Her horse sidestepped warily as Owen and Jon emerged from a thicket of dead grass beside them. "I am glad you are safe."

Verena ignored Owen's concern. He didn't seem particularly interested in her welfare as he ran from the arrows.

"I am unharmed," she replied curtly. Not waiting for his help, she swung herself from the saddle. Her guard cautiously drew their swords at the unfamiliar men. She hastily made introductions before blood was accidentally shed. "Are you returning to camp?"

"Nay," Jon pulled out a chunk of bread and handed it to Verena. Though her stomach growled in protest, she offered it to the injured Stuart first. The blood had begun to seep through his bandages and he was deathly pale. Seeing the soldier's condition, Jon took out a small bag of medical supplies and helped her change his bandages. "Lord Gundy sent us to track the Scots. We were getting close, but then we lost the trail."

"I would expect no less of the Old Lord's grandson," broke in Robert. He was still eyeing the newcomers with distrust, particularly Owen. They were like two wolves sensing a new threat to their pack.

"Be careful," warned Jon with his voice in a barely audible whisper. They crouched over Stuart, repairing the stitches that tore as Verena's horse unwittingly jostled him. "Gundy does not fully trust you after Scotland. He sent these men to watch over you and kill you should you try to run."

"I suspected as much, but how do you know?"

"Mary."

Mary told him this? Why would the assassin try to warn her? Verena wished she knew what motivated the strange woman.

"Where is she?"

"Helping Hadran deal with the nobles. She seems to have a lot of experience with that."

"I remember how Ivone was in Scotland. How bad is she now?" Verena could well imagine the chaos that ensued with so many egotistical nobles vying for command. If Cairn's intent was to create chaos, it looked like he succeeded admirably.

"Terrible," Jon confirmed. "I am in no hurry to return. The nobles are united in purpose, but they all have different ideas for the roles of their men. Ivone is worse now, if you can believe it. Now that she has attached herself to Gundy, she demands royal treatment and wants to be included in every decision. Before we left, Ivone threw a tantrum because her new chef couldn't find herring for a pie! It will be a miracle if they don't murder each other within a fortnight."

"Poor Hadran."

"Thank goodness for him! He suggested we help comb the forest with our superior tracking skills and get as far from the chaos as possible."

"Our superior tracking skills will be in question if we have naught to show for hours of searching." Owen had come up behind the pair and caught the end of their conversation. He roughly boxed Jon's ears, hastening him to his feet. "Away with you, lad."

She watched them disappear with a feeling of dread. She didn't want to return to camp. Soon Gundy would remember her and demand another sinister act from her. She shuddered imagining what that would be. Perhaps he would give her to one of his neighbors. The prospect was not appealing.

Chapter 50

The McPhersons disappeared as suddenly as they appeared. Many English soldiers crossed themselves in fear, remembering the sinister Old Lord. Several of the lords, led by Sir Reginald, wanted to push on, but Gundy insisted on a more sensible plan. He assumed by the hit and run nature of the attack that Cairn only had a small force in the woods and sent several groups of men to search for them. They stealthily combed the woods for any sign of Scottish footprints, but after several hours called a halt to the futile search. Cairn and his men simply vanished.

Setting up camp in a large, defensible circle with himself in the protected center, Gundy decided to rest and reorganize before pushing on. A makeshift hospital was set up in several large tents where Verena's guard brought the injured Stuart. He passed out again as they neared the camp, but he was still alive. If Gundy didn't try to move his army for a few more days he may survive.

A semblance of order had returned to the army by the time Verena's small group arrived. Her large tent had been set up by thoughtful servants complete with fresh water for bathing and food. Since the ever-watchful William and Robert insisted on staying with her, she grudgingly shared some of the meal with them. They were annoying and potentially dangerous, but she knew they were just doing their jobs.

The two guards sat down in the tent's main room while she went into the back to sponge Stuart's blood off her and change. The invisible servants had also provided her with a lovely new gown of green ermine-trimmed velvet which was indecently low cut, but came with thick wool undergarments to replace the ones she used as Stuart's bandages.

Stepping from behind the privacy curtain she felt like a different person. The appreciative looks William and Robert gave her exposed bosom proved the effort had been successful. Her hair had been swept up in an elaborate coif that was also stable enough to withstand heavy riding. She donned a comfortable pair of hose beneath her skirts and carried a small pouch of food and medical supplies in hidden pockets of her dress. Her knives were tucked safely into her sleeves and strapped to her thighs. Covering herself in a thick cloak she felt ready to face the day's challenges.

While she changed a servant came to tell her that Lord Gundy requested her presence as soon as possible. Still irritated that the guard's interference had drawn the McPherson arrows and nearly killed her, she didn't spare the waiting men more than a glance as she left. She was a spy and didn't want a posse of men following her about, but was forced to endure their company as she made her way to Gundy's tent.

The men stationed outside must have been given orders for her appearance for they quickly stepped out of the way as she approached as if she were indeed Gundy's long-lost relation. The English lord was preoccupied studying maps spread across a table, steadfastly ignoring Lady Ivone who sat with uncharacteristic humility in a corner of the room. She could detect a faint bruising on her cheek as if she had been recently struck. Mary, once again dressed in her 'George' clothing, stood behind Ivone with a stony expression. One gloved hand tightly gripped the pommel of a sword, but she dared not draw. More of Gundy's soldiers stood at rigid attention around the large tent. They tried to appear nonchalant, but they were eyeing Mary with distrust.

The tension in the room was palpable. Gundy's lusty indolence had vanished with their first skirmish with the Scots. Ivone may have allied herself with the powerful lord, but her darkening cheek clearly indicated he wouldn't tolerate her interference.

For a woman who spent years manipulating her late husband it was surprising that Ivone had so misjudged Gundy. She should have known she couldn't influence a man like him. Gundy was driven by selfish cruelty. He was using her as surely as Ivone was using him, though she didn't yet know the details of their alliance. Perhaps her presence would lend credibility to Gundy's claim when he had to explain his actions to the English king. If they married Gundy would have the excuse he needed to invade Scotland to 'protect' the property he would inherit.

What had Gundy offered Ivone in return—love and the chance to once again rule the McPherson clan? Ivone was a fool to think he would take the treasure, return her to power and then quietly withdraw to England. Judging by her stricken face Ivone must have quickly learned the folly of her plans.

Hadran stood near Mary watching Gundy with interest. There was a warning in his eyes that she couldn't decipher. Something momentous had happened in the tent prior to Verena's arrival and she felt like she had just walked into a trap. Though her fingers itched, she forced them away from her knives. If Gundy wanted to kill her he would have ordered his men to do so before. Gundy's deadly intensity as he focused his eyes upon her made her wish she had never come back to camp. He had been waiting for her and some innate voice told her she wouldn't like the reason why.

"Ah, Verena," said Gundy, glancing up from his papers. He nodded at her pristine appearance with approval. "Is the Scot in love with you?"

She jerked at his words. Did Cairn love her? He had certainly risked his life by coming to England.

"He never said the words, milord."

"I have been reviewing my scouts' reports and something continues to puzzle me." Gundy moved forward to stand before her He roughly grabbed her chin with his bony fingers, digging into her soft flesh until she flinched in pain. His eyes bored into hers as if forcing the truth from her soul. "We had no news of the McPherson's movements, no reports that he knew of my army's existence ... until you came to me."

"Milord?"

She had indeed wandered into a trap, one of her own creation. When she gave her report about her actions in Scotland Gundy didn't seem interested in the details, only her achievements and failures. Had he dangled the prospect of staying with Lord Reginald only to gauge her reaction? She should have known Gundy was secretly studying her and Verena's evasions had revealed far more than she wanted to say.

"You carry the McPherson's brat and refused to kill him."

"I didn't have an opportunity."

"Do you think me a fool?" Gundy leaned forward until his nose was nearly touching hers. Verena could smell his acrid breath fanning her cheeks. He must have at least one rotten tooth; the analytical part of Verena's mind couldn't help noticing. "You are in love with him and perhaps he is in love with you too. The McPherson followed you here."

"Nay, he knows the truth." Verena tried to shake her head, but Gundy held her tightly. She was terrified of what he might do if Gundy suspected Cairn truly cared for her. He could ransom her or torture her to hurt Cairn. "He imprisoned me in the dungeon and then attacked your army knowing I was here. He does not care for me."

"From what I have heard your captivity was hardly strenuous and as a servant you should have been traveling in the rear of my caravan where he didn't strike."

Casting about for help she saw Hadran's eyes were downcast. Had he told Gundy about her accommodations in Cairn's dungeon? A pang of sadness washed over her at her mentor's betrayal. Of course he was loyal to Gundy, but the spies had always taken care of each other. He should have known what such knowledge would mean to her and her unborn child.

"I agree," ventured Ivone. She gracefully rose from her chair and went to stand beside Gundy. Though Mary didn't move, the slight shift of her weight caused alarm bells to ring in the back of her mind. She wasn't the only person in danger here. An altercation had taken place between Gundy and Ivone, and Mary was not at all happy with the results. "I have seen them together in Scotland. My son surely fancies himself in love."

Long, manicured fingers were placed upon Gundy's arm. Ivone squeezed him slightly then raked her fingernails along his biceps.

"If he is willing to risk his life for her ..."

"He is not," Verena broke in, trying to sound flippant. She tossed her hair, freeing herself of Gundy's hold and ventured what Hadran called her 'endearing pout.' "I wish I were so skilled. When the McPherson discovered I was lying he banished me to the dark pit he calls a dungeon. It was the maid Rosie who brought me the blankets and food. If Cairn found out she would have been in the dungeon with me."

"She risked his wrath to help you?"

"An extra crust of bread and flea-ridden blanket wouldn't have made a difference to anyone. It merely soothed her conscience when she went to confession."

"Then why is he here now?" Gundy wanted to know. He shook off Ivone's arm, softening the rebuke with a rough pat on her rear.

"She is here," she replied, gesturing with her chin toward Ivone. From the corner of her eye she saw Mary stiffen and knew she said the wrong thing. Implicating Ivone in the Scots' attack didn't endear her to the lady's guard. "An army this large couldn't stay hidden for long. He is trying to protect his people."

Gundy paced the room in silence for a few moments. Verena still didn't know what he planned, but knew her life may very well depend upon his next decision.

"Let's say you are wrong and the Scot does care for you, what would he give to have his women safely returned? I thought one pot of honey would draw out the Scottish bear," Gundy nodded toward the livid Ivone. "But two will work even better."

"What do you mean?" Ivone demanded. "This wasn't part of our arrangement."

"Ah, but you see, my dear. I always intended to use you this way. What need have I of an independent Scottish wife?"

"I am French."

"That is hardly an improvement. Guards! Take them both to her tent and keep them there. We march at dawn."

William and Stuart instantly stepped forward to obey. They each grabbed her by the arm and quickly whisked her out of the tent while more men came forward to grab Ivone. Verena knew even if she overpowered her guards she was still in the middle of the English camp. She didn't have a chance of making it out alive, but Ivone didn't agree. She shouted and thrashed about like the meanest fishwife, calling Gundy names that made even him blush to the tips of his ears.

"Hadran!" she yelled, though her voice was barely audible over Ivone's shrieks. "What is the meaning of this? What does he intend?"

The old man turned away, refusing to answer. Nor did he move to assist her. When Mary stepped forward and unsheathed her sword, ready to plunge it into the belly of Ivone's attackers, he quickly stepped behind her. With a forceful tap of his sword's pommel, Hadran knocked her unconscious.

Chapter 51

Jon and Owen soon returned from searching the woods, but they were forbidden to talk to Verena. Her guards had taken up residence in their tent making the enormous contraption seem impossibly stuffy. They busied themselves preparing for tomorrow's journey, packing up everything except for the tent and a few blankets.

With William and Robert watching so diligently Jon couldn't approach close enough to whisper to her. He saw the tension in her shoulders when Hadran entered the tent and the way Hadran averted his guilty eyes from hers. Their small family of spies was rapidly falling apart.

The only time she was allowed to move from her position near the fire was when the unconscious Mary was brought in, tightly bound and stripped of weapons. It was Verena who ignored William's harsh bark of command to stay and ventured forth to check the ugly bump on her head. Mary's eyes drifted open while Verena probed her scalp, but after a few moments of confusion her gaze fastened on her with murderous intent. She couldn't be too badly damaged if she remembered everything.

"This is your fault!" spat Ivone. With a sigh she moved back to her assigned chair beside the brazier. She shrugged her shoulders, too weary to argue with the spiteful woman. Verena knew nothing of Gundy's plans and was as much a pawn in this as she. They were all prisoners, but what kind? Gundy may intend to exchange them for something or punish them to incite Cairn's rage.

"We should rest for the night," announced Hadran. His voice sounded weary and much older than his years. He had always seemed so strong to her as he spearheaded their adventures. Now he looked ancient. The stress of this journey had aged him remarkably in the last few days.

Good. She felt little sympathy for her former mentor. He was like Owen, solely concerned with his own advancement. It hurt to know he could treat her so callously, but she hid the pain behind a steely gaze. She was done feeling sorry for herself.

•

Verena lived alone long before she met Hadran. Her earliest memories were of running with packs of orphaned children through London's filthy streets, stealing anything she could get her grubby hands on and hiding from the royal guards. Meeting Hadran was a considerable upgrade, but he couldn't replace the father she had never known.

Though her early days were lonely, yearning for a real family and home, they made her strong. It was a hard life, but somehow she had found the strength to take care of herself. She needed to reclaim some of that strength now.

"We just returned!" cried Jon, interrupting the tense moment. "Don't we deserve a rest before our next assignment?"

"That is what tonight is for and I suggest you use the moonlight hours." Owen spread out a bedroll beside the fire. He had not said much since they left Scotland and she was puzzled by his behavior. Yesterday he had been anxious to enact his daring plan. Now he seemed unconcerned with their mission, but she knew better.

He was a wolf stalking prey, casually waiting for the right moment to strike. Owen never backed down or changed his mind. This added a new, deadly dimension to Gundy's games, a sinister threat he would be completely unprepared for. When it came, Owen's blow would plunge them all into chaos.

"You have no right to complain." Jon lifted one mud-stained sleeve, exposing a large, colorful new bruise. "You were resting comfortably on your mount while I had to shimmy up every tree in this forest. If you weren't so fat ..."

"Enough!" Owen rolled his shoulders, proudly showing them all how false Jon's remarks were. He bulged with muscles in thick, bumpy chords along his biceps and back. Ivone gulped audibly at the display, but she was used to Owen's preening. She much preferred Cairn's physique. He was tall, broad and perfectly proportioned like an ancient Roman statue she had once seen in a Flemish palace. Cairn's body never failed to take her breath away while Owen's bulky girth seemed crude.

One beefy hand grasped Jon's collar while another pinched the flesh of his thigh as Owen lifted the struggling boy high overhead. "Still think I am fat?"

"I wouldn't dare say such a thing in this position."

Jon's fearful glance moved about the tent and their astonished audience. If Owen wished he could snap the boy's spine like a twig. Thankfully after a few tense moments Owen set him down and roughly mused Jon's hair.

"I'll trust you to keep a civil tongue from now on."

Jon nodded, for once shocked into silence. Owen's hand had fallen to his throat, feeling the rapid beat of his pulse.

"I think you have frightened him enough for one night," said Hadran. He placed a restraining hand on each of them. "We have a long journey tomorrow and need to rest."

Jon quickly stepped away and began gathering his blankets. They had often joked like this in the past, but now there was a tension in the air. Owen's actions were not met with the usual laughter and boasting, but with an unnatural silence. This failed moment of fun spoke volumes of their changed circumstances: the spies no longer trusted each other.

Chapter 52

True to his word Gundy marched the massive army at dawn, despite a midnight attack on their baggage train. A continuous stream of fire arrows were shot at their supplies and the overzealous soldiers trying to save their grain actually helped destroy them by saturating the supplies with water. Without the ability to adequately dry their foodstuffs most of it quickly began to rot.

Gundy insisted to the grumbling lords that this was not a hindrance and would actually free the army to march faster without so much baggage. To the poor soldiers stripped to quarter rations and forced for forage off the frozen winterland, his words must have seemed ludicrous.

Luckily Hadran was much wiser than their lord and after the first attack insisted each of his spies carry several days of provisions in their saddlebags. This expedition was turning into a disaster and he wanted his people to be taken care of.

With the extra weapons she hid in her dress the day before she felt overloaded, but it was always better to be overprepared. The brightly painted litter was abandoned and she was now forced to ride sidesaddle on a mount tethered to Gundy's horse. Mary rode nearby, similarly anchored to one of Gundy's personal guards. Lady Ivone was also under guard, though she did her best to pretend otherwise. She was charming and gracious during their grueling march, determined to return to Gundy's good graces, but he seemed impervious. No woman, regardless of how charming, would make Gundy deviate from his plans.

"Your Scotsman is trying my patience," announced Gundy when another group of men returned empty handed from scouring the forest. Cairn's men were experts at attacking any trailing group of men and disappearing before reinforcements could arrive. Many of Gundy's scouts didn't return at all.

"I am sure he would say the same of you," she replied.

Gundy chuckled and adjusted himself in the saddle. The cunning lord wore an impressive suit of armor, painstakingly engraved with intricate symbols. Though the metal offered more protection than the padded linen most of his foot soldiers wore, the armor was much too nice for a battlefield. Gundy probably intended to give orders from a well-protected camp and not risk his life or expensive armor.

"If I knew you were so witty I would have summoned you to my side long ago."

Fighting the nauseating roll in her stomach as she pictured herself as Gundy's leman, she forced a smile. She would rather die than allow Gundy to touch her.

"Then you would have lost a valuable agent. Who would have secured the treasure if not I?"

"I'm sure it was ridiculously easy for you to gain the Scot's trust. With those big eyes you look like a nun on the way to confession. Tell me; were you as saintly in the bedchamber?"

"I was effective in my role." Verena wished she could spur her horse forward. She had no desire to speak of the passion she experienced with Cairn, particularly not to Lord Gundy. He could pull her into the woods and toss up her skirts if he so desired and no one would do a thing to stop him. When Gundy turned away to speak to a soldier she discreetly wrapped her cloak more securely over her low-cut bodice.

"I'm sure you were, but perhaps you are more suited for other duties. I should discover for myself how skilled you truly are."

"You forget, milord, that I am also a trained assassin."

The beautiful chestnut mare tossed its head as Gundy jerked on the reins. He stared at her for one perplexed moment before letting out a deep roar of laughter. He shook with mirth until tears coursed down his face. She gazed innocently ahead, ignoring the curious stares of the onlookers.

"I admire your boldness," said Gundy when he could speak again. "It is always the most brazen lasses that make the best lovers. It is a pity we weren't better acquainted before this venture."

"Servants are taught to obey." Ivone tried to nudge her mount forward and break into their conversation, but her guard kept pulling her back. They had a brief tug of war as she attempted to bring Gundy's attention back to herself. "A real woman must be independent otherwise how can you trust her sincerity?"

"A woman's sincerity should never be assumed," Gundy replied irritably. Ivone's vanity was beginning to annoy him. "I know Verena's motives so I can trust her to act in the way that is most beneficial to her. She needs survival, safety and money, all of which she obtains by my side. You on the other hand are motivated by ambition and greed —sentiments I know all too well. How long would your loyalties remain if another benefactor were to offer his protection?"

"I don't know what you mean, milord. I would never betray you."

Ivone lowered her head demurely and guided her horse away. There was something guilty in her expression that made her wonder if she had not already solicited the other lords for aid. She might have done the same if she thought they would help, but they were all firmly in Gundy's pocket—especially after the arrival of the McPherson silver.

"Of course not."

His tone was one of patronizing kindness. Their relationship had rapidly deteriorated in the few days since she joined the army, but it was to be expected. Though they shared ambition, they were too stubbornly independent to work together for long. If Gundy had not betrayed Ivone, she surely would have done the same to him as soon as the opportunity arose.

When they finally crossed the border into Scotland Gundy divided his army into three parts. The larger group encircled the castle in an impenetrable ring, beginning the siege. Another group was sent to wreak havoc on the countryside, burning and looting homes and killing anyone who had not taken refuge in the castle. Luckily Cairn was prepared for Gundy's arrival and had long ago brought his people into the castle's protective walls.

Verena was untethered from Gundy's horse and given to her former guards, William and Robert. Together with Mary, Ivone and a few other soldiers, they made their way deep into the Old Lord's forest. Mary bore this change with stoic silence, glaring at each of them as if calmly envisioning their disembowelment.

"Where are you taking us?" Ivone demanded, but the men ignored her. "Why won't anyone answer a simple question?"

"The Old Lord's tunnel," she guessed when no one spoke up. It was the only logical destination.

"Correct," William replied. It was the first word he said to her all day, though he had spent hours by Verena's side. Like Mary he had the look of someone intent on murder, but William was calm and composed; a stark difference to Mary's simmering rage. "The McPherson has been following us since the first attack. Gundy supposes he will follow us to the Old Lord's tunnel and try to stop us from entering."

"So you will lay a trap for him using us as bait," she finished. "How will you find the Old Lord's tunnel? You can't expect me to tell you its location."

"The old man, Hadran, told us it was in the big mound."

She winced at the mention of her former mentor. Evidently he told Gundy much more than his theories on Cairn's love. If Hadran was beside her right then she would have wrung his interfering neck.

Hours had passed since they separated from the main army, enough time for Gundy's men to set up an effective siege of the castle. Had Cairn decided to wait for his brother to return with reinforcements or had he attacked Gundy's forces alone? The first seemed the most likely. Cairn's men were skilled at evasion in the woods, but they couldn't hope to defeat him in a pitched battle.

They reached the Old Lord's burial mound and Robert swung her from the saddle. He handed the ladies shovels and ordered them to start digging.

"You cannot be serious!"

Ivone was aghast at the order. The hem of her fine velvet cloak was rapidly becoming soaked with mud despite the tall chopines she wore. Her fur lined gown was suited more for sipping wine in a solar than digging holes. She eyed the shovel as if it were a serpent.

"Make it look convincing."

"It would be far more convincing for you to dig for us," returned Ivone with asperity. "My son knows I do not work."

"You will work or I'll slice your pretty throat."

"I wouldn't do that," said Mary. She looked quickly around as if alerted to a noise in the surrounding forest. Catching her alarm many of the men drew their weapons, scanning the trees for danger. "Cairn could be watching right now. What would he do if he saw you murder Lady Ivone?"

"He would probably thank me." Several of the men snickered at the jest, but they didn't sheath their weapons. In a louder voice William began giving orders. "Alright men, we have wasted enough time. You three stay here and assist the women. We will return with more supplies."

Chapter 53

The soldiers with the cheapest armor were ordered to stay while William and the others pretended to leave. They were bait, like Verena, to make the excavation look convincing enough to provoke Cairn to abandon his hidden position in the woods and attack.

She and Mary set to work clearing the stones in front of the Old Lord's tomb, but Ivone refused to help. She insisted refined ladies didn't do manual labor and sat imperiously on a fallen tree, refusing to move no matter how the soldiers railed at her.

The men left behind wore patched and cheaply padded linen instead of metal armor. They were obviously peasants untrained in battle or tactics and thought this assignment would elevate them in Gundy's household. They reminded her uncomfortably of the English archers who met their end in these woods and the young lad who was killed after bringing poison to Cairn's table. They were all expendable. She would almost feel sorry for the soldiers if they didn't take every opportunity to ogle her cleavage and share crude jokes about what they would do to her when this was over.

"Gundy won't mind if we toss her skirts," said one. The soldiers were in a tight group to one side of the mound, encouraging each other to act. Despite their bold words, none of them seemed brave enough to try. "We would be done long before the others arrive."

"Speak for yourself," said another, scratching his crotch. "The wenches like me to take my time."

"What do you know about wenches?" asked the third. "You haven't touched a woman since you were sucking your dam's teats."

"That's not true! Before we marched Kate took me into her barn."

With the soldiers' attention on their boastful stories she turned to Mary and whispered a question that had been plaguing her for days.

"'Why did you warn me about Gundy's intentions?"

"This is not the time for such talk."

"I don't know if there will be another opportunity."

"Then you may question your Holy Father. You may meet Him soon."

"Tell me the truth," Verena insisted when Mary tried to turn away. She needed to understand the complex woman before they went any further. The people Verena thought she knew were constantly changing, eroding the bonds of their previous relationships. Perhaps if she understood Mary, the perplexing events of the last few days would begin to make sense. "I am tired of pretenses. Do you still intend to murder me?"

"Nay." The words were said grudgingly from a face twisted in distaste. "I could no more hurt you than cut out my own heart."

"Why?"

"Because of the babe you carry."

"You were a mother."

"Aye, long ago. I was working in the fields while my son played nearby. He wandered into the road while I wasn't looking and was trampled beneath the horse of an impatient young knight. For a while I went mad with grief. No one could console me, not my husband, or the priest. It was only when the knight offered a few coins to atone for our loss that I was able to think clearly again.

"That night I snuck into his bedchamber and slit his throat while he slept. I thought my life was over then, indeed, I wanted it to end, but Lady Ivone intervened on my behalf. I owe her my life."

What prompted the haughty woman to save Mary? Had it been kindness or opportunism? She doubted Ivone was capable of an altruistic act. She had spared Mary only to turn her into a slave.

"No matter what I feel for you, your babe deserves to live."

The contemptuous flick of Mary's wrist showed just what she thought of Verena, but her words lacked venom. That was much more than she expected from the gruff older woman.

Quickly she slipped a couple of knives to Mary. Unarmed the women had little chance of surviving the skirmish between the English and Scottish soldiers. They needed to work together to escape.

"I'll take Pockmarked and Squeaker. The others won't put up much of a fight."

The oldest of the group had a face covered in ugly red and white pimples. He was smaller than the others, but had the loudest mouth and carried two daggers in his belt. Squeaker wore an old green tunic that probably belonged to his father. It had been clumsily refitted to his slender frame, but he had not bothered to wash off the old sweat stains.

"What are you two conspiring about?" Rough hands grabbed Verena's shoulders and pushed her face forward into the burial mound. Taking advantage of her helpless position her attacker began to run his filthy hands along her backside, drawing up her skirts. "I like a wench on her knees."

The other two soldiers reached for Mary and tried to tackle her to the ground, but she was ready for them. She jerked one knee up, catching the first man in the groin. He collapsed on top of her in pain, but as she fell Mary reached around him to strike the second man in the neck with the knife. Taking advantage of his surprise, Mary rolled the first man off and jumped to her feet.

Verena meanwhile had brought one wooden chopine up and kicked her attacker between the legs. She then twisted sharply, elbowing him in the face and punching him in the kidney as she turned. He fell back in astonishment, roaring in pain.

She should have killed the soldier while he fumbled with her skirts, but a twinge of conscience had stayed her hand. Unfortunately her kindness had cost her the advantage of surprise. Now the soldier faced her warily with weapon drawn, realizing his quarry was not as helpless as he assumed.

"You are unnatural!" gasped her attacker. He had certainly never expected to find himself in a knife fight with a woman. He slashed wildly at her face and torso making her dance around the small clearing.

As Gundy predicted Cairn and a small band of Scottish knights exploded from the nearby trees almost as soon as the fight started. Cairn's faceplate was up, revealing a mask of fury that made even her retreat a few steps. He wore the McPherson's traditional coat of arms and looked nearly identical to the tapestry of the Old Lord hanging in the abandoned chambers. She half expected to see a grinning familiar following him into battle.

The Englishmen saw the berserker apparition and their wits deserted them. Half of the men turned to fight and the other began tripping over themselves to get away. Neither stood a chance. Cairn was a wild thing, slashing at the English as if he fought demons sent to carry away his soul.

She stood transfixed watching the graceful dance. She had often seen Cairn on the practice field even in the most abysmal weather, but she had never seen such rage. It was all she could do to stumble out of his way as Cairn reached her attacker. His sword flashed through the air, parrying the soldier's pitiful swing. He took a step backward and Cairn followed, intent on dismembering the man that dared to touch his woman.

Though she felt no love for the Englishman she didn't wish for his death. Before she could think of the stupidity of her actions, she grabbed a shovel and dove forward to parry Cairn's deadly downward thrust. The wooden handle snapped beneath Cairn's power and she had to jump back, falling over the Englishman to avoid being sliced open.

"Nay!" she yelled, throwing her hands wide to protect the dumbfounded soldier. Everyone in the clearing—including the English—looked at her as if she were daft. "Don't do this. He isn't worth it."

"Do you realize what he was about to do to you?" Cairn ground out. He grabbed her shoulders and thrust her aside. She reached for Cairn's arm to restrain him but he irritably shook her off.

"But he didn't. I am safe because of you. There is no need for this."

"He needs to be taught a lesson."

"He has."

The soldier in question had fallen backward onto the burial mound when she bumped into him. He lay there quivering, knowing there was no escape surrounded as he was by furious Scotsmen. Fergus took her by the arm and tried to drag her away, but she fought him, trying to twist out of his grip.

"Please don't do this."

Cairn was a knight. It was his duty to protect his people. She understood this and knew many had fallen beneath Cairn's sword in the heat of battle. So why couldn't she let him kill this one insignificant man?

"Gundy used him as he used me, and the little boy who served you wine, and the archers in the woods. No one else should die for that man."

The point of Cairn's sword dropped to the ground. His expression changed to one of such kindness she had to look away. Somehow it was easier to face him when Cairn was enraged. Now his pity made her want to squirm. How could he possibly understand the gnawing guilt she struggled with as more and more people were destroyed in Gundy's machinations?

The sword fell to the ground as Cairn gathered her into his arms. She ignored the uncomfortable bite of his armor and pressed herself tighter into his embrace, eager to feel Cairn's tenderness again. She should have run away with him when Cairn found her in Gundy's camp, but she was too stubborn, too afraid to trust. She vowed to never make that mistake again.

"There is so much I need to tell you." Verena's voice was muffled; her face was still buried in Cairn's shoulder.

"And I you."

As she lifted her head to speak, her lips were trapped by Cairn's. It felt too good to touch and taste him again. The stress of the past melted away as Cairn became her world. In the back of her mind she knew the danger was not over. She should tell him about Gundy's trap, but Cairn wouldn't let her go.

"This is such a touching sight I am loathe to interrupt," Gundy cackled as he emerged from the trees. "I knew you were being modest, Verena. The Scot looks ready to rip your clothes off. Perhaps I should let him ..."

Two score Englishmen stepped out from the forest led by Lord Gundy. At his side rode Hadran and Owen, armed with sinister looking crossbows and short swords. These were nothing like the other, uncouth soldiers. Before them stood the best of Gundy's army, knights handpicked for their bravery and skill.

"Come here, Verena," Owen said in a voice that brooked no disobedience, but she shook her head. She would no more follow her former comrade than jump into a pit of vipers.

"Your performance was inspired," continued Gundy as if Owen had not spoken. "A little show of danger quickly drew out the barbarians."

The muscles beneath her fingers tensed. For a moment Cairn's gaze turned thunderous as he realized her attack had been a show to force his hand. She was the succulent bait he couldn't resist. Verena had betrayed Cairn before, could he trust her now?

"I had no part of this," she insisted. She turned to Cairn, ignoring the English threat before them. "I will never deceive you again."

Cairn brushed his lips lightly over her brow before thrusting her behind his armored back.

"I know."

"Verena, come to me!" There was desperation in his tone as Owen ordered Verena to his side. The trap that she had unintentionally sprung on Cairn had sealed his fate. What interest had Gundy in taking prisoners when the McPherson castle would soon be his? If she didn't go with Owen she would share his demise.

"Nay."

"Verena, you stubborn girl." Hadran chided her this time, urging her to abandon her love. "Think about your future. Come to us."

"I have no future without him."

A tear fell softly down her cheek for her unborn child, but she angrily wiped it away. Gundy would never let her keep the baby. He would never allow her to escape his service. It was better to die now with the man she loved than to be forced back into slavery.

"If that is your wish ..." Gundy lifted a hand and the English drew their weapons. The outnumbered Scots prepared to fight to the death as the English encircled them. It was then Owen finally decided to make his move. Before anyone knew what he intended he slipped from his horse and mounted behind Gundy. One hand snaked around to pin his arms to his sides while the other held a wicked-looking knife to his throat.

"What are you doing? This is treason!" Gundy made a halfhearted attempt to struggle, but Owen's knife soon made him rethink any sudden moves. "I'll have your head for this!"

"I believe I'll have yours first," Owen drawled with glee. He let the blade press a little deeper until a small drop of blood trickled down Gundy's wrinkled flesh. "Drop your weapons."

Obediently the Englishmen dropped their weaponry to the ground in a loud shower of metal and leather. They were as perplexed by this turnaround as Gundy. During the last days of this mission they had frequently seen Owen in their lord's company.

They had no reason to believe he might mean their lord harm.

"Jon," barked Owen, delighting in his new position of power. "Gather their arms!"

Hesitantly Jon collected the discarded weapons. He didn't have complete faith in Owen, but they had been together so long it was difficult to disobey. He looked to Hadran for answers, but the old man merely watched.

"For the first time I am doing what I please!" Owen expertly twirled the knife before returning it to Gundy's quivering throat. "Like you I am taking my freedom, but I am much smarter than any of you! Now you shall obey me, not some noble. I will be your master."

"To what avail?" Verena asked when Hadran remained silent. If he wished to protect her, she would be jubilant, but he only wished to mold himself in Gundy's sinister image. She hated to see him become like the man she detested. "We cannot go on as we have before. Can't you see that?"

"We will do much better than before," insisted Owen. "No one will be safe from our intrigues. The crowns of Europe will cower before our powers, but I need you. I need you by my side."

"Nay." Verena shook her head sadly, knowing she could never return to the life she knew before Cairn opened her eyes to love. "This is where I belong. I'll never leave Cairn again."

"Then you shall die with him."

"Nay!"

Faster than she thought possible the knife in Owen's hand flew through the air. Verena had stepped forward while she spoke and now was completely exposed. Though Cairn thrust her to the side she knew it was too late. She saw her fate written on the flash of the blade.

They crashed to the ground in a painful heap. Cairn tried to cushion her as he fell, but the weight of his armor was suffocating. It took her a moment of disbelief to realize the knife had not found her after all. Looking around she discovered Hadran had planted himself firmly in her path and blocked the knife with his body.

"Hadran!" she shrieked. She tried to push Cairn off and run to her mentor, but Cairn wouldn't let her up. Chaos had broken loose in the small clearing when Owen released his blade. Seeing his chance to escape Gundy elbowed Owen sharply in the ribs and ordered his men to attack. He might have been saved, but Owen had more than one weapon on his large frame.

A small opening beneath his arm had provided Gundy's armor with flexibility of movement. Unfortunately his armorer had not anticipated Owen's skillful attack. Another knife was in his hand and thrust into the unprotected flesh before Owen was pulled from Gundy's seat.

The English soldiers grabbed their weapons and turned on the Scots, infuriated by their lord's betrayal and ready to take their anger out on anyone who happened to be near. Mary had long since grabbed the shocked Ivone and dragged her to the treeline. Jon was quick to follow their example when the English broke free.

Seeing the desperate situation Cairn gave a shrill whistle through his front teeth. The Old Lord's tunnel suddenly burst open, spilling dozens of Scottish and French knights into the clearing led by Cairn's brother Andreu. Seeing their comrades in danger they threw themselves into the battle. Though terrified for Hadran, she was smart enough to remain pinned beneath Cairn's armored bulk until it was safe to come out.

The fighting seemed to take forever while she waited to be released, but it only lasted a few minutes. The English were infuriated over the death of their lord, but not nearly as passionate as the Scots defending their homeland. Many of them turned and fled when they saw the Old Lord's crypt fly open.

When Cairn finally released her she took a deep breath and checked herself for injuries. She was amazed to discover that despite her rough adventures the baby rested comfortably in her belly. Only a tiny kick let her know the child didn't appreciate such activity.

"Did I hurt you?"

"Nay." Cairn's response was to once again crush her in his embrace. She would have been content to remain there forever if she wasn't beset by the need to breathe. "But you are suffocating me."

"I should do more than that after the scare you have given me." He was furious, but she knew his emotions were the outpouring of relief after battle. Some people cried, or laughed hysterically, but Cairn glowered, trying to rein in his emotions. Understanding the reasons behind his fierceness she tipped her face up and gently kissed away his frown.

Jon was at Hadran's side trying to staunch the bleeding with a rag. Verena knelt beside the old man, pulling out the medical supplies she had hidden in her skirt pockets. The knife was deep in his shoulder and she knew if she tried to pull it out he would likely bleed to death.

"Why did you do it?" she asked. She blinked rapidly to clear the tears that blurred her vision. Verena was so angry when she learned of Hadran's betrayal and then he nearly gave his life for her. She told herself Hadran wasn't her real family, but she couldn't imagine a father doing more than this dear, old man.

"I couldn't let him hurt you." The words were whispered as Hadran's strength seeped out like the blood staining Jon's cloth. He reached up to grasp her hand, but his grip was much weaker than it should be. She held him tightly, trying to squeeze some of her strength into him. "What I did before was for you. I knew how you felt about the Scot, but I have been with Gundy far too long. I thought it best to stay with him."

"You don't have to apologize. I need you to save your strength. I am going to pull this knife out and I don't expect you to like it."

"It is more than I deserve for my stupid meddling."

His melodrama forced a chuckle from Jon's clenched lips. "I hope you remember those words when you are on your feet again."

Long before they were finished sewing Hadran's wound he passed out from the pain. Cairn knelt by her side when he finished giving orders for the English soldiers. The surviving knights were to be held until the English armies dispersed. Without Gundy's leadership she had no doubt the truce between the bickering lords would soon dissolve. Gundy and his fallen knights were to be stored in the Old Lord's crypt until Cairn decided what to do with the bodies. It was an ignoble end to a man with such a high opinion of himself.

"Will he survive?"

She continued to tightly bind Hadran's wound, knowing if she stopped the slight tremble in her fingers would become uncontrollable. She tried to be the strong, capable agent Hadran taught her to be, but the strain of the last few days was more than she could bear. She thought she was going to die along with Cairn and her unborn child. The shock of her last minute reprieve turned her knees to jelly. Only by focusing on Hadran had she been able to keep the flood of emotions at bay and not completely disgrace herself before Cairn's men.

"That is up to the old man. I have done all I can."

"If anyone is stubborn enough to pull through this it is Hadran," Jon chimed in. "I have been telling him for days the McPherson would make a much better master than Gundy, but he wouldn't listen."

"Master?" Cairn reared his head in surprise, looking from one spy to the next. "What do you mean?"

"Just imagine what our skills can do for you."

"I believe you have done more than enough already," countered Cairn, running his fingers through his hair in exasperation. "I have no interest in Gundy's methods."

"But we've always been together and we earn our keep. Isn't that right, Mary?" Jon's young chin jutted forward impudently. Like Verena, he had been taking care of himself for a long time but he had grown to love his family of spies. His future was less than certain. Mary had been watching this exchange in silence with one arm around the terrified Ivone.

"You may stay as long as you wish," Cairn replied. "But I am no Gundy. If you truly wish me to be your 'master' I have a few rules for you. First, you are retired. Second, you must come to my wedding."

"Your wedding?" She was so startled she dropped the medical supplies she had been collecting.

"Aye, Verena. Will you marry me?"

"I cannot. I'm a peasant ..."

"Do you love me?"

"Of course."

Cairn pressed a soft, lingering kiss on her lips before continuing. "You are the person I want in my life and in my bed. I want our children to have your strength, intelligence and kindness. Your nobility is in your spirit. That means more to me than any pedigree. Say you will marry me."

For a long moment she couldn't speak as tears wracked her frame. She knew she was in love with Cairn, but never expected to marry him. What happened to the spoiled, selfish knight he was supposed to be? She realized long ago those words could never apply to Cairn. She nodded because her throat was still closed with tears.

The forest erupted with cheers as Cairn took her into his arms again. Even the baby kicked in appreciation.

"In that case," interrupted Jon when he could be heard above the shouts of the soldiers. He let out a shrill whistle and a young lad stepped forward, leading several packed horses into the clearing. "Consider this an early wedding present."

Andreu opened one of the sacks to examine the contents and swore loudly in surprise before pouring several silver coins into his hand.

"Remind me to invite you to my wedding," he teased. "If I ever find a lass as fair as our Verena."

"I may be able to help you with that. As Gundy discovered, the possibilities of my talents are endless, but they do not come cheaply."

Jon led Andreu into the Old Lord's tomb while boasting of his many exploits. Though he intended to stay with her, Jon was too young to retire and had no interest in becoming a shepherd or farmer.

"I'll speak to him," she said, noting Cairn's bemused expression.

"I wonder what would have become of the treasure if I had not allowed a group of enemy spies into my clan?"

"Some questions are better left unanswered. What will you do with your stepmother?"

"I will not see her harmed, but she has done too much to forgive. Andreu has a small manor in southern France where she cannot cause trouble."

Some people could cause trouble no matter where they were placed, but she wouldn't ruin the beautiful moment by pointing that out. She hoped Ivone's bevy of spoiled, aristocratic females would go with her.

Though Andreu's French soldiers and supplies had arrived before the English siege, there was much to be done before the McPhersons could feel safe. They had no guarantee the invaders would slip away once they learned of Gundy's death. There were more mouths to feed, but at the moment she was blissfully happy knowing that no matter what dangers appeared in the future, she would face them with the man she loved.

• • •

Lauren Marrero

While not traveling the world in search of adventure, Lauren Marrero resides in Glendale, California.

LaurenMarrero.com

You might also enjoy these Black Lyon titles ...

DEVIL IN A RED KILT
by Elysabeth Williams

For twenty years, Evan and Evie MacDonald were the couple "meant to be." Their marriage now in tatters, they're transported to thirteenth-century Scotland, landing on opposite sides of a clan feud. Faced with an ancient evil, the two must rekindle the "forever and ever" kind of love they once felt, and bargain for a bit of Fae magic to flip the hourglass right side up—before time runs out.

PIRATE UNMASKED
by Judie Kleng

Fleeing from an unwanted life in Crete, high-spirited Julie Sinclair decides her only escape is to disguise herself as a man and board The Black Hornet. Working as the ship's new cabin boy, she comes face to face with the perils of the high seas—and a torrent of new emotions in the ship's dashing young captain.

www.ingramcontent.com/pod-product-compliance
Lightning Source LLC
Chambersburg PA
CBHW050406260626
47156CB00003B/898